THE
LAST
CAMELLIA

Sarah Jio

ORION

An Orion paperback
First published in Great Britain in 2020 by Orion Fiction,
an imprint of The Orion Publishing Group Ltd
Carmelite House, 50 Victoria Embankment,
London EC4Y 0DZ

An Hachette UK company

1 3 5 7 9 10 8 6 4 2

Copyright © Sarah Jio 2013
First published by Plume, a member of Penguin Group (USA) Inc. in 2013

The moral right of Sarah Jio to be identified as
the author of this work has been asserted in accordance with
the Copyright, Designs and Patents Act of 1988.

All rights reserved. No part of this publication may be
reproduced, stored in a retrieval system, or transmitted
in any form or by any means, electronic, mechanical,
photocopying, recording, or otherwise, without the
prior permission of both the copyright owner and the
above publisher of this book.

All the characters in this book are fictitious, and any resemblance to
actual persons, living or dead, is purely coincidental.

A CIP catalogue record for this book is
available from the British Library.

ISBN (Mass Market Paperback) 978 1 4091 9081 3
ISBN (eBook) 978 1 4091 9082 0

Printed and bound in Great Britain by Clays Ltd, Elcograf S.p.A.

MIX
Paper from
responsible sources
FSC® C104740
FSC
www.fsc.org

www.orionbooks.co.uk

For my mother, Karen Mitchell,
who introduced me to camellias and all the other beautiful
and important flowers in the garden

Author's Note

Camellias are one of those flowers that don't get a lot of fanfare. They're not as beloved as roses. People don't get nostalgic about them the way they do about tulips or lilies. They don't have the fragrance of gardenias or the showiness of dahlias. They don't hold up very well in bouquets and, when in bloom, it isn't long before their petals brown and fall to the ground. And yet, I've always found camellias to be stunning in their quiet, understated way.

I don't remember the first time I noticed a camellia. I remember them growing in my grandmother's garden and blooming, one pink, one white, beside the entrance to my childhood home. Somehow, in my life, camellias were always *there*, gracefully swaying in the breeze.

They're old-fashioned flowers (trees, really). In Seattle, where I live, many of the homes built at the turn of the last century feature old camellias presiding over the front yards. In fact, when my husband and I bought our first home in Seattle—a 1902 Victorian—it came with a camellia. I still remember its enormous trunk and how it stood tall, with branches that reached up to our second-story bedroom window.

While you'll still find these gorgeous trees in modern-day gardens on occasion, camellias have stepped back to make room for more popular garden choices—rows of lavender, ornamental grasses, azaleas, and Japanese maples. Fashions change; garden preferences do too. And yet, I still have a soft spot for camellias.

When I set out to write this novel, I had an image in my mind of a single camellia tree with big saucer-size blossoms and shiny, emerald leaves. And then the rest of the scene came into view: row after row of camellias. An *orchard*.

I began to wonder if the camellia in this imaginary orchard could be a rare variety, perhaps even the last of its kind. And, as it turns out, a few very rare camellias do exist in real life—sequestered away in private gardens and public conservatories around the world, most notably in England.

When I close my eyes now, months after completing this novel, I can still see the gardens of Livingston Manor. I have to admit, it makes me a little sad to know that this place doesn't really exist, because I'd love more than anything to visit. I'd sit in the orchard and gaze out beyond the stone angel to the carriage house and admire the camellias.

I hope this story brings you closer to your own beautiful, private garden, whether it's right outside your door or tucked away in your heart.

SJ

My destiny is in your hands.

—The meaning of the camellia fl ower,
according to the Victorian language of fl owers

Prologue

A cottage in the English countryside
April 18, 1803

The old woman's hand trembled as she clutched her teacup. Out of breath, she hadn't stopped to wash the dirt from under her nails. She hovered over the stove, waiting for the teakettle to whistle as she eyed the wound on her finger, still raw. She'd clumsily cut it on the edge of the garden shears, and it throbbed beneath the bloodstained bandage. She'd tend to it later. Now she needed to come to her senses.

She poured water in the little white ceramic pot with the hairline crack along the edge and waited for the tea leaves to steep. *Could it be?* She'd seen a bloom, as clear as day. White with pink tips. The Middlebury Pink, she was certain of it. Her husband, rest his soul, had tended to the camellia for twenty years—sang to it in the spring, even covered its dark emerald leaves with a quilt when the frost came. Special, he'd called it. The woman hadn't understood all the fuss over a scrawny tree, especially when the fields needed plowing and there were potatoes to be harvested.

If he could only see it now. In bloom. *What if someone from the village finds it?* No, she couldn't let that happen. It was her responsibility to make sure of that.

Years ago, her husband spent sixpence on the tree, which was then just a sprout peeking out of a ceramic pot. The traveling sales-man told him it had been propagated from a shoot at the base of the Middlebury Pink, the most beautiful camellia in all of England, and perhaps even the world. The only known cultivar, which pro-duced the largest, most stunning blooms—white with pink tips—presided over the Queen's rose garden inside the gates of the palace. Of course, the woman hadn't believed the tale, not then, and she had scolded her husband for his foolishness in spending such a high price on what might be a weed, but in her heart, she did love to see him happy. And when he looked at the tree, he was happy. "I sup-pose it's better than squandering money on drink," she had said. "Besides, if it blooms, maybe we can sell the buds at the market."

But the tree didn't bloom. Not the first year or the second, or the third or fourth. And by the tenth year, the old woman had given up hope entirely. She grew bitter when her husband whispered to the tree in the mornings. He said he had read about the technique in a garden manual, but when she found him spritzing the tree with a mixture of water and her best vegetable soap, she didn't care that he said it would ward off pests; her patience had worn thin. Some-times she wished for a bolt of lightning to strike the tree, split it in two, so her husband could stop fawning over it the way he did. She thought, more than once, about taking an ax to its slim trunk and letting the blade slice through the green wood. It would feel good to take out her anger on the tree. But she refrained. And after the man died, the tree remained in the garden. Years passed, and the grass grew high around its trunk. The ivy wrapped its tendrils around the branches. The old woman paid no attention to the camellia un-til that morning, when a fleck of pink caught her eye. The single saucer-size blossom was more magnificent than she could ever have imagined. More beautiful than any rose she'd ever seen, it swayed in the morning breeze with such an air of royalty, the old woman had felt the urge to curtsey in its presence.

She took another sip of tea. The timing was uncanny. Just days ago, a royal decree had been issued notifying the kingdom that a rare camellia in the Queen's garden had been decimated in a windstorm. Greatly saddened, the Queen had learned that a former palace gardener had propagated a seedling from the tree and sold it to a farmer in the countryside. She had ordered her footmen to search the country for her beloved tree's descendant and to arrest the person who had harbored it all those years.

The woman stared ahead. She turned to the window when she heard horses' hooves in the distance. Moments later, a knock sounded at the door, sending ripples through her tea. She smoothed the wisps of gray hair that had fallen loose from her bun, took a deep breath, and opened the door.

"Good day," said a smartly dressed man. His tone was polite but urgent. "Upon orders from Her Majesty, we are searching the country for a certain valuable variety of camellia." The woman eyed the man's clothing—plain, common. He was an impostor; even she could tell. Her husband had warned her of the lot—flower thieves. Of course, it all fit. If they could get to the camellia before the Queen's footmen, they could command a fortune for it. The man held a page in his hand, rolled up into a tight scroll. Unfurling it with great care, he pointed to the blossom painted on the page, white with pink tips.

The woman's heart beat so loudly, she could hear nothing else.

"Do you know of its whereabouts?" the man asked. Without waiting for her reply, he turned to search the garden for himself.

The man walked along the garden path, past the rows of vegetables and herbs, trampling the carrot greens that had just pushed through the recently thawed soil. He stood looking ahead where the tulips had reared their heads through the black earth. He knelt down to pluck a bud, still green and immature, examining it carefully. "If you see the tree," he said, twirling the tulip in his hand, before tossing it behind him, "send word to me in town. The name's Harrington."

The old woman nodded compliantly. The man gestured toward the north. Just over the hill was Livingston Manor. The lady of the house had been kind to them, offering to let them stay in the old cottage by the carriage house so long as they tended the kitchen garden. "Better not mention my visit to anyone at the manor," the man said.

"Yes, sir," the woman said hastily. She stood still, watching as he returned to his horse. When she could no longer hear the *click-clack* on the road, she followed the garden path past the pear tree near the fence until she came to the camellia bearing its one, glorious bloom.

No, she thought to herself, touching the delicate blossom. The Queen could search every garden in the land, and the flower thieves could examine every petal, but she would make sure they never found this one.

CHAPTER 1

Addison

New York City
June 1, 2000

The phone rang from the kitchen, insistent, taunting. It might as well have been a stick of dynamite on the granite countertop. If I didn't pick it up after three rings, the answering machine would turn on. *I cannot let the answering machine turn on.*

"Are you getting that?" my husband, Rex, said from the couch, looking up from his notebook. He had an adorable fascination with old-school appliances. Typewriters, record players, and an answering machine circa 1987. But at that moment, I longed for voice mail. If only we had voice mail.

"I'll get it!" I said, jumping up from the breakfast table and stubbing my toe on the leg of the chair. I winced. One ring. Two.

The hair on my arms stood on end. What if it was *him?* He had started calling two weeks ago, and every time the phone rang, I felt the familiar terror. *Calm. Deep breath.* Maybe it was one of my clients. That horrible Mrs. Atwell, the one who'd made me redo her rose garden three times. Or the IRS. Let it be the IRS. Anyone would be more welcome than the person I feared waited on the other end of the line.

If I turned off the machine, he'd call again. Like a shark sensing blood in the water, he'd keep circling until he got what he wanted. I had to answer it. "Hello?" I said airily into the receiver.

Rex looked up, smiled at me, then returned to his notebook.

"Hello again, Addison." His voice made me shiver. I couldn't see him, of course, but I knew his face—the patchy stubble that grew around his chin, that amused look in his eyes. "You know, I don't care for your new name. *Amanda* suited you much better."

I remained silent, quickly opening the French doors and stepping outside onto the patio that overlooked a tiny patch of garden— rare for the city, but all ours. A bird chirped happily from the little camellia tree Rex and I had planted last year on our first wedding anniversary. I hated that he was trespassing on my private sanctuary.

"Listen," I whispered. "I told you to stop calling me." I looked up at the apartment building behind our townhouse, wondering if he could see me from one of the windows above.

"Amanda, Amanda," he said, amused.

"Stop calling me that."

"Oh, I forgot," he continued. "You're all fancy now. I read about your wedding in the paper." He clicked his tongue scoldingly. "Quite the fairy-tale ending for a girl who—"

"Please," I said. I couldn't bear the sound of his voice, the way it made me think of the past. "Why can't you leave me alone?" I begged.

"You mean, you don't *miss* me? Think of all the good times we had together. You remember the way we used to—"

"Stop," I said, cringing.

"Oh, I see how it is," he said. "All stuck-up now that you married the *King of England.* You think you're really something. Well, let me ask you this: Does your husband know *who you really are?* Does he know what you've *done?*"

I felt sick, woozy. "Please, please leave me alone," I pleaded, feeling my throat tightening as I swallowed.

He laughed to himself. "But I can't," he said. "No. You see, I spent ten years of my life in prison. That's a long time to think about things. And I thought a lot about you, Amanda. Almost every day."

I shuddered. With him behind bars, I'd felt a false sense of security. His incarceration, for two felony counts of money laundering and a lesser charge of statutory rape, had felt like a thick, warm blanket wrapped around me. And now that he was out, the blanket had been ripped off. I felt exposed, frightened.

"Here's the thing, baby," he continued. "I'm sitting on a very valuable piece of information. I mean, you can't blame me for wanting the same cushy life you have."

"I'm going to hang up now," I said, my finger hovering over the End Call button.

"This can all end well," he said. "You know what I want."

"I already told you I don't have that kind of money."

"You may not," he said, "but your husband's family does."

"No, don't bring them into this."

"Well," he said, "then I have no other choice." I heard the chime of an ice cream truck on the other end of the line. I remembered chasing after those trucks as a little girl, wide-eyed, hopeful. I don't know why; I never had a dollar for an ice cream sandwich, and yet they lured me still.

I pulled the phone from my ear and listened as the same notes sounded, a block away, perhaps. The melody struck terror in me. The truck was close. Too close.

"Where are you?" I asked, suddenly panicked.

"Why? You want to see me?" he said, amused. I could picture the menacing grin on his face.

My chin quivered. "Please, leave me alone," I pleaded. "Can't you just leave me alone?"

"It could have been so easy," he said. "But you've tried my patience. If I don't have the money by the end of the week, I'll have no other choice but to tell your husband everything. And when I say 'everything,' I mean *everything*."

"No," I cried. "Please!"

I walked around the building and peered beyond the fence at the side yard. The ice cream truck motored past, slowly. Children cheered and squealed as the melodic chimes poured through the loudspeaker, and yet, with each note, I became increasingly paralyzed with terror. "You have five days, Amanda," he said. "And, by the way, you look stunning in that dress. Blue's your color."

The line went dead, and I looked down at my blue linen dress, before turning to the street. The walnut tree in the distance. An old Honda with tinted windows and a rusty hood parked nearby. A bus stop that cast jagged shadows on the sidewalk.

I ran back to the house and closed the French doors, locking them behind me. "Let's go to England," I said to Rex, breathless.

He pushed his dark-rimmed glasses higher on the bridge of his nose. "Really?" He looked confused. "I thought you didn't want to make the trip. Why the change of heart?"

My in-laws had recently purchased a historic manor in the English countryside, and they'd invited Rex and me to stay there for the summer while they continued their travels throughout Asia, where Rex's father, James, was working. Rex, whose novel-in-progress was set in a manor in the English countryside, thought it would be perfect for research. And we both shared a love of old homes. From what his mother, Lydia, had said on the phone, the estate brimmed with history.

But the timing was off. My landscape design business had enjoyed a surge of activity, and I was juggling four new clients, including a massive garden installation on a rooftop in Manhattan. It was a terrible time to leave. And yet now I had no choice. Sean didn't know about the manor. He wouldn't find me there. The trip would give me time to think.

My eyes darted around the living room nervously. "Well, I don't. . . . I mean, I didn't." I sighed, collecting myself. "I've just been thinking it over, and, well, maybe we do need a getaway. Our anniversary is coming up." I sat down on the couch beside him, twirling a lock of his shiny dark hair between my fingers. "I could explore the gardens, maybe even learn a thing or two; you know everyone's crazy about English gardens here." I was talking fast, the way I do when I'm worried. Rex could tell, I know, because he squeezed my hand.

"You're nervous about the airplane, aren't you, honey?" he said.

True, I did have a bit of airplane fright, and my doctor had prescribed Xanax for such moments. But, no, Rex didn't know the real reason for my anxiety, and I could never let him find out.

There was a time when I believed I'd tell him the truth about me. But the longer I waited, the more it seemed impossible to open my mouth and utter the painful words. So I didn't. Instead, I hid behind my carefully crafted story. A girl from a wealthy family in New Hampshire whose parents had died in a car accident years ago. The money that had all been lost in a fraudulent investment scheme. Rex had believed it all, believed in *me*. He didn't wonder why I didn't get Christmas cards or birthday calls. He didn't ask if I wanted to visit my childhood home. He admired my strength, he said, that I could live in the present and not mourn the past. *If only you knew.*

I tucked my hand in his. "I'll be fine," I said. "And you said that the house would be the perfect place to really dig into your research—let's do it, Rex. Let's go."

He smiled, touching my cheek lightly. "You know I'd love to make the trip, but only if you're certain."

"I am," I said, shifting my gaze to the window and eyeing the rusty car parked on the street. I stood up and pulled the drapes closed. "The sun's so bright today." I continued, reaching for my phone, "I bet I can call the travel agency and get tickets for tomorrow."

"Really?" he said. "That quick?"

I forced a smile. "Why not? We might as well make the most of the summer."

"Well," he said, setting his notebook aside, "I'll phone my parents and see about arrangements. Wait, what about your clients?"

I winced inwardly, remembering the intricate boxwood-lined courtyard I'd planned for a client and the adjoining butterfly garden for her two little girls. I'd promised that the installation would be in place by the end of next week, for her daughter's birthday. My assistant, Cara, would have to oversee it all. She'd do a fine job, but it wouldn't be the job I'd do. The astilbes wouldn't be spaced perfectly. The hebe wouldn't be clipped into smooth spheres the way I'd envisioned. I sighed. I knew I couldn't stay, not with the dark cloud that hovered. I just had to make sure it didn't follow me to England.

"Ready?" Rex asked in the doorway the next evening. I'd managed to book us two seats on the nine p.m. direct flight to London.

"Yeah," I said from the doorstep, cinching my scarf higher on my neck. I took a few steps toward the cab waiting at the sidewalk, then froze.

Rex looked at me. "Is that the phone ringing?"

I shivered, looking back at the house. The ring was muffled but detectable.

"Should I run back and get it?"

"No," I said, hurrying to the car. "Let's not stop. We'll miss our plane."

CHAPTER 2

Flora

New York City
April 9, 1940

"Did you forget to pack your tweed coat?" my mother asked, looking frazzled. The wind had blown her gray hair into her eyes, and she swiped it aside with a flour-dusted sleeve.

"Mama," I said, smoothing my gray jacket. "I have this one. I won't need it."

"But that's much too light," she said. "It's cold in *England*, Flora."

"I'll be fine," I assured her. I knew my mother's concerns were greater than my choice of outerwear, and I could tell by the way she held herself that she was on the verge of crying. "Please, don't worry, Mama," I said, tucking my arm around her.

She buried her face in her hands. "I just wish you didn't have to go."

"Oh, Mama," I said, pulling a handkerchief from the pocket of my dress. My initials, FAL, appeared in the right corner, carefully embroidered in red thread. She'd just finished a fresh supply, pressing each cloth into perfect, stiff little squares mere hours before my departure.

"I won't let you waste a handkerchief on me," she said, sniffing. Papa tucked his in her hand. "Look at me carrying on this way." She sighed and reached for my hands, holding them up before her. "My little girl, all grown up."

I was their only child; my mother and father might have liked me to go on living with them forever, waking before sunrise to tend to the bakery below the apartment in the Bronx. Starting the dough at dawn, readying the pastry case for the breakfast crowd, I kept the place running with such efficiency it sang.

I wondered how they'd go on without me. Mama's wrists were getting tired, and her shoulder had all but given out from years hunched over the kneading board. And Papa's poor eye for business was just as concerning. Last week a schoolboy slipped his hand in the till and ran out with seven dollars. Papa didn't chase after him; he'd noticed the hole in the child's shoe and let him go. It would've been fine if we didn't have a leaky roof to fix or an electricity bill to pay. Mama always said that if he could, Papa would give every loaf of bread away. That's the kind of man he was.

And yet, someone had to keep an eye on the books. The little apartment above the bakery didn't pay for itself. In fact, last month the landlord showed up, angry and red-faced. Mr. Johnson had demanded payment for three months of back rent. I appeased him with a loaf of cinnamon bread and promised we'd pay.

I looked at the ship nervously.

"I'm so proud of you," Papa proclaimed, cupping my cheeks in his hands.

"Our little girl," Mama added. "Off to the London Conservatory to become a botanist."

I could hardly look at them, knowing the secret I kept. The deception was more than I could bear.

"She'll be running the place in no time," Papa chimed in.

I feigned a smile, even though my cheeks hurt. There was no job at the London Conservatory. No apprenticeship. It was all an elaborate tale I'd made up to hide the real reason for the journey. Yes, I had dreamed of becoming a botanist, my entire life, really. I'd thought a great deal about the various species of maple and rhododendron while braiding challah, and I'd successfully planted a wisteria vine in a large pot and trained it over the awning of the bakery. And at night, after we closed shop, I volunteered at the New York Botanical Garden. Sweeping up cuttings and fallen leaves hardly seemed like work when it provided the opportunity to gaze into the eye of a Phoenix White peony or a Lady Hillingdon rose, with petals the color of apricot preserves.

Yes, horticulture, not pastries, was my passion. I suppose Mr. Price knew that when he propositioned me at the bakery two months before.

"The name's Philip," he had said. "Philip Price." He slid a white business card across the counter. "I understand you work at the Botanical Garden in the evenings."

I nodded. "Yes, but how do you—"

"I'm looking for someone with a keen botanical eye," he said, popping a piece of roll from the sample tray into his mouth, "for an important job."

Mama had warned me about men like this, with hair so slick it glistened under the bakery lights. I shook my head before listening to his proposal. "No, thank you," I said quickly, bagging up his order of six cake doughnuts. He took a bite of one before handing me a crisp dollar bill. "My parents own this bakery," I continued. "I have to stay on to help them."

He looked around at the little bakery, his eyes stopping at the crack in the countertop, the peeling paint on the trim around the doorway. "So it's a profitable enterprise you have going here?" he asked.

I didn't like the tone of his voice, prying and condescending. "Well, we're not Rockefellers, if that's what you're asking." I frowned. "Mama and Papa opened this bakery twenty-three years ago. I grew up here."

"I see," the man said, his voice tinged with scorn. "How sentimental."

I turned back to the pastry case, annoyed.

"Listen," he said again, "I know your parents have fallen on hard times."

My eyes met his again.

"I hear that rent can be steep in this part of town," he said, dusting a bit of powdered sugar from his mustache. "You must be so worried about them."

I was. Papa refused to raise prices, on principle. But if they couldn't turn a profit, the bakery would have to close soon. I knew that. I turned back to the tray of scones I needed to box up for an order. "Will that be all, Mr. Price?" I asked. My family's financial problems weren't his concern.

"I can help," he said.

I smirked. "No offense, but we don't need any help."

"I can offer you a job," he continued. "A good one—one you are uniquely qualified to do."

"But I just told you, I work *here*."

The bells on the front door chimed. "Still have day-old

whole wheat on the rack, Flora?" Mrs. Madison, a regular, asked. The old widow lived on a frighteningly tiny pension, and Papa had instructed me to always give her fresh bread and charge her nothing for it.

"Yes, ma'am," I said, turning toward her with a smile. "Nothing but the finest." I handed her a loaf of whole wheat, still warm, and she fumbled with her pocketbook. "You go on now," I said with a smile. "Papa insists."

Her eyes smiled up at me. "Thank you, kindly, dear," she said, tucking the loaf into her shopping basket.

Mr. Price circled back, smiling. "Wouldn't you love to do that again and again, knowing that money didn't matter?"

I let out a sarcastic laugh. "Listen, sir," I said. "I'm not sure what you're getting at, but I think it's time you show yourself the door."

He reached inside his jacket and pulled out an envelope. I could see from the open flap that it was thick with cash. He slid it across the counter.

"You can expect ten times that when you finish the job," he said.

My mouth gaped.

"You have my card," he continued. "Call me when you're ready."

I opened the envelope, counting the bills, wide-eyed. It was enough to pay the rent and then some. He tipped his cap at me before turning toward the door.

I called him a week later after a debt collector roughed up Papa in the alley behind the bakery. He'd hobbled into the kitchen with a bloodied face.

"Mr. Price, this is Flora Lewis," I said in a shaky voice. "I'm ready to speak to you about that job."

"Good," he said. "I had a feeling you'd call."

The wind swept across my cheek on the dock, jarring me back to the present. No, Mama and Papa must never know the real story behind my journey to England. Mama wiped a tear from her eye. "I'm so proud of you," she said.

I kissed their cheeks before walking to the gangway and handing my ticket to a man at the bottom. As I took one last look at them, I felt a pang of guilt. Papa, with his kind smile and round face; Mama with her arthritic hands. *How will they get on without me?* Yet I knew that if I didn't leave, I would have flour under my fingernails forever. I longed to see the world beyond the bakery, if only to know that it existed.

"Promise me you'll be careful," Mama called to me from the dock as Papa walked toward me. "Promise me you won't stay away too long."

I nodded. A sheet of rain blew sideways, splattering my face with large droplets. "Good-bye," I cried. "I'll write you when I'm settled."

"Go on, honey," Papa said, tucking a cinnamon roll wrapped in wax paper into my pocket. "The ship'll leave without you."

I waved and walked on, this time without looking back.

"Sailing to England, all by yourself?"

I turned around to see a man leaning against the railing of the upper deck a few feet away. About my age, maybe a few years older, he wore a gray suit and a herringbone cap, which he tipped lower on his forehead. I might have nodded and walked on—after all, my plans were none of his business—but he smiled disarmingly. "I remember the first time I sailed across the Atlantic by myself," he said, walking closer, as if we were old friends. I liked the sound of his British accent, and I wondered what he was doing in New York. "I was nine years old, and scared out of my wits."

"Well," I said, stiffening. I hoped I didn't look how I felt: like a little girl who had become separated from her parents. "I'm not the least bit scared."

He nodded, eyeing my suitcase, but I quickly set it down behind me. Papa's old set wasn't exactly glamorous, but it was all we had. The canvas appliqué was worn and tattered, and the brass hinges had tarnished to a dull brown. "So, what brings you to England?" he said, taking off his hat and twirling it around his index finger.

My eyes darted. *What should I say?* "I, I—" I fumbled, "I'm going to be working at the London Conservatory."

His eyes widened with interest. "Oh? So you're a botanist."

"Well," I said, hoping he couldn't see how flustered I felt, "I—"

"My mother used to go up to the London Conservatory all the time," he said. "It's quite a place."

"Yes," I said. "Well, I should be—"

"Where will you be working?" he asked, taking a step closer. "I mean, in which greenhouse?"

"Ah," I stammered, "well, all over, I suppose."

He nodded, extending his hand. "I'm Desmond." His green eyes sparkled.

"Flora," I replied. As I took his hand, my ticket slipped from my grasp and fell to the deck.

Desmond knelt down and retrieved it. "So, let's see, you're on the—"

"Thank you," I said, quickly collecting the slip of paper

that revealed my humble cabin number, certainly far from the fancy stateroom he'd be staying in. "I'd better be going now."

A steward approached. "Miss, may I help you find your stateroom?"

I nodded, gazing up at the enormous ocean liner.

"See you around," Desmond said, donning his cap again and tipping the brim once more, as he ascended the nearby stairs to the upper deck.

"Are you in first class?" the steward asked skeptically, eyeing the stairs where Desmond had disappeared.

"No," I said. "I believe I'm in, er, third class."

He grunted, then pointed to another steward, this one younger, who led me down a flight of stairs, and then another, deeper into the bowels of the ship. We walked down a dingy, poorly lit hallway, until he stopped in front of a nondescript door. "Your cabin," he said, without emotion. Inside, there was a bed with a shabby coverlet and a small table on which a single withered yellow chrysanthemum languished in a glass vase of cloudy water. The room measured about the size of the bakery storeroom, but I indulged in the very first space I could claim as all mine as if it were a penthouse. I sighed contentedly. "Thank you," I said a little too enthusiastically. The steward nodded and left.

I pressed my nose against the tiny porthole. The glass fogged up, and I wiped it with the sleeve of my dress until I could see the pier outside. I watched for some time, until a horn sounded, and the engine began to rumble and vibrate as the ship pulled out of the harbor slowly, as if it were reluctant to begin the journey. But the ship gained speed, and I watched as a fogbank swallowed up the city in a slow and steady gulp.

What did my mother say? Yes, "Keep your purse with you at all times. There are thieves on those traveling ships." *If she only knew.*

I had promised to meet Mr. Price that afternoon, so I ventured out the door and followed the blue-carpeted walkway down one turn and then another. "Excuse me, sir," I said timidly to a crewman. "Would you please direct me to the promenade deck?"

He eyed me with amusement. "So you fancy the finer quarters, do you?"

My cheeks flushed. "Well, yes—I mean, no," I said, flustered. "I'm meeting someone there."

He shrugged, pointing to the stairs. "Suit yourself."

I met Mr. Price on the promenade deck, and he instructed me to sit beside him. "I'm glad you came," he said, looking me over. "You didn't tell your parents about our arrangement, did you?"

I shook my head. I didn't like his speaking of Mama and Papa. "Of course I didn't."

"Good," he said, before taking a long sip of his martini. A bit of it sloshed over the side of the glass when he set it down on the table in front of him. "Anyone else?"

I thought of the man I'd met earlier, Desmond. But I decided not to mention him. "No," I said.

Mr. Price nodded. "So, I've already told you that you'll be acting as the nanny at a manor in the countryside. But I haven't told you exactly what you'll be doing there."

I listened expectantly.

"I run an international ring of flower thieves," he said.

I gasped at the phrase. As if plucked from the pages of a novel, here was the ringleader, sitting beside me with a smirk on his face.

"Of course, we don't exactly like to think of ourselves as *thieves*," he said smiling with lamblike innocence when he detected my startled expression. "We are simply the *brokers* of fine flowers. Some of the prized specimens in your beloved New York Botanical Garden came from the men I work with. The fact is, flowers are a commodity like any other. If someone's willing to pay, we're willing to deliver."

I nodded cautiously. All I could do was think of the roses, the lilies, the rare gardenia in the east wing—were they all acquired by dishonest means, uprooted from someone's personal flowerbed in the cover of darkness? It seemed so sad, so wrong. My cheeks burned. "Mr. Price, how on earth can you—"

"No point getting into all those details," he continued. "Leave the sausage-making to me. All you need to know is that a client has his sights on a rare tree that he believes is planted somewhere on the grounds," he explained. "A camellia. He's willing to pay a fortune for it, and your job is to find it."

"I don't understand," I said. "You want me to find a *tree*? Couldn't anyone do that?"

"No," he said. "It's a private estate, and it's difficult to get on the property—unless, that is, you're a trusted employee."

I nodded, even though I felt a pit in my stomach.

"Here," he said, digging into his suit pocket and producing a wrinkled envelope with a photograph inside. Even in black-and-white, the camellia was a stunning specimen. I flipped it over to read the words "Middlebury Pink."

"It used to be in the royal garden at Buckingham Palace,"

Mr. Price continued, "but for whatever reason, no seeds were saved, and it was lost over the years. According to my researcher, the last known tree of its kind may be at Livingston Manor."

I didn't take my eyes off the photograph. "Why doesn't your client just go there and get it himself?"

"It's not quite that easy," he said with an amused grin. "There are at least a hundred varieties of camellias on the property. Apparently the tree has a very short blooming window." He lit a cigarette. "Since you're engaged as the new nanny to Lord Edward Livingston's children, you can stay on until it blooms. It's the perfect ruse. No one will suspect a nanny—until the tree is discovered missing, and by then you'll be long gone."

"But I know nothing about children," I said, feeling a panicked flutter in my chest. "How can *I* do this?"

"Just do it," he said. "Gain their trust, then inquire about the camellia. Find it and write me." He handed me a card with a London address. "Don't telephone. Someone could overhear."

I nodded. "But, I don't understand. What does this man want with the tree?"

His eyes narrowed, then he shrugged. "What the hell," he said. "You might as well know." He yawned. "Some higher-up in the Third Reich wants it. For his mistress."

"The *Third Reich*," I said, horrified. My stomach churned. "But, how can you . . . how could I . . . ? Surely I can't—"

"Listen, Miss Lewis," he said sternly. "Technically, you're not doing anything wrong. All you have to do is find the tree, report back, and then you get your payment. Simple. In and out. Leave the rest to me."

"But—"

He set down his martini glass, fishing an olive from its depths. "You care about your parents, don't you?"

I nodded, remembering the way the debt collector had bloodied Papa's face.

"And you'd like to see them out of debt, with more time to rest and relax, wouldn't you?"

"Yes," I muttered, dabbing my eye with a handkerchief.

"Then *find the camellia*."

Restless in my cabin, I decided to go for a walk around the ship. The breeze had picked up, but I didn't feel like going all the way down to my cabin to get a coat. Instead, I sat down on a bench on the west side of the ship, where the wind wasn't quite as bad, and pulled out my sketchbook and a pencil. I thought about the camellia I had been hired to find, and as I did, I drew its delicate petals, its big rounded leaves. *Can I really go through with this?*

"Oh, hello again." I looked up to see Desmond walking toward me.

I quickly tucked my sketchbook back into my purse. "Hello," I said quickly.

"You must be freezing out here," he said, sitting down beside me. "Here," he continued, slipping off his coat. "Wear this."

"I'm fine," I said. "I actually like the fresh air."

He tucked his coat around my shoulders, and I was grateful for its warmth.

"I insist. My mum didn't raise me to stand by while a young lady shivers beside me."

I steadied myself as the ship jostled to the right. "It's always rocky on the first few days," he said. "It'll even out soon."

I nodded.

"I saw you on the promenade deck earlier," he said. "Your boyfriend?"

I shook my head. "No," I said adamantly, hoping he hadn't heard any of my exchange with Mr. Price. "He's a—"

"I, I mean," Desmond stammered, "it's none of my business, of course, but I—"

"He's a business associate."

"Oh," Desmond replied. "From the conservatory?"

"Yes," I said quickly.

The sun was beginning to set. The horizon took on a peach hue. "Have you always lived in London?"

Desmond took off his cap and scratched his head for a moment. "Yeah," he said. "Well, mostly in the countryside. But my father keeps a home in London."

I nodded, imagining the world he came from—so different from mine.

"So what were you doing in America?" I asked.

He smoothed his sandy blond hair. "Oh, just sorting out some business affairs."

I nodded. I couldn't exactly expect him to reveal details about his life if I wasn't being frank about mine.

The boat sloshed along the sea, swaying like a cradle, and we sat in silence for a few moments.

"Can I confess something to you?" he finally said.

I turned to him and nodded.

"When I was in New York," he said cautiously, "I almost decided to stay." His eyes remained fixed on the horizon.

"Why didn't you, then?" I asked.

He shrugged. "Duty. I joined the British army six months ago. I'll be shipping off soon."

"Oh," I said, feeling a pang of worry. In the bakery, I'd been able to compartmentalize the war, to let it exist only in the headlines of the newspapers. But now? It stood before me in a gray suit, shoulders dusted with raindrops.

"I felt so free in New York, so unencumbered," he continued. "I was tempted to leave it all behind and stay." He smiled at me. "Start over, you know?" He shook his head. "But I have to finish what I started."

I nodded, thinking about the camellia, the lies I was about to tell. "I know what you mean."

Just then, music began to play from the direction of the upper deck. "Oh, I almost forgot," he said. "The Captain's Welcoming Ball is tonight. Did you see the invitation?"

My cheeks flushed. Of course, third-class passengers, I was sure, had not received the same invitations slipped under their doors. "Yes," I said, momentarily ashamed of myself. But then Desmond took my hand, and all concern melted away.

"Let's go," he said. "Together."

"But I'm not dressed appropriately," I said, looking down at my simple blue dress. "I didn't pack anything formal."

"Nonsense," he said. "You look perfect as you are. Besides, we don't have to go in, if you don't want to. We can just catch a little of the music and champagne from the lobby."

"Well," I said, "I—"

"Good," he replied. "It's a date."

Ladies in formal attire bustled by us, on the arms of smartly dressed gentlemen. I felt out of place, and I wondered what Mr.

Price would think of my presence here. I looked around, hoping not to find him in the ballroom.

"Good evening, sir," a steward said to Desmond, before turning to me. I thought I detected a look of surprise on his face, but I tried to ignore it. "Good evening, madame," he said. "Champagne?"

"Yes, thank you," Desmond said, swiping two filled glasses from the steward's tray and handing one to me.

I studied the way the bubbles skipped and danced in the glass flute. Desmond took a drink, and I followed. It was my first taste of champagne, and I liked it. The moment I'd finished the glass, a steward appeared with a fresh one. I felt warm all over, and when Desmond suggested we get some air outside, the cold wind didn't have near the sting as it had earlier, especially with his jacket draped over my shoulders.

The band began playing a slower song, and Desmond smiled. "Care to dance?"

"Yes," I said, feeling light and uninhibited. I wondered what Mr. Price would think, but I banished the thought.

Desmond pulled me closer to him, and we swayed to the music under the starlit sky. He looked up and pointed overhead. "Look," he said. "That one's trying to communicate with us."

I grinned. "Oh, is it?"

"Yes," he replied. "The stars have their own language, you know. If you're careful, you can learn it."

"All right, Aristotle," I said. "So what's this star trying to say?"

He stared up at the sky for a few moments, watching the star sparkle.

"And?" he said. He nodded his head to himself, then looked back at me. "Just what I thought."

"So you're not going to tell me?"

"Can't," he said, grinning.

"You're something else, you know," I said, stealing a sideways glance at him. I leaned my head against his chest, and we swayed together like that for a moment, before I felt a tap on my shoulder.

I looked up to see Mr. Price.

"Excuse me, Miss Lewis," he said territorially. "It's getting late. Don't you think you ought to be finding your way back to your room?"

I dropped my hands to my side and took a step back. "I was only—"

"Miss Lewis," Mr. Price said, giving me a stern look.

I turned to Desmond. He looked confused, concerned. "He's right," I said. "It's getting late. Thank you for the lovely time tonight."

Desmond nodded, despite his obvious disappointment, and I turned to leave, following Mr. Price to the blue-carpeted staircase ahead.

"Miss Lewis," Mr. Price said when he'd deposited me at the door to my cabin, "I suggest you keep to yourself for the rest of the trip."

"Yes, sir," I said. He walked down the long hallway, and when he rounded the corner, I slipped my key into the door, but turned around quickly when I heard a *psssst* coming from behind me.

A woman, a few years older than I, peeked her head out

from a door across the hall. "Excuse me," she said. "May I have a quick word with you?"

"Me?" I said, a little confused.

She stepped out into the hallway, closing the door to her cabin behind her. "Yes," she said. "It's important."

I nodded. "OK."

She walked toward me. "We can't talk here," she said. "Inside your cabin."

We slipped into the room, and I closed the door behind me.

"You're working with Mr. Price," she said, "aren't you?"

I shook my head. "I don't know what you mean."

"You don't have to pretend," she said. "I know all about him. I used to work for him."

I gasped. "You did?"

"Yes," she said. "I saw you talking to him on the upper deck today, and I figured you're one of his new girls."

"Well, I . . . well, yes," I said, finally confessing. "But you don't understand, I have to do this. For my family."

"That's what I thought too," she said with a knowing smile. "But there are other ways."

I shook my head. "I'm already committed. I can't turn back now."

"You can," she said. "Just think about it. Believe me, you don't want to get mixed up with this man. I'm still trying to untangle myself."

I nodded.

"My name's Georgia."

"Flora," I replied.

"Nice to meet you, Flora." She turned to the door, before looking back briefly. "I recommend that you stay in this room for the rest of the voyage. Tell the steward you're ill and have your meals brought down to your room. The less you see Mr. Price, the better. And then when we dock, you can disappear into London. I can help you find the funds to get back home."

I thought about Desmond, my father, and the men who had threatened him. Georgia's plan seemed implausible, but I nodded again. "And, please, whatever you decide to do, don't tell Mr. Price that you saw me."

CHAPTER 3

Addison

I felt a gentle nudge on my shoulder. "Honey," Rex whispered into my ear. "We're here."

I opened my eyes, letting the scene outside the cab's window come into focus.

I gasped. "You didn't tell me your parents bought *Buckingham Palace*!"

Rex grinned. "It's pretty great, isn't it?"

"*Great*'s hardly the right word," I said, unable to take my eyes off of the manor. "It's *grand*." Three stories, built of intricate stonework, towered above us. Light green ivy, trimmed into submission, spread out over the masonry. I noticed a dormer window on the third floor and thought I saw the ruffle of a curtain, before my eyes met Rex's again. "Didn't you say the house was empty?"

"Well, yes," Rex said, stepping out onto the gravel driveway. "Aside from the housekeeper." He grinned. "Father said she came with the place."

"Oh," I said, scooting toward him on the seat, before taking his hand as he helped me outside. I felt the crunch of gravel underfoot.

Rex turned to me. "Shall we go in?" He hefted the bags from the driver's arms and set out toward the entrance.

The cab driver cleared his throat, and I turned around. "Oh, I'm so sorry, did my husband forget to pay the fare?"

"No, ma'am," he said quickly, lifting his hat and rubbing his forehead nervously as he eyed the old house. "It's just that, well . . . you do know about this old place, don't you?"

I frowned. "Know what?"

Rex was too far ahead to hear our conversation.

"My mum's the superstitious type," he said, taking a step closer to me and gazing up at the facade curiously. "She said it's the only place in Clivebrook she wouldn't dare step foot in." He shook his head cautiously, eyes fixed on the manor. "Well," he said, tipping his cap and smiling nervously. "Don't mean to worry you."

"What was that all about?" Rex asked once I'd caught up to him.

"His mother thinks the house is haunted," I said, eyeing the pair of stone lions bracketing the front steps.

"Haunted, huh?" Rex strode up the steps, then suddenly turned to me and said, "Boo!"

I jumped back, startled. "Stop!" I cried.

Rex set the bags down and took me in his arms. I could tell by his serious expression that he was no longer joking. "You OK, Addie?" he asked, searching my face.

"Of course I'm OK," I said, more defensively than I had planned. "Why?"

"You've seemed a little jumpy these past few days."

"Sorry," I said a little self-consciously. "I guess I've had a lot on my mind, with the trip and all."

He pressed his nose against mine. He'd always been stellar at reading me, like the day I came home from work feeling sick. "You're getting a migraine," he had said. I asked him how he knew, but he just shrugged. "Your eyes change right before you get one." I nodded now, feeling my chest tighten when I thought of the phone calls, when I thought of *him*, but I forced a smile.

"You're sweet," I said, "but everything's fine. Really, I couldn't be happier that I'm here." I weaved my hand into his. "With you."

He kissed my wrist lovingly, but concern lingered in his eyes.

An old woman stood before us, as if she'd materialized out of nowhere. Her wispy, chin-length white hair was tucked behind her ears, revealing a drawn face, with dark, sunken eyes and hollow, colorless cheeks. She wore a navy blue dress with sleeves that puffed slightly at the shoulders and a crisp white apron tied around her waist. She kept her hands clasped in front of her. "Welcome to Livingston Manor," she said dutifully, through thin lips that formed a brief, uncomfortable smile before the corners of her mouth turned downward again.

"Thank you," Rex said, holding out his hand. "I'm Rex Sinclair, and this is my wife, Addison. You must be Mrs. Dilloway? Father said you've been working here since the 1930s. Quite impressive."

"Yes," the woman said without emotion. She looked at me curiously, and I wondered how I compared to the other women who'd visited the manor years ago, ladies with impeccable wardrobes and grooming, no doubt. I bit the edge of the ragged cuticle on my left thumb. I wished I'd remembered to put on a bit of lipstick before we arrived.

Rex nodded. "And is it just you running the place?"

"Myself; the cook, Mrs. Klein; and the boy I hire on occasion to tend the garden," she replied. "Oh, and a girl who comes in on Saturday to help with the laundry," she said, casting a stern glance at me.

Rex dug his toe in the gravel, smashing an ant before looking up at Mrs. Dilloway curiously. "My father said you intend on staying on, and you're most welcome to, but I want you to know that my wife and I can mind the house just fine on our own," he said. "What I mean is, if you'd like the summer off, you're most welcome." I knew what Rex was getting at. She ought to be retired, not changing bed linens.

"Mr. Sinclair," she said stiffly, "Livingston Manor is my home. It will always be my home. So, with respect, I ask that you please honor my wish to remain in service here."

Rex nodded. "Then it's settled."

Mrs. Dilloway exhaled. "Now, let's go in."

My cell phone buzzed in my pocket, but I ignored it.

CHAPTER 4

Flora

April 11, 1940

On the second morning of the voyage, when I was green with seasickness, I heard a knock at my door.

"Yes?" I called from the bed, too weak to get up. Besides, it was probably just a steward delivering breakfast. He could chuck the tray over the side of the ship as far as I was concerned. I'd never felt so miserable, and I was feeling increasingly wary about the job ahead of me.

"Flora?" I recognized Georgia's voice, muffled by the door.

I sat up in bed. Vertigo instantly set in, and I steadied myself on the bedside table, then quickly smoothed my hair.

"Flora, are you in there?"

I looked at my face in the oval mirror on the wall. Pale and plain. I hadn't bothered to dress. Georgia knocked again, this time louder, more determined.

"Just a minute," I called out, reaching for my pink robe on the hook near the door. I turned the doorknob and pressed my nose to the opening.

"Oh, good," she said. "I was getting worried." She barreled past me.

She looked at me as if seeing me for the first time. "Are you well?"

"No," I said, feeling annoyed.

"I thought you might like some reading material."

"Yes," I replied. "I've been staring at this wall for far too long."

"Good, then," she said, depositing a regal-looking dark blue leather-bound volume in my hands. I turned over the spine, reading the words: "*The Years* by Virginia Woolf."

"I think you'll like it," Georgia said. "I read it the first time I traveled from New York to London.

"Anything to take my mind off this seasickness." I opened the book to the first page. "It was an uncertain spring," the first line read. *Yes*, it was.

April 14, 1940

Having nothing to do but read for the rest of the voyage, I finished the book on the final day at sea, and it wasn't until the last page that I flipped back to the beginning and saw the inscription Georgia had written on the inside cover: "Flora, the truth of the matter is that we always know the right thing to do. The hard part is doing it. Love, Georgia."

I tucked the book into my bag, and as I packed my suitcase, I thought of how much I'd changed even in the short time of the voyage. In New York, there was a right and a wrong. But now? Now, even despite Georgia's prodding, I had come to realize that maybe sometimes there's a gray. I hated what I was about to do, but I had committed to it, for Mama and Papa. And now that I was this far along, I couldn't turn back, even if Georgia believed I could.

I pulled the brim of my hat lower on my forehead and ventured out, first collecting my train tickets from the front desk, then finding my way to the debarkation deck. Mr. Price had arranged for a cab to take me to the train station, where I'd board a train to London, and from London I'd take a cab to Clivebrook, to the manor. Part of me hoped to see Desmond once more, but I'd heeded Mr. Price's advice and had kept to myself the rest of the voyage. I wondered if Desmond had looked for me, but there was no sense in thinking about him anymore. I had a job to do, and I'd never see him again.

I was happy not to find Georgia on the train from Liverpool to London. I'd already made up my mind. As I stared out the window at the foggy countryside whizzing past, I smiled at a young mother across the aisle, who had just pulled a loaf of bread from her bag. She broke off a piece and handed it to her tiny son, seated next to her. He wore a cap and overalls and promptly stuffed the chunk in his mouth. She then held up the loaf to me. "Care for a bit of bread, miss?"

I noticed the patch on the elbow of her dress and shook my head with a smile. "No, thank you. You're very kind, but I'm fine. I ate breakfast on the ship."

The little boy peeked at me from beside his mother and smiled. *What would they think if they knew what type of person I really was, if they knew I was coming to their country to help commit a crime?* I bit the edge of my lip. I wouldn't be stealing, exactly. Mr. Price had said I was only to identify the rare camellia and report back. That was different, I told myself. And yet the guilt grew in me like a cancer.

When the train arrived in London, I gathered my bags and walked to the street, slowly, on leaden legs. I retrieved the address from my purse. Livingston Manor, 11 Westland Drive, Clivebrook. *This is it.*

A cab pulled up. "Need a lift, miss?" the driver shouted from the window.

I looked up and forced a smile. "Yes," I said, glancing at the card in my hand. "Can you take me to Clivebrook?"

"Sure thing, miss," he said, jumping out to pick up my bag.

Inside the cab, I leaned my head back against the seat and sighed. I pulled the envelope from my purse and removed the photograph of the rare camellia.

The driver started the engine and turned the car out to the street slowly, before applying his brakes suddenly. "Miss," he said, regarding something in the rearview mirror. "Do you know him?"

"Who?" I said, turning around.

Desmond stood on the sidewalk, waving his arms at the cab. He must have seen me getting into the car. He looked a little sad standing there. I wanted to jump out and run to him, but what would I say? And if I told him the truth, what would he think?

"Would you like me to turn back, miss?" the driver asked.

I clutched the photo tighter in my hand. "No," I said, waving to Desmond, mouthing the words "I'm sorry."

"No," I continued. "Please don't stop."

"Yes, ma'am," he said, applying his foot to the gas pedal.

CHAPTER 5

Addison

Mrs. Dilloway showed us to our room, a large suite overlooking the garden. "This used to be Lord Livingston's private quarters," she said. "Of course, after he passed, it was redone for Lord Abbott during the years he stayed here." Her eyes full of memories, she ran her hand along the dark trim before quickly snatching it back. "You'll find towels in the bath," she continued. "Can I have Mrs. Klein bring anything up for lunch?"

"We're fine," Rex said. "We grabbed a bite in London."

I walked to the side window and looked out at a grove of trees. Spots of color pushed through the emerald leaves, some pink, others red, a few bits of white. The effect was stunning. "Very well," Mrs. Dilloway said, turning to the door.

"Wait," I said. "The orchard. It's lovely. The trees—they're camellias, right?"

Mrs. Dilloway pursed her lips. "Yes."

"I've never seen so many planted together that way," I said, pausing to admire them. They were past their blooming season, of course. Some bloomed later, some earlier, but the vast majority of camellias are best in early spring, when the air is crisp. Still, even with the few flowers that remained, it was easy to envision the orchard at its peak, like the Queen's painted rose trees in *Alice in Wonderland*.

"Will that be all?" Mrs. Dilloway asked curtly. I could tell she wasn't used to conversation.

I nodded, turning back to the window.

I felt Rex's hand on my waist as he nestled in beside me. He gestured toward the mahogany bed with its perfectly smoothed duvet and gave me a mischievous smile. "We are the lord and lady of the house now."

I pulled away. "Not now, honey," I said quickly. "We have so much unpacking to do."

"Oh," he said, wounded. He sat down on the bed and fumbled with the collar of his shirt.

No matter how happy we were or how much we loved each other, there would always be the giant elephant in the room, the one that followed us everywhere, reminding us of the fact that Rex wanted children and I never would. I forced a smile. "How could we, anyway," I said, planting a kiss on his cheek, "with that housekeeper poking around? Tonight?"

Rex's smile returned.

"This place is perfect for your research," I said, changing the subject. "Did you see that spooky old back staircase when we came up?"

"Yeah," he said. "The servants' staircase?"

I nodded. "It's like the ones in the old murder mysteries, where the killer escapes."

"The house does have a distinct Alfred Hitchcock feel to it, doesn't it?" He set his jacket on a side chair. "I can hardly believe my parents got it for such a steal—fully furnished."

"What's the story of this house?" I asked, looking up at a painting of a stern-looking yet handsome man on the wall. "How strange that a family would sell all of their heirlooms."

Rex shrugged. "From what my mother said, Lord Livingston died in the sixties, and Mrs. Dilloway stayed on to take care of one of his sons. The poor fellow had some kind of complications from a childhood illness. His condition worsened over time."

"So he died?"

"Yes," Rex said. "Last year, which is when the family put the home on the market. Mum said it was the strangest transaction. The lawyer who handled the estate insisted that all the furniture and art—everything—stay with the house."

"Weird," I said, tracing the edge of the mahogany side table. "You'd think that the family would have at least some sentimental attachments."

"I guess not," he said. "My father said something about one of the heirs." He scratched his head as if trying to recall the details. "He hadn't talked to his father in years before he died. Some family feud, I guess."

I thought of what the cab driver had said about the house. "Rex, do you think something *happened* here?"

"Who knows?" he said, grinning a little. "Maybe the housekeeper has a pile of bodies stashed in the basement."

"Shhh," I said. "What if she hears you?" I began unpacking the clothes from my suitcase and setting them inside the dresser on the far wall. "Besides, I feel a little sorry for her. Imagine having to work as a housekeeper in your eighties."

Rex shrugged. "Father offered to pay her a generous severance when he bought the house, but she insisted on staying on," he said.

I looked around the room, surveying the antique furniture,

the crystal chandelier overhead. "She must feel protective of this place."

Rex cocked his head to the right. "That, or she's hiding something." He pulled out his notebook and jotted something down. "See, it figures. Why else would someone stay in service for the better part of a century, even after everyone in the family has died or moved on? This is novel material."

"Now you're talking," I said. He had piqued my curiosity too. I walked to the window, looking out over the rolling hills and gardens that led to the orchard. I felt a pang of homesickness then. I'd miss the lupines, the asters, the rare poppies I'd planted from seed a few months back in our tiny New York garden. It would be a symphony of beauty and color for . . . the squirrels.

I sat down at the dressing table, pulling a comb through my light brown hair. I'd worked so hard to secret my past away, and now, like a rabid, caged animal, it growled and threatened. I twisted my wedding ring around my finger.

"I think I'll have a shower," Rex said, rummaging through his suitcase. "Did you happen to pack my razor?"

"Sorry," I said. "I didn't."

"Oh well. I'll just take a car into town and pick one up. Need anything?"

"No," I said. "I'm fine. Wait, no—chocolate. I need chocolate."

Rex grinned and reached for his coat on the side table. "See you in a few," he said.

After he'd left, I looked up at my reflection in the enormous gilded dressing room mirror, wondering how many countesses and the like had gazed at their faces in the very same Edwardian looking glass—curled, corseted, and trimmed in lace, no doubt. I eyed my scraggly gray Gap cardigan and black cotton leggings and felt a shiver of embarrassment. There it was again, that deep-seated fear that had hovered since childhood, the one that whispered, "You're not good enough."

I willed away the thoughts as I grabbed the remote and turned on the TV, listening to the latest headlines on CNN. More unrest in Israel. A helicopter down in Iraq. I turned it off quickly, and walked to the large paned window that overlooked the gardens. I tucked back the yellow and white toile curtains, pressed into sharp pleats. Lydia's decorator, who'd recently styled Nigella Lawson's London flat, had encouraged her to preserve the traditional look of the old house, and I was glad to see that my mother-in-law had given in. The daughter of a developer, she intended to renovate the home and use it as a weekend residence. But her initial plan to gut the centuries-old manor and give it an open, minimalist feel just didn't seem right. It would be the equivalent of putting a white picket fence around a Frank Lloyd Wright. Thankfully, she'd been talked out of such a dramatic overhaul. But there would be a renovation. Rex said an architect had been drawing up plans. I hoped they would preserve the integrity of the house—and the gardens.

Outside the window, Rex stood in the driveway in front of an old-fashioned car. Probably a Rolls-Royce. His father collected them, and Rex had been delighted to find one in the garage at the manor. A woman approached, and I leaned in to get a better look. Her blond hair was cropped into a blunt bob, and she wore sunglasses. I leaned in closer. *Who is she?* She spoke to Rex. He shook his head, looking back at the house. They exchanged a few more words, before she handed him a large envelope and walked to a blue convertible parked in the driveway. Rex climbed into the old car. Each started their engines simultaneously. I touched the glass and watched as the cars motored away. *Probably just someone who works at the house.*

I waited for Rex to return, but after a half hour, I ventured downstairs by myself. Mrs. Dilloway had offered a tour of the manor, but where was she now? The antique wall clock's ticktocking pendulum penetrated the silence that pervaded the decorous space. Passing intricate paneling, ornate moldings, and paintings depicting pastoral English life, I walked through the foyer and entered a room on the east side. A cabinet beside a window caught my eye. Its hardwood doors had been painstakingly carved in a floral design. I reached out to touch one of the glass knobs and tried to tug the door open, but it jammed. I tried again, pulling a little harder this time, and the knob released into my hand. Someone cleared their throat behind me.

My cheeks reddened when my eyes met Mrs. Dilloway's. "Oh, hello," I said guiltily. "I was just admiring this cabinet. I'm afraid I've broken the knob. I'm very sorry, I'm sure I can—"

"Give it to me," Mrs. Dilloway said stiffly. She walked toward me and collected the knob, depositing it into the pocket of her dress. "I'll have it repaired."

"I'm sorry," I said again.

"No harm done," she said, though I could read her face. She didn't trust me, and she didn't want me skulking about the manor, opening cabinet doors that, for all intents and purposes, were to remain shut. "Now," she said, glancing at the stairs. "Would you like to see the rest of the house?"

"Yes," I said. "But maybe we should wait for Rex. I know he wanted to have the grand tour." I turned to the window, a little annoyed. "I'm not sure what's taking him so long. He only needed to pick up a razor."

"Oh," Mrs. Dilloway said. "Yes, your husband called to say he would be in town for another two hours. He had some, what did he say, *business* to attend to."

"Business?" I shook my head. What type of business would Rex have in town, right after we arrived? "I don't understand. Did he give you any details?"

"He didn't say," Mrs. Dilloway said slowly, staring at me curiously, her hands resuming the clasp she had fronted when we arrived.

"That doesn't make any sense," I said under my breath. "Why didn't he call my phone?" I dug my cell out of my pocket and realized that the battery had died.

I followed Mrs. Dilloway to the doorway, before stopping suddenly in front of a bookcase. I realized I had left my book on the plane. "Maybe I'll grab something to read," I said. My eyes met Mrs. Dilloway's. "That is, if you don't mind?"

"Of course not," she replied, even though her face told me that she did mind, perhaps very much.

I pulled a blue leather-bound book from the case, and read the words on the cover: "*The Years* by Virginia Woolf." "How strange," I said. "My assistant, Cara, was just telling me that I must read this book while I am in England. The characters are the kind of people who would have lived in a house just like this." I followed Mrs. Dilloway back into the foyer, where our eyes met. There was a slight smile, just a flash, and then she pursed her lips.

"What is it?" I asked, hoping I hadn't offended her.

"It's nothing," she said, pausing. "I seem to have forgotten the sound of an American accent." She looked momentarily amused. "You remind me of someone who came to stay here a very long time ago."

CHAPTER 6

Flora

"Here we are," the driver said, as he pulled into Clive-brook. "What was the address again, miss?" The village was smaller than I'd expected, with just a smattering of shops along the main street and a fountain at the center of town. A green awning caught my eye. The sign on the door read: HAROLD'S BAKERY. My stomach growled.

"If you don't mind," I said, "I think I'll stop here and grab a bite."

"Sure thing," the driver replied.

I paid the fare and walked to the bakery, examining the strange-looking pastries in the window before venturing inside.

"Good day," an older woman said from behind the counter.

"Hello," I replied.

"Visiting from out of town?"

"Yes," I said. "I'm from New York."

"Fancy that!" the woman exclaimed, turning to the back room. "Harold!" she shouted. "Come out here!"

A moment later, a stocky man with a round belly appeared. He smiled at me warmly.

"She's from New York," the woman said. "If only Elsie were here. She dreamed of traveling to New York." She pointed to a framed photo on the wall above a tub of icing. "Our daughter. Disappeared four years ago. The police's theory is that she ran off to London with some chap," she said, shaking her head solemnly, "but she wouldn't do that. Not our Elsie."

"I'm so sorry," I said, "for your loss."

The smile returned to the woman's face. She looked at her husband lovingly. "And here I am going on about her again, Harold. I said I wasn't going to do that anymore. No sense dredging up the past. Elsie wouldn't want that." She looked back up at the photo on the wall. The young woman's soft blond hair curled around her face. She looked like a cherub.

"So tell me, *miss*, what brings you here to Clivebrook?"

I smiled nervously. "Just . . . visiting."

"Well," she said, handing me an apricot scone, "I hope you enjoy your stay here."

I smiled and thanked her. Outside, the wind picked up, and I quickly fastened the top button of my coat, thinking of Mama and Papa and missing them deeply. *If something happened to me, would they keep my photo hanging in the bakery?*

I walked along the sidewalk to the train station, where a driver wearing a black suit and tweed cap leaned against a parked cab. He swung a pocket watch on a chain in a circular motion. "Where to?" he asked as I approached.

I looked down at the scrap of paper that Mr. Price had given me, hesitant, even after coming this far, to go through with the plan. "Livingston Manor," I finally said. The words sounded cold and foreign as they crossed my lips.

The man arched his brows and eyed me curiously. "Going up to the big house, are you?"

"Yes," I said.

"An American?" he said, amused.

"I am."

"And what brings a pretty girl like you to Livingston Manor?"

"A job," I said stiffly. I didn't like his arrogant tone.

"Well, I hope they're paying you well," he said with a sniff. "It would take a lot of dough to get me to take a job there, especially after, well, everything."

"What do you mean?"

"The lady of the house died last year," he said, leaning in closer and lowering his voice to a whisper. "Something's not quite right up there." He shook his head. "My brother does odd jobs, handyman work," he said. "Well, he was up at the manor in February fixing a window on the second floor, and he said he heard the sound of a woman crying in the eaves of the house. Like a—"

"Well," I said. A chill crept down my spine. "I don't believe in ghosts."

"You will when you see this place," he said. "But, suit yourself."

He lifted my bag, then eyed me curiously again. "What did you say your business was at the manor?"

"I'm the new nanny," I said.

The driver smirked.

"What's so funny?"

"I'm just surprised, that's all."

I folded my arms. "Why?"

"Nothing," he said with an amused grin.

The car pulled up in front of the manor cautiously, then sputtered to a stop, as if the engine had no interest in motoring any closer to the property. The sight nearly took my breath away. The ivy-covered stone facade with ornate cornices and exquisite detailing looked like a page torn from a history book. Three stories high with five visible chimneys, it was far grander than I'd imagined, and as I took a step toward the entryway, my heart fluttered in anticipation.

"Should I wait here?" the man asked.

I shook my head. "Wait? Why?"

He looked at me as if I was a very foolish woman. "In case you change your mind."

"No," I said. "I'm not going to change my mind."

The driver retrieved my bag from the trunk and set it down with a thud a few paces ahead, all the while looking up at the manor with diffidence. "Well, that's as far as I'll go," he said. "Good luck to you, miss."

I nodded, tucking a few bills into his hand—the last of my money. "Thank you, but I make my own luck." It's something Mama would have said.

As the car motored away, I lifted my suitcase and turned around quickly when I heard the crunch of gravel behind me.

An older man, perhaps sixty, with a regal-looking face approached. Tall, with a slightly protruding belly, he wore a black suit and stared at me curiously. "Good day, miss," he said. "And you are?"

"Flora," I replied. "Flora Lewis." What was it Mr. Price had told me to say? "The agency sent me," I said quickly, as if to prove that I had business here and wasn't loitering on private grounds. I smoothed a wrinkle in my dress as he looked me over.

"Why, yes," he said, flashing a disarming smile. "Of course. The new nanny." He held out his hand. "I'm Mr. Beardsley, the butler. How do you do?"

"Very well, thank you," I said a little nervously.

"I will apologize now," he said, lifting my bag from my hand, "for the state of the gardens."

"I don't quite understand," I said.

"You see," he replied, eyeing my suitcase. I hoped he didn't see the patch Mama had sewn onto the side. "We're a bit short staffed at the moment, and I'm afraid things aren't going to improve in that department anytime soon."

"Oh?"

He cleared his throat. "We had a *situation* with our gardener," he continued. "He was let go, which is why the gardens look the way they do. It is a great disappointment to me that they have fallen into disarray."

I nodded. "If I may say, the grounds don't look that bad." The azaleas were overgrown, yes, and maybe the boxwood could use shaping, but everywhere, green lushness prevailed. A wall of rhododendrons lined the walkway, bloodred. I could smell their light, woody scent in the afternoon sun.

"You're kind to say so, Miss Lewis," he said. "But it wouldn't be up to her Ladyship's standards." He spoke in a hushed voice, as if the laurel hedge might have ears. "She cared about each petal. And they cared for her." He sighed. "The gardens simply haven't been the same since she passed last year." He pointed to the walkway ahead. "Well, let me take you inside." He stopped to pick up my bag. "I must tell you," he continued, "I didn't expect an *American*."

"Oh," I said, surprised, "didn't the, er, agency tell you?"

"I'm afraid they left out that detail," he said.

"I hope it won't be a problem, sir."

"No, no," he said, the corners of his eyes softening to reveal kindness I was starved for. "Let me show you to your quarters so you can freshen up before you meet his Lordship and the children."

I followed him past a knot garden, where boxwood had been planted in a square formation. They looked a bit scraggly, as if in need of a proper clipping. Mr. Beardsley stopped and knelt down to pick up a large pink flower blossom lying on the pathway, marveling at it momentarily before tucking it into his pocket.

I wanted to stop and linger in the gardens, to soak up the beauty all around, but I followed Mr. Beardsley through a side door and descended a set of stairs. "Of course, given the nature of your duties, you won't spend much time down here, aside from sleeping, but please know that you are always welcome in the servants' hall."

I nodded as a plump young woman, barely eighteen, approached. Her curly red hair sprung disobediently from her white cap and fell around her round, rosy cheeks. "Excuse me, Mr. Beardsley," she said, tugging at her white apron nervously. I noticed a smudge of soot near the pocket. "May I have a word with you?"

"Yes, Sadie?"

"It's just that, well, sir . . ."

"What is it?"

"It's Mr. Nicholas, sir," she continued. "He's made off with the flour sack again."

Mr. Beardsley frowned. "Again?"

"He has, sir," she said. "And he's scattered it out in the library. The bookcase looks as if it's had a dusting of snow." She giggled, then quickly covered her mouth with her hand before speaking again. "Mrs. Dilloway says it's ruined Lord Livingston's volume of Shakespeare. She's worked herself into a frightful tizzy, I'm afraid. She said she doesn't know what to do about that boy, that next thing he'll do is burn the house down, and—"

"Fortunate for us all, then, that the children's new nanny has arrived today," Mr. Beardsley replied. "Sadie, allow me to introduce you to Miss Lewis."

Sadie smiled warmly. "It's a pleasure to meet you, miss," she said.

"You as well," I said. "Please, call me Flora."

She nodded. "I'll just be going now," she said, before retrieving a basket of washing at her feet.

"Sadie," I said, ignoring Mr. Beardsley, who'd already begun walking ahead. "Are the children really . . . that bad?"

She nodded. "We've gone through three nannies since January," she whispered, studying my face, before smiling again. "I hope you stay. I like you."

"Thanks," I said with a grin.

I caught up with Mr. Beardsley, and we proceeded down a hallway to the kitchen. "This is Mrs. Marden," he said, "the cook." A large, gruff-looking woman sat at a table near the stove peeling potatoes intently. "Mrs. Marden, this is Miss Lewis, the children's new nanny."

"Another one?" she said, without looking up.

"Yes, Miss Lewis was sent by the agency and we are quite grateful to have her."

"Well," she said, tossing a freshly peeled potato into a cauldron of boiling water, her eyes meeting mine for the first time. The hot water splashed up in the air, and I lurched back to avoid getting scalded. "Better not get too comfortable. It's only a matter of time before this place gets the best of you." She looked me over. "No offense, but I'd be surprised if you have it in you to last past dinner."

Mr. Beardsley cleared his throat. "The job is not without challenges, but I'm sure Mrs. Marden will agree that it also has its rewards. You won't find a finer home for miles. And Mrs. Marden's cooking is, of course, a perk."

The woman smiled smugly as she began chopping vegetables. She paused to hold up a scrawny carrot, crimped at the end. "They're bitter," she said. "I don't know how I'm expected to manage with ingredients like this. Since Mr. Blythe left, the kitchen garden has suffered. Everyone blames the cook. 'Tisn't fair, I tell you. A proper kitchen must have a proper garden. 'Tisn't right."

"Thank you for voicing your concerns, Mrs. Marden," Mr. Beardsley said. "We shall continue this discussion another time."

She turned back to the vegetables and grumbled something under her breath.

I followed Mr. Beardsley down another corridor. He pointed to a door on the right. "This will be your room," he said. "I hope it will be satisfactory."

Inside was a simple twin bed, a dressing table, a chest of drawers, and a wardrobe. I peered out the window to see a distinguished-looking man standing alone on the terrace, gazing out to the gardens.

"That man," I said to Mr. Beardsley. "Who is he?"

"Oh," he said, cinching his tie nervously. "His Lordship must have returned early from London. Well then. I must be going. Please wash and be ready to meet the children in an hour. Mrs. Dilloway, the housekeeper, will be in the drawing room at two o'clock."

I nodded as he turned to the door. "Wait," I said, without taking my eyes off the lush landscape outside. "Those trees in the distance. The ones with the flowers. Are they . . ." My heart fluttered a little. "Camellias?" I thought of Mr. Price's words. *Identify the Middlebury Pink, and then go home. In and out.*

Mr. Beardsley sighed, looking momentarily pained, before he spoke. "Yes. They were Lady Anna's prized possessions."

"They're beautiful," I said, turning back to the window. There were so many of them. *Will I be able to locate the Middlebury Pink?*

"Indeed," he said, allowing the smile to return to his face. "Well, I'll leave you now. See you at two."

After the door closed, I turned to the window and gazed out at the camellia orchard, with its rows of elegant trees with showy blossoms in shades of pink, white, and scarlet. A cold wind seeped through the window frame, filling the air with an eerie, high-pitched hum. I shivered, wondering about the camellias and their secrets.

CHAPTER 7

Addison

Mrs. Klein, the cook, stopped us on the landing of the stairway. Her cheeks bright pink, she motioned to Mrs. Dilloway.

"I'm sorry to bother you two," she said. "Mrs. Dilloway, you're wanted on the telephone."

"I'm afraid we're a bit old-fashioned," Mrs. Dilloway said, turning to me. "There aren't any lines installed on the second story. I'll have to take it in the kitchen."

"That's fine," I said, following her downstairs, where I waited in the drawing room on a blue velvet couch with carved mahogany feet, which reminded me of an old claw-foot bathtub I'd had in my first apartment after college, the one I'd rented before I met Rex at the fund-raiser for the New York Botanical Garden. Life had been less complicated then. I sighed, looking down at the book in my hands. *The Years.* I rested my elbow against the arm of the couch and cracked the spine. It had the feel of a book that hadn't been touched in decades, creaking, as if to say *ahhh.* A waft of musty air hit my nose, punctuated with something else, something floral and pleasant. I thumbed past the title page, brittle, water-stained, until I came to the first chapter, simply titled "1880." I read and then reread the first line:

"It was an uncertain spring."

The line resonated with me as if I'd read it a thousand times, only I hadn't. I let my mind wander to New York and the frightening shadow that hovered over me there, which is when I noticed something written on the inside cover. A bit of the blue ink had run, but I could still make out the words. The two lines puzzled me: "The truth of the matter is that we always know the right thing to do. The hard part is doing it."

Who was Flora? And Georgia? And what had she meant by these words? I fanned the pages of the book, as if the answer lay buried inside the volume, which is when something fell out of the book onto my lap. I picked up the small square and turned it over to take a careful look at the treasure in my hands—a black-and-white photograph of a variegated camellia with a single bloom so breathtaking, I let out a little gasp. Before I tucked the photograph back inside the book, I noticed there was another stuck to it. Carefully, I separated the two images and discovered the portrait of a handsome young soldier, in uniform. He stood at the base of a staircase, smiling as though he may have loved the person standing behind the camera, perhaps very much. I recognized the paneling in the backdrop. The foyer at Livingston Manor.

I heard footsteps behind me, and I quickly tucked the photographs back inside the book. "Oh, thank goodness it's you," I said, grateful to see my husband standing in the doorway.

He planted a kiss on the top of my head. "Did I miss anything exciting?"

"Yeah," I said. "Look what I found."

He took the book in his hands, then shrugged.

"Look inside," I said. "At the inscription."

"Flora?"

"Yeah," I said. "I wonder who she was."

"Maybe she was Lord Livingston's wife," Rex offered.

"Perhaps," I said. "Or his daughter." I pulled out the photograph of the camellia blossom again and studied it carefully. "Why do you think this photo was left here?"

"Bookmark, maybe?"

I shook my head, remembering the photograph of the rose that hung above my desk at home. "No, I think this flower had some sort of significance to her."

"Maybe," Rex said, sitting on the sofa.

I nodded. The light from the window filtered into the room, beaming off Rex's dark hair and illuminating his tan skin and hazel eyes. He was handsome. Sometimes, I worried, too handsome. "Did you get your razor?"

He looked momentarily confused, but then he nodded. "Oh, yeah," he said, rubbing the stubble on his chin. "Yes, got it."

"What took you so long?" I asked, standing up. "Mrs. Dilloway said you had business in town?"

"Yes, paperwork for my father," he said. "It couldn't be filed from China, so I had to sign for them with a notary." He pointed to the driveway. "A courier brought them to the house just before I left."

"Oh," I said, remembering the woman in the blue convertible.

Mrs. Dilloway suddenly appeared in the doorway. "Pardon my intrusion," she said, her voice steeped in formality that didn't fit the decade, or perhaps even the century. "If you would like to accompany me, I will begin the tour now."

We followed her up the stairs, and I marveled at the enormous crystal chandelier above. Its chain appeared perilously dainty for the weight it carried. The steps creaked underfoot as we made our way to the second floor. Above the landing hung a painting of a beautiful woman. Her blond wavy hair framed her pale face like a halo. Below the hollow of her neck, a locket rested. I leaned in closer to examine its floral design—a detail I might otherwise have missed—and felt as though she was looking at me, really looking at me. Those eyes. I knew their expression. Lonely. Troubled. Trapped. I looked away, but my gaze ventured back to the canvas. The woman clutched a flower in her right hand. A pink camellia. I recognized the familiar petal structure and the shape of the leaf. I squinted in the dim light. Could that be blood on the tips of her fingernails? I rubbed my own nails. *Probably just a shadow.*

"Are you coming, Addison?" Rex called from down the hallway.

"Coming," I said, collecting myself, and yet unable to look away from the painting. "Wait, Mrs. Dilloway—who is the woman in the portrait?"

She walked toward me reluctantly. "That is Lady Anna," she finally said. "She was Lord Livingston's wife." Mrs. Dilloway closed her eyes tightly and then reopened them. "She was just a girl of eighteen when she first came to the manor," she continued, surveying the painting as though she hadn't permitted herself to look at it in a very long time. "It hasn't been the same since she . . ." She turned away quickly. "Let's continue on."

Lady Anna. I'd felt a vibe the moment I'd set foot on the property earlier that day, a certain presence that lingered in every door's creak, in every bit of wind that blew up from the garden and whistled through the windows. I imagined her standing at the end of the long corridor, watching us, such strange, modern people, poking about her house, handling her belongings, staring up at her portrait. What did she think of us, this lady with a locket around her neck and a camellia in her hand? And why did she appear so sad?

"The Livingston children occupied this wing," she said, pointing down a dark corridor.

"Children?" I asked. "How many?"

"Five," she replied, before shaking her head. "I mean four."

I shot Rex a confused look.

She stopped at a set of double doors at the end of the hall. The hinges creaked as she opened them and turned to Rex. "That dreadful decorator of your mother's hasn't gotten to this room yet." Her face revealed a moment of warmth. "It's just as the children left it." Mrs. Dilloway looked pleased. "They spent many happy hours here."

I walked to the bookcase and examined the storybooks inside. As a girl, I had dreamed of having stacks of books at my disposal— stories to get lost in, other worlds to live in when mine was so bleak. It's why I went to the library every day after school—that and because there usually wasn't anyone waiting for me at home.

I sighed, running my hand along the books' spines, but I sensed Mrs. Dilloway's apprehension, so I stepped back. I had the feeling that we were touring a museum that she alone curated.

"Should we keep going?" I asked, inching toward the doorway.

"Look at this!" Rex exclaimed, calling me over to a toy chest by the far wall. He held a tin airplane. Its red paint had long since eroded. "This is one of those old windup models," he said. "A friend of mine collects these. They're rare. It must be worth a fortune."

Mrs. Dilloway eyed the plane protectively until he'd set it back down on the toy chest. "It was Lord Abbott's," she said. "One of Lord Livingston's sons." She turned and walked out the door, which was our cue to follow.

"Did I say something wrong?" Rex whispered to me.

I shrugged, and we quickly proceeded into the hallway behind Mrs. Dilloway.

"The guest quarters are down that way," she said. "It's where visitors stayed when the Livingstons entertained. Now," she continued, "I must go check on the drapes on the third floor. That infernal decorator had them installed last week and they're so thin, I fear the light will destroy Lord Livingston's paintings."

I turned to follow her up the stairs, grasping the railing, but Mrs. Dilloway placed her icy hand over mine. "There's nothing of importance up here," she said.

"Oh," I said quickly.

"I'll see you both this evening," she said in a dismissive tone.

After she'd gone, Rex turned to me. "That was strange."

I nodded.

"Addie," he whispered, "she talks about Lord Livingston as if he's still *alive*."

CHAPTER 8

M rs. Dilloway greeted me in the drawing room at one. "Hello, Miss Lewis," she said from the doorway. Could this really be the housekeeper? She didn't look much older than I. Her light brown hair was pulled back into a tidy bun, without a single hair askew. Her face, with high cheekbones and a regal mouth, looked wiser than her years. She had a formal way about her, and yet there was softness, too. I wondered if we might become friends.

"Hello," I said.

She smiled at me curiously. "Did you expect someone else?"

"No, no," I stammered. "It's just that, well . . ."

"I know what you're thinking," she said with a brief smile. "I am quite young to be the head housekeeper of such a great house. But I can assure you that I am well suited for the job. Her Ladyship, rest her soul, would have no one else running things."

"Of course," I said. "I don't doubt that at all."

Mrs. Dilloway's face softened, a good-faith attempt to erase our awkward start. "Well," she said. "I am relieved that you've finally arrived. I'm certain that one more day of over-seeing the children might do me in." She smiled again and turned to the staircase. "I'm afraid you have your work cut out for you."

The light fixture above our heads began to rattle, which is when we heard the thunder of footsteps stampeding down the staircase. I set my hand on the side table to brace myself. "They sound like a pack of rhinoceroses," I said nervously.

"Rhinoceroses would be easier," she said under her breath. "Children!" she cried as they clamored their way down the stairs. "You know your father does not permit running in the house! And Mr. Abbott, remove yourself from the banister at once."

A blond-haired boy peered around the corner.

"Mr. Abbott," Mrs. Dilloway continued, "please come in and meet your new nanny, Miss Lewis."

"We don't want a new nanny!" another boy, this one younger and dark-haired, bellowed from behind his brother.

"Mr. Nicholas," Mrs. Dilloway said, "that is no way to speak of Miss Lewis, who has traveled a great distance to see you. Please be polite and tell her hello."

Nicholas stuck out his tongue before sinking into a wing-back chair near the window. "I won't tell her hello. And you can't make me either!"

Mrs. Dilloway gave me a knowing look. "Miss Katherine and Miss Janie?" A dark-haired, serious-looking young girl appeared, with a towheaded tot waddling behind, a bedraggled doll clutched in her hand. "Will *you* greet Miss Lewis?"

I knelt down in front of the girls and smiled awkwardly. "Hello," I said to the older one. "Tell me, how old are you?"

"I'm ten," she said. "And Janie is two." She sighed discontentedly. "And you are *not* our mother."

"I'll leave you now," Mrs. Dilloway said, smiling to herself as she walked out the door.

Abbott kept his arms folded tightly across his chest.

I stood up and moved to the sofa. "I've come here to take care of you, and I hope we can be friends," I said nervously. I hated misrepresenting myself to these children, especially after what they'd been through and knowing that I wouldn't be staying long. But I needed their help to find the camellia in the orchard. "Do you think we can?"

"I don't like to make friends with girls," Nicholas piped up.

"Neither do I," added Abbott.

I folded my hands in my lap and sighed. The old grandfather clock on the wall ticked and tocked. "All right," I said. "I see."

"I'm your friend," little Janie said in a sweet voice, melting the icy silence. She walked over to me and planted herself in my lap, running a chubby hand along my cheek. I couldn't help but smile.

"Thank you," I said to the little girl.

Katherine shrugged with an annoyed look that far surpassed her ten years. "Janie doesn't know what she's talking about," she huffed. "She's only a baby."

"No," the tiny child protested. "I'm a big girl."

"Katherine's right," Nicholas added. "Janie doesn't even remember Mother."

Janie looked at me and then down in her lap, crestfallen.

"It's OK, honey," I whispered before turning to the older children. "As you may already know, I'm from America. We're a little less formal there, so I have to ask you: Must I refer to you as Lady and Lord? I don't mean any disrespect, but, well, it sounds so stiff and formal. And you're children, after all."

"Well, I, for one, hate the title," Abbott said, finally unfolding his arms from his chest.

"Me too," Nicholas said, looking relieved, then thoughtful for a moment. "Could you call me Nicholas the Great instead? I read about a comic book character called that."

"Nicholas the Great it is, then," I said, smiling.

"You may call me Lady Katherine," Katherine said with an air of annoyance. "And we don't need a nanny. We can take care of ourselves."

Abbott smirked. "Mr. Beardsley arranged for you to come, didn't he?"

"Yes," I said. "I believe he did."

"Mr. Beardsley is a mean old booby!" Nicholas exclaimed, crossing his arms across his chest.

"Now, Nicholas," I said, trying very hard to stifle a laugh. "I mean, Nicholas the Great." His smile revealed one missing front tooth. "I don't think it's very nice to call Mr. Beardsley a"—I placed my hand over my mouth, but the gesture failed to repress the laughter that seeped out—"a booby."

Nicholas smiled. "You think he's a booby too, don't you?"

The room went quiet in anticipation of my response. I peered over my shoulder to see if Mrs. Dilloway was near; she wasn't. I smiled, and looked back at the children. "I suppose you might say he has one or two booby qualities."

The children laughed—all but Katherine, who frowned, busying herself with the ribbons in her hair.

Janie looked up at me from her perch in my lap. "Booby," she said with a giggle.

I smiled. This wasn't going to be easy, but so far, so good.

"The children take their tea at three," Mrs. Dilloway said in the servants' hall later that afternoon. "Nicholas and Abbott have riding lessons straight after, and Katherine and Janie have piano lessons. The lessons are a terrible bore to Katherine, who'd much rather be out riding with her brothers."

I nodded as she walked out to the hallway. "If you don't mind my asking, why isn't she permitted to ride with her brothers?" I asked Sadie, seated beside me.

She sighed. "Lord Livingston won't allow it. Not since Lady Anna died."

I lowered my voice. "Did she die in a riding accident?"

"No, no," Sadie replied. "My stars, if only it had been a riding accident." She clutched a rosary around her neck and sighed. "Since she passed, Lord Livingston hasn't been the same."

"How so?"

Sadie looked left and then right, as if she worried the teacups in the cupboard might be spies. "He's cross now," she said. "Closed off. Well, I suppose he's always been, but now it's different—much worse. The day she died, the children lost two parents, if you ask me. He hardly pays them any attention. It's a pity."

I leaned in closer to Sadie. "How did she die?"

She shrugged. "No one knows, really. They found her body out there." She paused, lowering her voice to a whisper. "In the orchard."

I covered my mouth. "That's just terrible," I said. "I suppose Lord Livingston must have loved her a great deal."

Sadie looked conflicted. She took a bite of her roll and didn't finish chewing it before speaking. "I guess you could say so, but she wasn't happy here, Lady Anna. Never was. She never warmed to the moors, the isolation. She missed America. Of course, Lord Livingston tried to make her happy." She gestured toward the window. "He brought in every plant, tree, and shrub you could ever imagine. Rare ones, too. You should have seen the gardeners parading through here with flowers pulled from the depths of the Amazon forest." She sighed. "And that orchard. He helped her find all of the camellias. My, did she love the camellias. No expense was spared when it came to Lady Anna's gardens. But, you know, they could never compare to her gardens in America." Sadie nodded to herself. "I'll never forget seeing her face one day when she received a letter from America. You'd think her heart was about to break right there."

"Didn't she go home to visit?"

She shook her head. "Lady Anna was from a wealthy family. From what I gather, his Lordship needed a fortune to save the manor. And her father wanted her as far away from Charleston as possible."

"Why?"

"The rumor is that she fell for some boy who was poor and not suitable for her. So they sent her to England. But what Lord Livingston didn't realize is that you can't keep a wife, a human being, under lock and key. Not even in the company of the rarest flowers in the world. She longed for her life in Charleston, but Lord Livingston wouldn't hear of it. And after the children were born, her fate was sealed. She couldn't leave. It broke her, I think."

"No wonder the children are so troubled," I said, shaking my head. "What they must have endured!"

Sadie nodded.

"You said they found her in the orchard?"

"Yes," she continued. "She and his Lordship had a row that morning. It was a bad one. I know, because I was scrubbing the floors outside of the drawing room. She ran out, and I could see that she'd been crying. She took her tea on the terrace with that awful gardener Mr. Blythe, and then she went for a walk in the gardens. They found her down there that night."

"What happened?" I gasped.

"No one knows," Sadie said in a hushed voice. "But it's never sat well with me. His Lordship fired Mr. Blythe on the spot." She sighed. "Only the sweet Lord Jesus knows what went on in that orchard," she continued. "Poor Lady Anna, she—"

"That will be all, Sadie," Mrs. Dilloway said from the doorway. How long had she been standing there? Neither of us had noticed her.

"Yes, ma'am," Sadie said quickly, her cheeks reddening. "I was only telling Miss Lewis about—"

"Yes, I know what you were discussing with Miss Lewis— things that should not be spoken of," she said. "Now, it's time you get started on the bedrooms. The washing is ready to be collected. Get on with it, please."

"Yes, ma'am," Sadie said, jumping to her feet.

Mrs. Dilloway cast a disapproving look toward me and then turned on her heel.

"What's America like?" Sadie asked in the servants' hall later. It wasn't really a hall, but that's what they called it. The room contained a long table with a bench on one side and chairs on the other.

"Oh, it's fine, I guess," I said.

"I've never been fond of Americans," Mrs. Marden said, casting a glance toward me. "But I do like the accent. Lady Anna had such a way of talking." The cook frowned as though recalling something unpleasant. "I take it they don't eat stew in America?"

"I'm not sure what you mean," I said, flustered.

"You hardly touched your lunch today," she added with a smirk.

"I'm sorry," I said. "I haven't had much of an appetite since leaving home."

The cook was a large woman, in both height and girth. She wore her gray hair short, and when she smiled, which wasn't often, she revealed a crooked front tooth. "If you don't like my cooking, you can just say so. No point in beating around the bush."

"I don't mean that at all, ma'am," I said, flushing. To compensate, I pointed to the breadboard on the table. "That's a fine loaf you've got there."

Mrs. Marden arched her eyebrows. "And how would *you* know?"

"I know bread," I said. "I grew up in a bakery."

"My, my," she said, as though my comment had added fuel to the fire. "A baker's daughter has taken up residence in Livingston Manor."

Mrs. Dilloway cleared her throat. "Mrs. Marden, perhaps she can give you a few pointers on your scones."

The cook smirked and turned to her bowl.

A large man with dark hair and a prominent Adam's apple appeared in the doorway of the servants' hall. He was so tall, he had to stoop below the doorway as he passed through. I watched as he stopped at a basin by the window to wash his hands before joining us at the table. He looked up as he reached for the soap, and our eyes met, but he turned away without smiling. Dirt-tinged water streamed from his hands.

"Miss Lewis, this is Mr. Humphrey, Lord Livingston's chauffeur," Mrs. Dilloway said as the man sat down, helping himself to a slice of bread. "Mr. Humphrey, Miss Lewis is the new nanny."

He nodded. "What do you think of them?"

"I'm sorry?" I asked.

"The children," he said, spreading butter on the thick slice of bread with a firm hand. Dirt remained under his nails from the apparently unsuccessful scrubbing.

"Oh, yes," I said. "I hope they'll warm to me, after all they've been through."

He grunted something between bites, before taking a drink of tea. "Watch out for the eldest one," he said. "That boy carries a pitchfork, I tell you."

"I don't know if I'd go as far as to say that," I said.

"Well," he harrumphed. "Say what you want, but that child is the devil incarnate."

"Miss Lewis," Mrs. Dilloway interjected, "Mr. Humphrey's just smarting because he thinks Abbott gave the car a flat tire last week."

"What makes you think he did that?"

Mr. Humphrey leaned back in his chair. "I know a guilty face when I see one," he said. "Besides, you should have seen his smirk when I had to patch the tire."

"Maybe he's just misunderstood," I said. "Maybe his brother and sisters are too. After all, they only recently lost their mother."

A silence fell over the room, and I felt my cheeks growing pink.

"Miss Lewis," Mrs. Dilloway began, "if you don't have an appetite, why don't I show you the house?"

I nodded. "That would be lovely, thank you."

We walked up the stairs, through the doorway that led to the foyer. Mrs. Dilloway walked straight to a gold sconce on the far wall and polished it with her sleeve. "That Sadie," she huffed. "She always neglects these fixtures." She took a step back to examine the sconce, then frowned. "Lord Livingston doesn't like to see fingerprints."

I glanced around the foyer, open to three stories. The walls were dressed in elaborate wood panels and decorated with paintings of people engaged in foxhunting and horse-riding and other scenes of life in the English countryside of centuries past. I thought of Desmond suddenly, wondering if he came from a home like this.

"It's quite something, isn't it?" Mrs. Dilloway said proudly.

"Oh, yes," I replied.

"I remember my first day here. I'd never seen anything more beautiful in all my life."

"I can see why," I said, marveling at the space. "It's so different from where I come from."

"You will come to love it as I have," Mrs. Dilloway said confidently.

I gazed up at a painting of a stiff-looking man with a dog seated at his feet. I thought of Papa with his easy smile and rosy cheeks. "What's Mr. Livingston, I mean, er, Lord Livingston like?"

Mrs. Dilloway eyed the painting affectionately. "He's a complicated man," she said. "He—" The front door flung open and a large yellow Labrador retriever barreled in. His light fur was all but covered in a thick layer of mud. He wagged his tail, and dropped a rubber ball at my feet. A moment later, Abbott and Nicholas appeared sheepishly, their pants mud-stained.

"Mr. Abbott! Mr. Nicholas!" Mrs. Dilloway scolded. "Where have you been?"

"We only took Ferris on a walk to the rose garden, ma'am," the elder boy said.

"Boys, your father forbade you," she continued. "Why must you disobey him?"

"It was Ferris's fault," Nicholas said. "He ran away. We had to go after him."

Mrs. Dilloway plucked a pink petal that had affixed itself to the mud on Abbott's shirt. It was much too large to be a rose petal. "I see you haven't been truthful with me," she said, eyeing the petal. "You've been in the orchard again, haven't you?"

The orchard.

He nodded guiltily.

"Mr. Abbott, you are twelve years old. You know better. Now, run upstairs and get in the bath. You too, Mr. Nicholas. There's just enough time to wash and get this foyer cleaned before dinner. You're very lucky that Miss Lewis and I have soft hearts and won't mention it to your father. Now, be off with you."

The boys disappeared up the stairs, and Mrs. Dilloway sighed. "I'll get Mr. Humphrey to wash Ferris," she said. "If he insists on keeping a dog, he must bathe him. I told Lord Livingston a dog was a bad idea, but Mr. Humphrey convinced him." She sighed. "You check on the boys. Make sure they scrub behind their ears and that their clothes are pressed for dinner.

I'll present you to Lord Livingston at six in the dining room. Servants don't eat with the family, but the nanny is the exception."

"Yes, ma'am," I said, walking upstairs. On the landing, a white sheet covered a large object that had been propped against the balusters. I lifted the corner to find a painting of a woman clutching a pink flower. Her sad eyes pierced mine, and I marveled at the emotion the artist had captured with the paintbrush. *Please*, she seemed to cry, *help me*. I shivered, quickly tucking the sheet back over the canvas before anyone saw me.

CHAPTER 9

Addison

"There's a concert in the park in town tonight," Rex said that evening. "Want to go?"

"Are you asking me out?" I said, grinning.

"I am," he replied with a big smile.

We took the old Rolls-Royce and parked it along the street and walked to the park. Tables were set up in front of a small stage, where couples, young and old, were hovering over pints of beer, smiling, talking, whispering things into one another's ears.

"You find us a table," Rex said, kissing my cheek lightly. "I'll go grab the beers."

I chose a table toward the far right and sat down. While I waited for Rex to return, I noticed an older couple sitting at a nearby table. They held hands and gazed into each other's eyes, seeming to speak a language all to themselves.

"For you," Rex said, setting a pint of amber ale in front of me. A bit of the froth had spilled over the side. I slurped it up.

Rex took a drink, then leaned back in his chair. "So I was thinking," he said. "In a novel, would the villain be the secretive housekeeper type—"

"You mean, like Mrs. Dilloway?"

He nodded. "Or a dark horse, like that guy over there." He pointed to an older man in a dark suit seated on the other side of the park. A chocolate Labrador sat at his feet.

"No, never the guy with the dog," I said. "Dogs hint at a person's goodness."

"Not unless it's there to throw the reader off," Rex said. "A way to make a character *seem* good."

"You may be onto something there," I said, taking another sip. "So you're thinking of adding a new character to your novel?"

"Maybe," he said, a little cryptically. "But I do have an idea."

"What?"

He leaned in closer. "What if I start over, write a murder mystery about a family in an old manor house like the very one we're staying in? A mystery that spans generations."

"I think it's brilliant," I said.

Rex planted his chin in his palm and smiled. I loved it when he looked at me that way, as if the earth's very orbit depended on my approval. "Will you help me?"

"Honey, you're the word guy," I said.

"But you're so good at plot," he continued. "Remember how you helped me work out the turning point, where the character leaves New York—"

"And realizes he left behind the love of his life?"

Rex nodded. "The story wouldn't have been the same without that scene."

I shrugged. "I just knew they were meant to be together, that's all. The reader would have hated you for separating them."

"That's just it," Rex said. "You realized that. I didn't."

"Well," I said modestly. "I guess all those years reading Nancy Drew paid off, that or my love of rom coms."

"You have a sixth sense for these things," he said. "And I think, with your help, this novel might be the one."

I squeezed his hand. "Then I'm your girl."

The band took to the stage, and I watched as a man fiddled with the cord attached to his guitar. "Want another beer?" Rex asked.

"Sure."

"Be right back," he said, jumping up from his seat.

I watched him disappear through the crowd to the beer tent. The sun had set, and the candles on the tables lent a warm, orange glow to the surroundings. I admired the old linden tree in the distance. I followed the curve of its branches with my eyes, which is when I noticed a shadowy figure slip behind the tree's trunk. My stomach lurched. *No, it can't be him. . . . Or can it?* I searched the crowd desperately until I saw Rex returning with a beer in each hand and a smile that made my fears momentarily vanish.

The next morning, Rex took to the drawing room with a stack of books he'd found in the bedroom, including one about ladies' fashions in prewar Britain. "You know you're just going to flip right to the lingerie section," I said, grinning.

"Wait, there's a *lingerie* section?" he asked playfully.

I snatched the book from him and flipped to the back, to a page detailing the various kinds of petticoats of the time. "For your reading pleasure," I said, laying the book in his lap.

Rex grinned. "I guess I had something a little *different* in mind when you said 'lingerie.'"

I wanted to take a photo of his face just then. That boyish grin. That look of love, of contentedness. Couldn't he see? We didn't need children to complete us. We were already complete. I had my flowers and plants, and he had his writing. Wasn't that enough? Didn't he love the ebb and flow of our life together just as it was? The way I'd race home for dinner with a basket brimming with vegetables from the market or a handful of herbs from a garden project, eager to read the pages he'd written that day. Didn't he love, as I did, the quiet mornings we spent in our garden, sipping espresso and discussing our latest venture to a flea market in Queens or an antiques shop in Connecticut? Once we carted an enormous painted dresser to a taping of *Antiques Roadshow* only to find that the piece was made in China. I grinned at the memory.

Rex set the book aside and looked up at me. "So, say I set a mystery right here at the manor," he said. "An entirely new book. Who would the cast of characters be?"

"Well," I said, "the overbearing Lord of the house, of course, and his sad, mysterious wife."

Rex scribbled a few notes in his notebook.

I looked out the window to the orchard beyond. "Maybe she spent her time in the gardens because of her sadness? Maybe the flowers gave her a sense of peace."

"I like it," Rex said. "And the housekeeper—she's in on something. Maybe she has a thing for the Lord?"

"Maybe," I said. "There might be others, too. Like the children in the nursery. The other household staff." I eyed the copy of *The Years* I'd left on the side table. "And then there's Flora."

Rex looked momentarily confused. "Flora?"

"Yeah," I said. "I found her name right here in this book."

"Who is she?" Rex asked.

"I don't know. But I'd like to find out."

"Me too," he said, turning back to his notebook.

I heard a rattling sound outside. "The wind is picking up," he said.

I walked to the window and looked outside, where great sheets of rain fell. "Too bad," I said. "I was hoping we could go out to the gardens today."

"Maybe it'll clear up this afternoon," he said.

"I hope," I said, picking up the copy of *The Years*. "I think I'll go upstairs for a while and let you get some research done."

From the stairway, I looked down the hall of the west wing, toward the nursery. I could almost hear the laughter of children of centuries past. Had they been happy here? How could they not have been, with that dollhouse, all the toys, and the well-stocked bookcase?

I turned toward the east wing, where a mahogany double door beckoned on the right. I hadn't noticed this room before; Mrs. Dilloway had skipped the east wing when we toured the manor. I walked closer, looking around me before placing my hand on the knob. I turned it, slowly, unsure whether it was locked. To my surprise, it wasn't.

The door creaked a little as I pushed it open and slipped past the threshold. Inside, the air felt cold on my skin, and I shivered as the room came into focus. I wished Rex were standing beside me. The drapes had been pulled shut, but I could see, even in the dim light, that this bedroom had once belonged to a woman—a woman of great importance. Not a single ripple was evident on the lace-trimmed floral bedspread, and the large wardrobe on the opposite wall had been propped open, revealing an array of gowns inside.

I walked to the dressing table, examining a set of brushes and a mirror engraved with the letters AML. Had this been Lady Anna's private chamber? I looked at myself in the old mirror, which had a jagged crack at the center. Had Lady Anna looked at her reflection in this very same mirror the day she died? I touched my finger to the lightning-bolt crack in the glass.

I could still hear the rain falling outside. It pelted the window glass. And as a gust of wind howled through the cracks of the trim, a distinct floral scent hit my nose—the heady, musky scent of lilac, maybe—as if there might be a woman standing there behind me, a woman who had recently spritzed perfume on the nape of her neck. My heart beat wildly in my chest as I spun around, which is when I noticed the vase of flowers on the dresser. Freshly cut peonies and a few sprigs of purple lilac peeked out of a large crystal vase. Had Mrs. Dilloway left them here? Why? For whom?

I walked to the dresser to have a closer look, and I saw a book resting atop a lace cloth. Larger than a diary, it appeared to be a scrapbook or album of some sort, with various items tucked inside. I turned to the first page and squinted to read the handwritten inscription: "The Camellias of Livingston Manor; Compiled by Anna Livingston."

My eyes widened. Inside were dozens of pressed blossoms. Faded and paper-thin, each had been glued to its own page alongside handwritten accounts of the date and origin, with detailed planting and care information. Beside the "Petelo Camellia" bloom, Lady Anna had inscribed: "Edward surprised me with this little tree on my birthday. It came from Vietnam, where it was found in a low-lying forest at the foot of a mountain. Its bright yellow petals cheered me instantly. It reminded me of one I saw in the conservatory in Charleston so many years ago."

So Lord Livingston had brought her rare camellias to cheer her up. Why had she needed cheering? I was fascinated by the variety of camellias in the book. Reds, pinks, whites. Variegated hybrids. Camellias from all over the world.

I paid particular attention to the notes that edged each page. "Didn't get sufficient sunlight in the north end of the garden. Moved to west, where soil is better. More drainage." Suddenly a peculiar pattern emerged. Every top right corner was marked with a series of numbers. I flipped back to the Petelo's page and studied the code: 5:3:31:2:1. Below it, letters spelled out "L. sussex Hertzberg." Botanical taxonomy code, probably. But these words didn't apply to this camellia or any camellias I knew of.

I read through the book, until I came to the last page, which had been torn out. The only proof of its existence was a jagged remnant. *Who took it? Why?* Anna's book had been meticulously put together. Surely, she hadn't torn the page.

I heard footsteps on the staircase outside, and I hurried back out to the hallway, closing the door carefully behind me. I tucked the book under my arm as I walked back down the corridor to the staircase, which is when I nearly collided with Mrs. Dilloway.

"Ms. Sinclair," she said, readjusting the rose stems in her hand. "May I . . . help you?"

"Yes," I stammered, attempting to obscure the book from her view. "I mean, no. I'm fine."

"Of course," she said with a tinge of suspicion in her voice.

I ran back to the bedroom and was happy to find Rex seated on the bed inside. "There you are," he said, looking up from his book.

"I was in the east wing," I said, sitting down beside him. "I found a room."

"Oh?" His curiosity was piqued.

"I went inside. It was open. Rex, it was the strangest thing. It had to have been Lady Anna's room. Mrs. Dilloway keeps it as if she's still alive. All her clothes, her things. Even fresh flowers in the vase."

"Now *that* is creepy," he said.

"I know." I set the camellia book on the bed. "And look what I found."

"What is it?" he asked, taking the book into his hands.

"She kept a record of all the camellias on the property, with the strangest notations. And see the last page? It's been torn out."

Rex studied the book for a moment, then shrugged. "Maybe one of the camellias died and she didn't need to keep the page?"

I shook my head. "No, some of the others died in a snowstorm in 1934," I said. "See, look at this one. It says so right here on this page. This is different."

He scratched his head and then froze as he was struck with an idea. "What if this is some sort of code?"

"That's what I was thinking," I said. "You know, this could all turn out to be one pretty fantastic novel."

Rex smiled at me suddenly. "Thanks," he said.

"For what?"

"For believing in me. You know my parents hate this novel thing. They'd much rather I go back to the investment firm."

"But you were miserable in that job," I said. Rex's happiness, however, wasn't exactly at the top of his parents' list of priorities. In their view, a successful executive befitted the Sinclair name; a struggling novelist did not.

"Well," I said, "see what they say when you hit the *New York Times* bestseller list."

Rex grinned. "We've almost burned through our savings," he said. "I guess I'll have to figure out a backup plan if this book thing doesn't pan out." He shrugged.

I shook my head. "No. Give it more time. My business is taking off. And"—I paused to choose my words carefully—"your parents would always help if it came to that."

"I won't take their money," he said. It was a sore spot with him. After they'd bought us the townhouse in New York, there were strings attached. My father used to always say, "I brought you into this world, and I can take you out." But with Rex's parents, it was more like, "I gave you a life of privilege, and I can take it all away." They meant well, of course. But there were expectations to visit the family at Christmas and Easter and again for his grandmother's birthday. That was manageable, I suppose. But when his mother suggested that he convert me to the Anglican Church (she even sent him a membership card in the mail, partially filled out with my name at the top), he drew the line.

"I won't let them help us," he said proudly. "I know it might sound idealist, but when we have children . . . I mean, if we have children, I want them to know that their parents worked for what they have."

I looked at my feet. "Rex, but I thought we decided—"

"Decided what?"

I sighed. "That we were going to table that discussion for now."

"I can't, Addie," he said. "I want children—with the woman I love. I can't deny that. And I don't want to act as if it doesn't matter to me."

I stood up and walked to the window, my heart beating faster.

"I wish you'd tell me," he said.

I spun around. "Tell you what?"

His eyes clouded with worry. "What it is you're keeping from me," he said. "Sometimes I watch you while you're sleeping, and I think that if I stare at you long enough, I'll be able to read your mind."

We'd had this conversation dozens of times before, of course.

I'd managed to appease him each time. I'd tell him things that made him feel better, that it wasn't him, but me. That I couldn't picture myself as a mom, and I didn't think motherhood was for everyone. But when I looked him in the eye, I know he didn't buy it. I know he believed there was more to the story. And there was.

I turned away. I couldn't hold his gaze for fear that my eyes would project the hurt, the pain I kept buried inside. Sometimes I suspected that Rex *could* read my mind, as evidenced by small, silly moments, when he'd finish my sentences or come home with spring rolls and pad Thai at the precise moment I was dialing the restaurant for takeout. And then there was his uncanny knack for knowing when I was getting a migraine. Could he read my mind now? Could he see the anguish I'd kept hidden for half of my life?

He stood up and reached for his messenger bag. I turned around and watched him tuck his notebook and a few books inside. "I think I'll head to that café in town and do a little writing there," he said.

I nodded. I hated seeing him hurt, but I didn't know what else to say. I could only watch as he slung the bag over his shoulder and walked out to the hallway, closing the door with a gentle click behind him.

I laid my head on the pillow, thinking about Rex for a long time, before I heard my laptop chime from the bedside table. Rex's parents had wired the room for Internet use, and I'd almost forgotten that I'd plugged in the laptop the night before. I lifted the computer into my lap and pulled up my e-mail account. There was a message from a client and one from my assistant, Cara, letting me know that the butterfly garden had been successfully installed. She had attached a photo. The astilbes had been planted too close together, but besides that, she'd pulled it off.

I didn't want to think of my own life then, so I let my mind turn to the gardens of Livingston Manor, in particular the camellias and the book kept by Lady Anna. I decided to compose an e-mail to one of my former professors, Louise Clark, director of horticultural studies at New York University. Last fall we'd exchanged e-mails about a rare pink lilac that had turned up in the garden of one of my clients in Brooklyn. Maybe she knew something about camellias.

Hi, Louise,

How are you? I'm spending the summer in England with my husband, Rex, at a manor owned by his parents. It's gorgeous, and absolutely otherworldly. You wouldn't believe the gardens, in particular the old camellia orchard out back. That's what I'm writing about. I found an old book here, with information about the camellias planted on the grounds. I recognized most of them. Some are quite rare. I'll have to send photos if this rain ever stops. In the meantime, I have two questions: 1) Have you heard of a variety called the AnnaMaria Bellweather? I didn't recognize the name, and the bloom is gorgeous—a big pink blossom with a dark pink center. And 2) You don't, by chance, know anything about any rare varieties that might have turned up in England in the 1920s or '30s? Anything I should keep my eyes out for? I don't know where I'm going with this— just a hunch. A page was torn out of the garden scrapbook. I can't help but wonder if it recorded an important variety. Anyway, I hope this note makes sense. I'm jet-lagged. Thanks so much, Louise! Warmest wishes from England, Addison

P.S. Oh, forgot to mention: On each page, there is the strangest code next to the flower entries. For instance, on the Petelo, there are the numbers "5:3:31:2:1." And below it are the words "L. sussex Hertzberg." Any idea what this could mean?

I sent the e-mail and then turned back to the camellia book, reading through its pages again, until I heard my computer chime fifteen minutes later. I eagerly opened Louise's response.

> Hi, Addison! So good to hear from you. This will be a quick reply since I'm off to a meeting with the board shortly, but I couldn't resist writing you back. Your discovery is an exciting one, indeed. First, I did a search for the AnnaMaria Bellweather in the database, and it appears to be a variety named after a woman from Charleston in the early 1900s. From what I know, all the debutantes wanted camellias named after them. It was considered a great social honor. But there were only so many to go around. This Miss Anna Bellweather must have been quite something. As for your other question— the rare camellias—oh yes. There is one in particular that you must Google. The Middlebury Pink. About fifteen years ago there was some renewed interest. I'm recalling an article in the *Telegraph*, I think. You'll have to poke around. But anyway, it's believed to be extinct. Maybe it is, maybe it isn't. But what a coup if you were able to locate it! A plant lover's dream! As for your botanical code, you have me stumped. I thought it might be Vienna code, which was used more often in England early in the century, but it doesn't quite make sense. It must be a personal way of referencing plants that the gardener used. As for the "L. sussex Hertzberg," I can't find any reference in any of the databases. A mystery! Now, off to finish these papers. Best wishes, Louise
>
> P.S. Keep me posted!

I immediately pulled up Google and typed in the words *Middlebury Pink*. Hundreds of entries came back. I combed through the articles, learning all I could about the stunning variety with white petals tipped with pink. It appeared in botanical history books, but its existence had eluded gardeners for decades, and many considered it merely a myth. And then, in a blog post written by a botanist at the London Conservatory, I read that the last known variety had been seen at Livingston Manor in the 1930s.

I ran to the window, looking out at the orchard, where the misty air clung to the hillside. Had the Middlebury Pink survived after all these years?

"Hey," Rex said as we walked in from the driveway late that afternoon. I had gone out to greet him. "You wouldn't believe the research I packed in today."

I grinned. "Oh?" I was happy to see him smiling again after the difficult conversation we'd had earlier.

"Yeah," he said. "I think I've completely mapped out the setting for this book." He touched his index finger to his forehead, as if remembering some detail. "And you know what? The strangest thing happened in town today."

"What?"

"I met a guy from *New York*," he said. "From the Bronx."

I shivered. It had to be a coincidence.

"I wish I could remember his name," he continued. "It was Tom or Shawn, or something like that. He said he was here visiting an old girlfriend. Anyway, small world, huh?"

"Yeah," I said, nodding, feeling the old terror creep back.

In an instant, my mind turned to the summer of 1985, to the night that changed my life forever. I had just turned fifteen. It was hot, unbearably so. The leaves on the floor of Greenhouse No. 4 at the New York Botanical Garden crunched under my feet. Sean handed me a shovel and said, "Dig."

"You OK, honey?" Rex asked, placing a hand on my arm.

I blinked hard, quickly pulling myself together. "Yeah," I said, clutching my stomach. "I don't think I'm quite used to these rich English meals, that's all."

Rex nodded. "You need some air. You've been cooped up in the house all day." He reached for the newspaper on the side table near the door and tucked it under his arm. "Let's go sit on the terrace for a while."

I followed him outside, where we nestled into two chairs under an awning. The rain had finally stopped, and the ground seemed to ooze gray mist. Rex thumbed open the newspaper, and looked up a moment later. "Look at this," he said. "Our little village seems to be the center of an unsolved mystery. A girl from Clivebrook went missing in 1931." He pointed to a black-and-white photo of a young woman with dark hair and kind eyes. "Apparently this is the anniversary of her disappearance."

"How sad," I said, taking the newspaper in my hands. "And creepy." I read the caption. "Lila Hertzberg, abducted on the second of January in 1931, was never found." *Hertzberg. Where have I heard that name before?*

Rex looked up from his book. "I know. It sounds like Clivebrook had its very own Jack the Ripper back in the day. I was talking to the owner of the café yesterday, and he said there were other women who disappeared in the 1930s," he said. "One named Elsie. I had a babysitter by that name when I was young. She used to get into my mom's boxed wine after we were in bed." He smiled to lighten the mood. "I don't know what I find more disturbing, the unsolved abductions or the boxed wine."

I forced a smile as a raven dipped down from the sky and landed on a stone urn on the terrace, boldly cawing at us like a ghost from my past. I clapped my hands together and the bird retreated, defiantly.

Rex's cell phone began ringing, and he pulled it from his pocket. "Better get this," he said, walking along the pathway toward the front of the house. He waved to me as he pressed the phone to his ear, a gesture that said, *I'll only be a minute*. I listened as his voice trailed off, getting fainter with each step. "Did you find it?" he asked. "Good. I'm coming over now. I want to see this. . . . Yes, of course. . . . No, she doesn't. . . ."

When Rex was out of sight, I decided to go back inside. The breeze had picked up, and I needed a sweater. I passed a stack of mail on the entryway hutch. A tan envelope caught my eye. In the upper left-hand corner, I read the name "Lord Nicholas Livingston." Wasn't that one of the children who had lived here? It was addressed to my father-in-law. Surely, Rex's father wouldn't mind my opening it—it could contain important information that he needed to know about. I picked it up and walked to the drawing room, casting a glance toward the door before running my hand along the edge of the envelope to tear it, hastily pulling out the letter inside.

To Mr. Sinclair:

I am Nicholas Livingston, a former resident of Livingston Manor. There's something of great importance that I would like to speak to you about. If you would kindly ring me at my office in London, we can discuss the matter. Please don't speak a word about our correspondence to the household staff, especially Mrs. Dilloway.

Best regards,

Nicholas Livingston

What could he possibly have to say to my in-laws, and why didn't he want it shared with Mrs. Dilloway? I heard footsteps behind me and hastily tucked the letter into the pocket of my jeans before I turned around to find Mrs. Dilloway in the doorway.

"Oh, hi," I said nervously.

"Do you and Mr. Sinclair prefer dinner served at six or six-thirty tonight?"

"Oh, no," I said. "I meant to talk to you about that. We're going to grab dinner in town tonight."

"Yes, of course," she said stiffly, before holding up an envelope. "This came for you."

"For me?" I asked, as she handed me a FedEx envelope. I eyed the label, with an overnight sticker on the edge. "I don't understand," I continued. "I didn't tell anyone I was going to be here."

The old woman looked at me curiously before turning toward the door. "Well, I'll leave you now," she said.

I sat on the sofa and held the envelope in my hands, waiting for the click of her heels to fade before I tore the flap open. My heart beat faster. I had recognized the handwriting on the envelope and felt the familiar sick feeling in my stomach. *How did he find me here?* Inside was a slip of ruled paper, the kind with frayed edges, torn carelessly from a spiral-bound notebook. *"Hello, Amanda."*

I crumpled the page and leaned my head back against the sofa, remembering, as much as I desperately wanted to forget.

Fifteen Years Prior

"State your age for the record," the officer said to me, emotionless. He sat at a gray steel desk, piled high with folders. A phone rang insistently, but he ignored it. "Miss Barton," he said again. "Please do not waste my time. You can see I'm very busy here."

I looked at my feet.

"I'll ask you again, and if you don't cooperate, it's juvenile detention for you," he barked. I recognized that familiar tone, just like my father's. The anger that went zero to sixty in seconds, the transformation into a monster. When I was little, I didn't know what brought it on, or how it happened. He would be normal one moment, and the next, he'd be tugging at his belt, chasing after me with that wild look in his eye. Mama said he was sick. Still, it didn't give him permission to do what he did.

"You runaways never learn," the officer said. "You think life's more exciting on the streets, but then you mess up, and we have to institutionalize you." He tapped his pen on the side of the steel desk. "Just in case you're hard of hearing, I'll give you one more chance to explain yourself, before you get juvenile detention—this time for sixty days. State your birth date for the record."

I picked at my bleeding fingernails, gnawed down past the nail beds. Couldn't he see that I *wanted* to be sent to juvie? I looked him straight in the eye and didn't say a word.

He slammed his clipboard on the desk and stood up. "Stan! Book her!"

"Oh, there you are," Rex said. "Sorry I took so long."

"I'm in no rush," I said a little defensively. "Anyway, who was on the phone?"

"Just my father's business manager. I have to sign off on some architectural renderings for the house."

"Oh," I said.

"Hey, why don't we go see the gardens? The sun's out, finally, and I know the walk will cheer you up."

"I'd love that," I said, smiling again. "Let me grab my jacket."

I tucked my cell phone and the camellia book into my backpack and followed Rex out onto the terrace that led to the garden pathway. The boxwood hedges that lined the walkway had been sorely neglected over the years, but I tried to imagine what they would have looked like in their prime—clipped into perfect submission, no doubt. Now, however, they appeared overgrown and ragged—bushy in some places, yellowed and anemic-looking in others. Poor things, like old ladies deprived of weekly visits to the hair salon. I longed to get my hands on a hedge trimmer and give them a haircut.

Yes, the property had become overgrown, but there was so much promise here. Good bones, as they said about houses. With a bit of pruning and replanting in places, the gardens could be grand again. My fingers practically itched to get started.

Rex and I followed the path past an ailing rose garden, but I stopped for a moment to pluck a sprig of ivy that threatened to suffocate an old tea rose. In theory, ivy is quaint, charming even. But I'd seen too many gardens destroyed by the vine, which has become an invasive weed in some parts of the world. It creeps in slowly and then quietly covers flower beds with its snakelike tendrils until all the life below has been snuffed out. I knelt down to plunge my fingers into the soil below the rose's overgrown canes, which probably hadn't been pruned in at least a decade, until I found the base of the ivy's root. Stubborn and determined, it held on tightly, but I fought harder, pulling until I held the entire scraggly root in my hand. Invasive plants were like all evil things; the only way to ensure that they wouldn't return was to face them head-on, battle it out, and win. Anything else was only a temporary fix. I sighed, thinking of my own life. I was letting the weeds grow all over me. They were threatening my happiness and, in some ways, my life. So why couldn't I face them?

"Can't resist a little weeding, can you?" Rex said with a smile.

I stood back to examine my work. "That's better," I said.

When the sun disappeared behind a cloud, the horizon took on a dark cast. I felt a raindrop on my cheek and quickly pulled the hood of my jacket over my head before we trudged down a soft slope, lower into the valley of the property. I stopped when my eyes met a stone statue nearly completely covered by ivy. I set down my bag and pulled the vines aside.

"Here, I'll help you," Rex said. Together we uncovered the face of a stone angel. Rex untangled the ivy's clutch on her wings, and I pulled the vines free from her body. "There you are," I said to the stone beauty. "That's got to feel better." Before I stood up, I noticed a few sprigs of purple pushing out near the base of the statue. I leaned in to have a closer look. Deadly nightshade, or rather, *Atropa belladonna*. "Rex!" I said.

He leaned in closer. "What is it?"

"It's called *Atropa belladonna*," I explained. "It's a highly poisonous plant." I remembered the story of a gardener who had been hospitalized after accidently rubbing his eye with a finger contaminated with the nightshade's sap. Even in small doses, the plant was noxious, and potentially lethal. "Remind me to tell your parents to keep an eye out for this." Rex's younger sister had small children.

The wind picked up. I felt it seep through my coat, and I shivered.

"Should we turn back?" Rex asked.

"No," I said. "Let's see the camellias." Past their normal blooming season, the trees had shed many of their blossoms, but the ones that remained were vibrant and showy, like the finale of a fireworks show. Up close, the trees did not disappoint. I stared up in awe at a yellow blossom, touching its petals lightly and breathing in the balmy, lemony scent. I pulled out Anna's book, flipping to the page with the Petelo camellia.

"Do you think this is it?" Rex asked.

I nodded, studying the notes Lady Anna had left, before comparing the petal structure. "This has to be it," I said. "But this numeric code? What do you think it means?" 5:3:31:2:1. "Maybe a location?" I counted the rows of trees, five in total. "Yeah, this is the fifth row, if you count from the east." I turned around to reassess my bearings.

"And the tree is third from the front," Rex said, his eyes meeting mine. "I think we cracked it."

"Almost," I said. "But what do the last numbers mean?" I walked to the next tree, stopping to admire its dark, emerald green leaves, so shiny and smooth. I picked up a pink blossom that had recently fallen to the ground and referred to the book again. The AnnaMaria Bellweather. But there were only two digits beside it—5:4—and no cryptic botanical name. "This doesn't make any sense," I said to Rex.

We walked through each row of trees. Some had fared better than others, and I paused to touch the carcass of a tree that appeared to have burned at some point in its history. Its bare, jagged branches had been charred on one side. Probably lightning. I hoped it wasn't the Middlebury Pink.

"Drat," Rex said when the rain began to increase in intensity. He pointed to an old outbuilding in the distance, and we ran to it, taking cover under its eaves. The roof sagged with moss, and the old rusty weather vane creaked on its axis. I peered through the dark window, using the sleeve of my jacket to wipe away the condensation so I could get a better look, which is when I thought I detected movement inside. "Hello?" I said, hearing my heart pound inside my chest.

"What is it?" Rex asked.

"Honey, I think there's someone in there."

He looked spooked, but I could tell he was putting up a brave front. "Nah," he said.

I recoiled when I thought I heard door hinges creak. Frightened, I turned back to the pathway, picking up my pace to a sprint and then tripping on the root of a tree. I let out a cry of pain as I landed on my elbow.

"Addison!" Rex called from behind me. "Are you OK?"

Blood dripped from my arm when Rex found me a moment later. "Oh, honey, you're hurt."

"Sorry," I said from the safety of the hillside. I could see the roof of the outbuilding below. Its sagging moss roof practically blended into the orchard. "I got a little spooked."

"Come on," he said, helping me up. "Let's get you bandaged up."

Rex and I left our muddy shoes by the door, and walked to the foyer, where I hung up my coat.

"I see you've been out in the gardens," Mrs. Dilloway said from the stairway.

"Yes, we have," Rex said. "Though it wasn't the best day for a walk."

"No," Mrs. Dilloway said. "Not at all."

I felt her eyes boring into me as we walked to the stairs. And then it hit me. *Hertzberg.*

I spun around. "Rex, did you leave the newspaper on the terrace?"

"I think so," he replied.

Mrs. Dilloway shook her head. "I brought it in when it began to rain," she said, pointing to the side table. "There."

A few raindrops had soaked the paper, but I could still make out the type. I tucked it under my arm and walked toward the stairs. I didn't stop until Rex and I had made it to the second floor and had closed the bedroom door behind us. I laid the newspaper out on the bed, and set the camellia book beside it. The article stated that Lila Hertzberg had been abducted on the second of January in 1931. I turned to the Petelo page in the camellia book. The remaining digits read "31:2:1." I gasped. *It must be a date.* I scanned the article, reading about Lila Hertzberg. She was born in Sussex. *Sussex.* I reread the cryptic botanical name below the code: *L. sussex Hertzberg.* Rex's eyes met mine. "My God," I said, shaking my head gravely. "What have we just found?"

That night, Rex took me to Milton's, the pub in the village. "What will it be, spiced beef sandwich or fish and chips?" he said, setting the menu down.

"Well, I know what you're getting," I said, smiling as I pushed the menu aside and took a sip of the wine that the waiter had just uncorked and poured. Rex could never pass up the fish and chips.

Neither of us could shake the discovery we'd made in the garden today. "Rex, I don't know what to make of things in the orchard."

"Me either," he said, rubbing his head. "But do you think the abductor would really lay out this information?"

"I don't know," I said, taking another sip of wine. "Maybe it's his calling card." I nodded to myself. "Or maybe Lady Anna was trying to piece it all together."

"I'd vote for the latter," he said. "Maybe she knew something sinister was going on at the manor. Maybe she was looking for clues, and she found them in the orchard."

I refolded the napkin in my lap. "Do you think Mrs. Dilloway knows anything?"

"Oh, I'm sure she does," Rex said. "She's lived at the manor so long, she's bound to know something."

I sighed. "But getting her to talk is the real challenge. I've never met anyone so tight-lipped."

"Hey," he said. "Let's take off our detective hats for a bit and enjoy the night." He reached for my hand. "What do you say?"

"OK," I said, cracking a smile.

He drew my arm toward him and ran his finger lightly against my skin until he stopped at my watch. "You know something crazy?" he asked, cocking his head to the right. "I don't think I've ever seen your bare wrist."

I pulled my hand back instinctively.

He looked momentarily astonished. "I've just realized that I've seen every square inch of you," he said, before slipping his finger between my wrist and my watch, "but I've never seen *this* wrist."

I sat up quickly, tucking my arm behind my back. "Of course you've seen it."

"Just the same," he said, gently pulling my arm back to him. His intentions were romantic, playful, and yet they struck all the wrong chords. "Let's take it off." He fingered the clasp of the watch, pulling it away from my skin enough to reveal the scars I so desperately wanted to keep hidden. "My God," he said, gasping. "What happened?"

"Nothing," I said, snatching my hand back. "They're . . . just chicken pox scars."

"Oh," he said, still taken aback. "I didn't know you had the chicken pox."

"Well, I did," I said, grateful to see the waiter coming with our dinner. "And now you know."

CHAPTER 10

"**K**nock, knock." Mrs. Dilloway peered into my room. I'd
left the door cracked, not wanting to appear reclusive.
The children were busy with their lessons, so I decided to take
the opportunity to write a letter home. Mama and Papa would
be eager to hear that I'd arrived safely. I set my pen and stationery aside and looked up at the door.

"Oh, hi," I said, tucking the pen and paper inside the desk
drawer.

"Do you have everything you need?"

"Yes," I replied, gathering courage to inquire about the
gardens. "I was just wondering if . . . well . . . if I might gather
some of the camellias for an arrangement," I continued. "Before they're finished blooming."

"I'd advise against that," she said quickly. Before I could
offer a reply, she clasped her hands together. "Now, since our
tour was interrupted, shall we continue?"

"Thank you," I said. "Yes."

Upstairs, Mrs. Dilloway led me past the drawing room,
pointing out the broom closet, where she said Nicholas

sometimes hid, and the dumbwaiter, where Janie was known to disappear to from time to time. We walked by the dining room, the parlor, the sitting room, and then made our way up the stairs to the nursery. It was a grand room, with enormous leaded glass windows overlooking the gardens and rolling hillside. I imagined them flung open in the summertime, with the floral scent of the gardens wafting in. I walked past a dollhouse as tall as Katherine, nearly tripping on a wooden block.

"Mind your step," Mrs. Dilloway said. "The children are dreadful about picking up after themselves."

I eyed a large bookcase to my right. "Do they like stories?"

"They used to," she said.

I pulled a picture book from the shelf. "Oh, I adore Beatrix Potter," I said. "Do you think they'd like me to read to them?"

Mrs. Dilloway shrugged. "You could try. But the last nanny didn't have much luck."

I sat down on the sofa near the bookshelf. "May I ask you something?"

"Of course."

"Is there something I need to know, about what happened to their mother? Sadie said that—"

"You'd do well to not listen to housemaid gossip, Miss Lewis," she said, frowning. "Rehashing the past will do nothing for the children. They've been through a lot this past year, more than children should have to endure."

I nodded.

She turned to face me as I stood up. "Shall we continue on?"

"Yes," I said, following her out the door.

We walked along a dark corridor. "These are the children's bedrooms," she said. "The girls' rooms are here, and the boys occupy the rooms on the right."

I counted five doors. "This other room," I said, walking to the last room on the right and reaching for the doorknob. "Whose is this?"

Mrs. Dilloway's hand reached the knob before mine. "Just a spare bedroom," she said quickly, turning to another flight of stairs.

"But what about the hall down there?" I asked, pointing to a dark corridor ahead.

She looked thoughtful. "The east wing belonged to Lady Anna," she said, appearing lost in memories. "Her bedroom, dressing room, and study."

"Oh," I said, embarrassed by my inquiry. "I, I—"

"It's fine," Mrs. Dilloway said. "You ought to know, for the children's sake. They used to love to greet her there in the mornings. It used to drive his Lordship mad the way she'd let them jump on the bed. She was never formal like him."

As she spoke, her eyes looked sad, distant. I longed to know more about Lady Anna. I peered down the corridor, feeling a magnetic pull. Before I could advance, I felt Mrs. Dilloway's cold hand on my wrist.

"Please," she said, indicating the staircase that led to the third floor. "There's something I need to show you."

I followed her up the stairs, gazing up at the domed ceiling, with its ornate trim work and painted murals depicting angels, animals, and the countryside in bloom. *What must it be like for the children, to live in a veritable museum?*

Mrs. Dilloway indicated a door ahead. "Miss Lewis, can I trust you with a secret?"

"Of course," I said, a little confused.

When we got to the door, she produced a brass key from the pocket of her dress and inserted it into the lock. "It's a bit stiff," she said. The lock released and she turned the knob. The door creaked loudly as she opened it. "The hinges have gotten a little rusty over the years." Her voice was thick with disappointment. "It's this blasted country air. It's a wonder we're not all rusted to our cores."

I stared ahead, beyond the doorway and Mrs. Dilloway. "Come in, Miss Lewis," she said, sensing my hesitation.

A ray of light beamed into the dim hallway, and she looked both ways, cautiously. "Quickly," she said. "We mustn't be seen."

As soon as I stepped inside the space, Mrs. Dilloway closed the door behind us with a hurried click. Light streamed down through the glass roof overhead. I followed her into the space, pushing a wayward vine from my view. It immediately sprung back and cheekily smacked me in the face. "What is this place?" I asked, in awe.

"The conservatory," she said, then lowered her voice. "Lady Anna's conservatory." She walked a few paces farther. "It's quite a sight, isn't it?"

I was too awestruck to speak. Vines of bright pink flowers danced over a wrought-iron arbor. I recognized them immediately as the very same variety, bougainvillea, that grew in Greenhouse No. 4 at the New York Botanical Garden. Just beyond, two potted trees stood at attention—a lemon, its shiny yellow globes glistening in the sunlight, and what looked like an orange, studded with the tiniest fruit I'd ever seen.

"What is this?" I asked, fascinated.

"A kumquat," she said. "Lady Anna used to pick them for the children." She reached out to pluck one of the tiny oranges from the tree. "Here, try for yourself."

I held it in my hand, admiring its smooth, shiny skin.

I sank my teeth into the flesh of the fruit. Its thin skin disintegrated in my mouth, releasing a burst of sweet and sour that made my eyes shoot open and a smile spread across my face. "Oh, my," I said. "I've never had anything like it."

Mrs. Dilloway nodded. "You should try the clementines, then. They're Persian."

I walked a few paces farther, admiring the potted orchids—at least a hundred specimens, so exquisite they looked like Southern belles in hoop skirts. On the far wall were variegated ferns, bleeding hearts, and a lilac tree I could smell from the other end of the room.

Mrs. Dilloway watched me quietly. "She would have liked you," she said. "Lady Anna."

I gave her a quizzical look.

"She didn't care for most of the nannies," she said. "It's why I've brought you here," she continued. "I need your help."

"With what?"

"Sit," she said, indicating a stone bench to our left. I obeyed, and she sat next to me. "You see," she continued, looking around at the expansive conservatory. "After her death, Lord Livingston hasn't been able to face this place. He gave all of the servants strict instructions to leave it be."

"But the plants," I said, covering my mouth, "they'll all die."

She nodded. "I couldn't live with myself knowing that Lady Anna's prized flowers and plants were perishing right above our heads. Besides, I made Lady Anna a promise, and I'm bound to that."

"What did you promise?"

She smiled to herself, a sad, private smile. "To look after her gardens." She sighed. "It hasn't been easy." She placed her hand over her heart. "Do you know anything about flowers, Miss Lewis?"

"Yes," I said quickly, before worrying that I might sound too eager. "I mean, a little."

"Good," she said, sighing.

I followed a vine with my eyes. It had crept along the wall up to the glass ceiling. "Passionflower?" I said, pointing up at it.

Mrs. Dilloway nodded. "She loved to see it in bloom."

"I can't understand why Lord Livingston would want to be rid of all this beauty," I said, entranced.

She clasped her hands together. "Sometimes I think that when Lady Anna passed, his Lordship felt that all the beauty in the world had died with her. He can't so much as look at a flower in the garden these days. He asked Mr. Humphrey to take out the tulips, and I fear that the camellias are next."

I gasped. "He wouldn't destroy them, would he?" I said, picking a yellowed leaf from the ground and crinkling it between my fingers.

"I don't know," she said, standing up. "But I haven't the time to tend to it anymore with the pressing needs of this household. I need you to look after it. Water the plants. See to it that weeds don't take over. Prune back the branches now and then, that sort of thing."

My eyes widened. In some ways, it was a dream come true. A conservatory filled with exotic plants at my disposal? But the responsibility was too great. I stood up, shaking my head in polite protest. "Mrs. Dilloway, I'm really not suited for the job. I only have an amateur knowledge of plants."

She ran her hand along the edge of a light green fern, so delicate it looked like a swath of French lace. "Lady Anna didn't have a stitch of botanical training either," she said. "But she loved these plants like they were her children. She listened to them. She let them teach her. That's all you need to do." She turned to me. "Can I count on you?"

I took a deep breath. "Well, I—"

"Good," she said. "The water spigot is over there. Pruning shears are in the closet. Careful not to bang about. His Lordship could hear you. His bedroom and terrace are directly below."

My heart beat faster at the thought of being found skulking around his dead wife's forbidden garden. "Maybe I shouldn't—"

"Oh," Mrs. Dilloway continued, "there's one more thing. One of Lady Anna's necklaces, a locket, has been missing since her death. I always thought I'd find it here, but it hasn't turned up. If you see it, well, bring it to me immediately."

"Yes," I said. "Yes, of course."

She turned back toward the door, and I followed as she walked past the citrus trees, which gave off a sweet, heady scent in the sunlight. She paused to pluck a few kumquats before passing through the flower-covered archway and continuing on to the door. As she reached for the doorknob, I tapped her shoulder. "The necklace," I whispered, sensing that there might be more to the story, perhaps much more. "Why is it so important?"

She looked at me for a long moment. "It's not so much the necklace itself," she said, "but what's inside it."

I nodded.

"Here," she said, reaching and tucking the kumquats into the pocket of my dress. "For later."

I smiled.

"Don't speak a word of this, now," she said. "To anyone."

I followed her down the staircase, where Mr. Beardsley stood in the foyer. "Mrs. Dilloway," he said, wiping his brow with a handkerchief. "Come quick. There's been a *situation*."

CHAPTER 11

Addison

My eyes shot open at two a.m. I sat up, gasping for breath. In my dream, I saw Sean again. I looked over at Rex, sleeping peacefully beside me. *It's just a dream. It's only a dream.* But when I closed my eyes, all I could see was his face.

Fifteen Years Prior

My aunt Jean lit a cigarette in the car and blew a cloud of smoke toward me. "You don't say much, do you?"

I folded my arms, gazing through the smoky air out the window at the trees along the roadside.

"Well," she said, "you'll like New York City." She wore a blue bandanna around her head. Turquoise earrings dangled from her ears. Before she died, Mama had called her older sister a hippie. She took another puff of her cigarette and smiled. "The apartment's small," she continued, "but it'll grow on you in time."

She meant well, I knew that. She hadn't had to take me in

when the caseworker discovered the situation at home. After Mama had died, Daddy started drinking.

"I heard what he did to you," Jean said cautiously. "Sweet child. You've been through so much."

"He didn't mean it," I said quickly, touching the scar on my temple. "It was the booze."

"Well," she said. "Nobody's going to hurt you anymore."

I nodded, wondering about New York City. I'd never ventured far from our home in the Adirondack Mountains. Mama had been afraid of the city and the people who lived there. I studied the tattoo on Jean's forearm, a butterfly. They were as different as two sisters could be.

"Listen," she said, extinguishing her cigarette on the dash. An ember of ash rolled onto the carpet. I pushed the tip of my shoe against it. "You know you can talk to me, don't you? About anything."

I bit my lip and nodded.

We passed cow pastures, a church, and a junkyard with hundreds of rusted-out cars splayed out along the road. "My sister and I weren't close," she said. "You know that, of course. God, to think of what she must have told you about me." She sighed. "Well, that's all behind us. Now I only hope that we can be friends." She turned her eyes from the road to me briefly and smiled.

I turned back to the window. We drove for another hour, maybe more. I must have dozed off, because when I opened my eyes, tall buildings stood outside the car window. "We're almost home," Jean said. "I'm glad you got some shut-eye."

She pulled the car in front of a brick building. A shirtless man sat on a stoop smoking a cigarette. He shouted something at a woman walking by. A dog barked in the distance.

I reached for my backpack on the floor and clutched it tightly as I stepped out of the car, following Jean up the steps in front of the building to a stairwell, where a crushed Coke can lay in the corner next to a crumpled bag from McDonald's. A fly buzzed around me, and I swatted it away. The smell of urine lingered.

"We're six floors up," Jean said. "The elevator's been out for a year. It's a hike, but you'll get used to it in time."

Out of breath, I followed Jean out of the stairwell onto the sixth floor. She stopped at a door halfway down the hall and inserted a key. "Mama's home," she called into the apartment. Until that moment, it hadn't occurred to me that Aunt Jean ever had children. If she had, my mother had never spoken of them.

A cat leapt off of the back of a couch, and Jean scooped the ball of fur into her arms. Near the door, the contents of a plastic grocery bag spilled out onto the floor—disposable baby diapers and a bag of apples. "Sean!" she screamed. "Where are you?" I heard heavy metal music coming from a back bedroom. "That boy," Jean said under breath. "I told him to watch Miles." A toddler sat, wearing only a soggy diaper, in front of the TV. She knelt beside him. "You OK, sweetie?" He didn't break his gaze from the TV screen.

She laid the boy down on the rug and changed his diaper before wiping his dirty mouth with a baby wipe. "I take in foster kids from time to time," she said. "I see it as a calling. That, and the extra one hundred and thirty dollars a month helps pay the bills." She scooped the boy up from the floor and plopped him in her lap. "This is Miles. He doesn't talk much. He came from a terrible home situation. He's three, small for his age."

I nodded.

Jean picked up a teddy bear a few feet away. The head had been torn off. She looked at Miles before frowning in the direction of the back bedroom. "Did Sean do this?"

The child nodded, then looked down at his lap.

"Sean!" Jean shouted. "I tell you," she said to me, "I'm at my wits' end with that boy. I thought I could change him, but you know, I think that some kids are just born mean."

A moment later a boy a year or two older than I, at least sixteen, maybe seventeen, appeared. His greasy, long dark hair hung around his face. He wore dark jeans and an AC/DC T-shirt.

"Another?" he smirked.

"This is Amanda," Jean said. "My *niece*. She's come to live with us. And, Sean, you will treat her with respect, do you hear?"

Sean didn't say anything. He just looked at me and smiled, a smile that frightened me to my core.

The next morning at breakfast, Mrs. Dilloway set out a tray with eggs, bacon, fruit, and scones in the dining room. "I hope this will be sufficient for you," she said stiffly, turning to look at me. "Mrs. Klein isn't used to cooking for Americans."

"I beg your pardon," Rex said playfully. "I may live in the U.S., but I'm a Brit through and through."

I cleared my throat. "What he means is the food is fine, thank you." I admired the array of fruit in the crystal bowl and helped myself to a scoop, before pointing to what looked like a tiny orange. "Is that a—"

"A kumquat," Mrs. Dilloway replied, looking at me curiously.

I stabbed the little fruit with my fork and took a bite, filling my mouth with its tart juice before turning back to my book.

"What are you reading?" Rex asked.

"*The Years*," I replied. "The book I found in the drawing room."

"Oh, yes," he said. "Mrs. Dilloway?"

She looked up from a tray she was about to shuttle back to the kitchen. "Yes?"

"Do you know if there was ever a woman by the name of Flora who lived at the manor?"

The carafe of orange juice teetered on the tray, and she set it down quickly before it fell to the floor. "Why do you ask, Mr. Sinclair?"

Rex pointed to the book in my hands. "Her name is written here," he said.

Mrs. Dilloway looked out the window, as if envisioning a scene from the manor's past.

"Was she one of the Livingston children?" Rex asked.

She shook her head. "She was employed as a nanny here a very long time ago," she finally said. "Now if you'll excuse me," she continued, wiping a spot of orange juice on the table with a cloth from her dress pocket, "I'll just step out to get the tea."

"So Flora was the nanny," Rex whispered after Mrs. Dilloway had gone. "Adds a whole new dimension, don't you think?"

I nodded. "It's odd that Mrs. Dilloway seems so affected by the recollection of her."

After breakfast, we went back upstairs, and I fanned the pages of the book again, which is when I noticed something I had missed in the upper corner of the inside cover. "F. Lewis," written in blue ink. Now I had Flora's last name. I pulled out my laptop and, on a whim, began searching for a Flora Lewis from the 1940s. A needle in a haystack, I knew that, but maybe I'd get a lucky break.

I scrolled through a list of search results, getting nowhere, until a Wikipedia "Unsolved Mysteries" link caught my eye.

"Find anything?" Rex asked, leaning over the laptop.

"Look at this," I said, pointing to the screen. Partway down the page, a headline read, AMERICAN NANNY VANISHES IN ENGLAND. I clicked it and read a scanned copy of a *New York Sun* article dated November 13, 1940.

> New York resident Flora Lewis, 24, was last seen at Livingston Manor in Clivebrook, England, where she'd been hired to care for the children of Lord Livingston, a widower and London businessman. Her parents, who could not be reached for comment, own a bakery in the Bronx. Local woman Georgia Hillman remembers Flora as a bright, kind young woman. "I met her on the ship to England," she said. "I'll never forget her." Anyone with details of Lewis's whereabouts are urged to contact the New York Police or notify the authorities in England immediately.

So Flora went missing? I remembered Lila Hertzberg and shook my head. "This isn't good, Rex," I said. "What the heck do you think happened to these women?"

He leaned back against the pillows, staring into his notebook. "Wait, what did you say the friend's name was—the one quoted in the article?"

I turned back to the screen. "Georgia Hillman."

Rex's eyes lit up. "It's the same name in the book," he said, reaching for *The Years* and turning to the first page. "See, she wrote the inscription."

"Hmmm," I said, turning back to the laptop. "Maybe I can find her." I googled the name and keyed through the search results until I found a woman with the same name quoted in an article about the opening of a retirement home in Manhattan. I searched for the number of the retirement home, then called it on my cell phone, waiting for two rings, then three, and four.

"Roosevelt Senior Living," a woman's voice chirped.

"Yes, hello, I'm calling to see if a Ms. Georgia Hillman lives at your facility."

"We don't give out resident information," she said, sounding a little annoyed.

"Oh, of course," I said. "Then can you simply pass along a message?"

"Sure," she said.

"I'm hoping that Ms. Hillman can call me," I continued. "I need to speak to her about something important." I gave her my cell phone number before hanging up. *What are the chances that she'll even call? That she even lives there? The newspaper article is seven years old.* "So much for that," I said. "She's probably deceased."

I turned to my laptop when I heard the chime of an incoming e-mail. I didn't recognize the sender. Not at first. Then I clicked the message open and my heart sank.

> I saw your husband in the village at a café. I almost told him everything. But I'm going to be patient, Amanda. I understand that your in-laws are in Asia. It takes time to wire that kind of money, so I'll give you the benefit of the doubt. But not for long.

Rex lay beside me, peacefully thumbing through a history book as my heart raced. *Dear Lord. He's here. He's really here.*

CHAPTER 12

I wondered what Mr. Beardsley seemed so anxious about, but there wasn't time to investigate. The children were waiting in the nursery. Abbott sat on the window seat, looking out to the gardens. Nicholas lay facedown on the floor, in protest. Katherine, sporting a permanent frown, tugged at her curls as she stood near the dollhouse, where Janie sat playing happily.

"Nicholas," I scolded. "You'll ruin your clothes."

The boy sat up reluctantly, at a snail's pace, before standing and shuffling to the window seat by Abbott. "Hey!" Abbott cried, giving his younger brother a hasty shove. "I was here first."

"Come now, boys, there's room for the both of you," I said.

Mrs. Dilloway had explained the children's schedule earlier. His Lordship had taken them out of boarding school, so their days were filled with a chorus of tutors and lessons, with very little playtime, except on weekends, and only for an hour in the afternoons.

I kept an eye on the clock; the children would need to be dressed and ready for dinner by six. I felt a pit in my stomach, knowing I'd be meeting Lord Livingston for the first time, and I didn't want there to be any hiccups.

Abbott sighed, pressing his face against the window. Outside, the countryside was awash in gray. Rain splattered against the window. "Why must it always rain here?"

Janie ran to my side. "It's only thunder, honey," I said, smoothing her silky blond hair with my hand.

"I don't like thunder," she said. Her blue eyes clouded with worry and her little mouth turned down at the corners. She was a beautiful child. I wondered if she took after her mother.

"What should we do to keep our minds off of it, then?" I asked, glancing cautiously at Katherine, who sat on a nearby sofa with folded arms. "Katherine, do you have any suggestions?"

"It's *Lady* Katherine," she said sharply.

Nicholas flung a rubber ball in the air; it bounced off the roof of the dollhouse. "You're not a lady yet," he said teasingly.

"I *am* a lady," she said. "I'm ten years old, and Father said I am to be called Lady Katherine by the servants."

"Miss Lewis isn't a servant," Nicholas piped up.

"Yes, she is," Abbott countered.

"Children," I said, raising my voice over their shouting. "Please, stop arguing. You may think of me however you like. But I am your nanny, and I am here to look after you. Like me or don't, but please, do not shout at one another."

Katherine sighed and turned to face the bookcase. She reached to a high shelf, and the sleeve of her dress fell back to her elbow, revealing a dozen wounds, jagged and raw.

I gasped, and rushed to her side. "Katherine, what happened to your arm? Did you get hurt?"

She quickly covered her forearm with her sleeve. "It's nothing," she snapped.

"Let me see it," I said. "Did someone hurt you? Please, I—"

"I'm fine," she barked. "I only fell in the garden. It's nothing."

I touched my hand to her arm, gently. "But I only want to help—"

"Please," she said, wrenching her arm away from me. "I told you it's nothing."

Abbott picked up a comic book and buried his nose in it, and Nicholas sulked. I turned to little Janie, who held a doll with flaxen hair in desperate need of a brushing. I would have to get through to Katherine, but it wasn't happening now. "Let's see about this dolly's hair," I said, reaching for a hairbrush on the floor near the sofa.

I turned to Katherine. "Do you like dolls?"

"No," she said, without looking at me.

"Katherine doesn't like anything," Abbott said with a smirk.

"You know nothing about me," she said in protest.

"She used to like to look at the flowers," Nicholas added. "With Mother."

Katherine made a disgusted face at her brother. "Don't speak of Mother in front of *her*!"

"Why not?" Nicholas countered.

I looked at Katherine again. "You like flower gardens, then, Katherine?"

She didn't answer.

"I do too," I said. "In fact, when the rain clears, I was hoping that you children could take me on a tour of the gardens.

Maybe tomorrow." I hated to think that I was using the children to lead me to the camellias, but I had to find a way into the orchard without being too conspicuous.

"Father doesn't like us to go into the orchard," Katherine said, snuffing out the idea.

"Why?" I asked, remembering a similar warning from Mrs. Dilloway.

"Because Mummy—"

Katherine elbowed Nicholas in the side. "Ouch!" he cried.

"He doesn't know what he's talking about," Katherine added, rolling her eyes.

"Please," I said. "Let's stop all this bickering and amuse ourselves properly." I glanced at the bookcase a few feet away. "Who likes stories?"

The older children didn't answer, but little Janie walked to my side and leaned against my leg. "I do," she said with a smile.

"Good, then," I said, selecting a book from the shelf at random. "We shall read."

I felt Katherine brush my side as she pushed past Nicholas to secure a preferable seat on the sofa. "Excuse me," she said briskly before nestling next to a pillow, returning her arms to a folded position. Nicholas sat beside her, and Abbott lay on his side on the rug and let out a yawn.

"Now," I said, turning to the first page before glancing at the clock. "Just enough time for a nice story before we dress for dinner."

"Children!" Mrs. Dilloway scolded. "Quickly, take your seats before your father arrives." I thought of Papa at home in the bakery in New York, with flour under his nails and a big jovial smile, and felt sorry for these children. No one should fear their own father the way they did.

Nicholas and Abbott scrambled into their chairs. They looked sharp in their dinner suits, like little men. Katherine sat across the table, smoothing an imaginary wrinkle from the sleeve of her pale yellow dress before giving me a mischievous smile. Of all the children, she worried me the most.

Mrs. Dilloway indicated a seat at the end of the long table, much too large and lonely for four children and their father. "Miss Lewis, you may take your seat here, near Janie. She needs assistance being fed."

"Yes, ma'am," I said, scooping Janie into my arms and depositing her into the seat beside mine as Mrs. Dilloway left the room. I felt as if we were all part of an elaborate theater production just before the curtain rises.

Abbott tapped his knife against his plate, and as if on cue, Nicholas picked up his fork and began with the water glass.

"Really, you two," Katherine huffed. "Must you always act like barbarians?"

Janie squealed with delight, and in an attempt to join her brothers' dinnertime percussion ensemble, she reached for the spoon at her place setting and knocked her crystal water glass to its side. Water soaked the tablecloth before the glass spun to the ground, missing the rug and landing on the hardwood floor, where it shattered in jagged shards.

"Oh dear," I said, quickly kneeling to attend to the mess. As I did, a hush fell over the dining room. "Tin cups would be much more sensible for children of your age. I shall talk to Mrs. Dilloway." I concealed the shards of crystal under the table.

"There," I said, rising to my feet. Your father will never know. It will be our little secret."

My cheeks reddened when Lord Livingston entered the dining room. Tall and thin, his temples kissed with gray, he still looked a great deal younger up close. I could see where Nicholas got his good looks. He was the spitting image of his father; I wondered if Abbott resented the resemblance.

He cleared his throat.

"Welcome home, Father!" Katherine cried.

He nodded at her formally, then turned to Mrs. Dilloway, who approached the table carrying a domed serving platter. "Who," he said, waving a finger at me, "is *this*?"

"This is Miss Lewis," she replied nervously. "The children's new nanny. She arrived yesterday."

"Pleased to meet you, sir, I mean, er, Mr. . . ." I said.

Mrs. Dilloway looked momentarily pained. "Miss Lewis is from America, your Lordship," she said, as if to get the matter over with swiftly, efficiently.

He handed Mr. Beardsley his coat without taking his eyes off me. "Indeed," he said wryly. "I may not know how children are raised in America, but at Livingston Manor, no one drinks from *tin* cups."

"Why, yes," I stammered, "yes, of course. I only thought that the children could—"

"The children," he continued, "will learn to drink from glasses like ladies and gentlemen."

"It's just that, with all due respect, sir, little Janie is only two, and—"

"I'm well aware of my daughter's age, Miss . . ."

"Miss Lewis, sir," I said. My cheeks burned, and I thought I heard a giggle from Katherine's direction. "Yes, sir, I mean, your Lordship."

Lord Livingston sat, and I followed.

"Papa, I can jump my horse over the river now," Nicholas boasted.

"No you can't," Abbott interjected. "You missed that jump by a good three feet."

Nicholas looked down at his lap, then back up again at his father, ignoring Abbott. "You could come riding with me in the morning and see for yourself."

"Not tomorrow, my boy," he said. "I have business to attend to in the morning."

Nicholas sank back into his chair as Mrs. Dilloway ladled a thick, orange-colored bisque into the bowls in front of us.

"Would you like to hear me play the piano after dinner, Father?" Katherine asked sweetly. "I can play Minuet in G now."

"Very good, Katherine," he said. "But I'll be retiring right after dinner. Another time, dear."

"Yes, Father," she said with a disappointed sigh.

I fed Janie a spoonful of soup, and she happily lapped it up, oblivious to the disappointment of her siblings.

"And how do you like your accommodations here, Miss Lewis?" Lord Livingston asked, dabbing a napkin to his mouth.

"Very well, thank you," I said. "You have a beautiful home."

"Yes," he said stiffly. "It's been in the family for generations."

"The gardens are particularly lovely," I added. I clenched my fists, wishing I could retract the statement. Mrs. Dilloway glared at me from the corner of the room.

"Well," Lord Livingston replied, "you can expect some

changes to the property this fall. The camellias are coming out." He set his fork down with such force, I wondered if he'd chipped the china. "All of them. The ground is too damp now, but by next spring, before the rains, they'll be leveled." He cut into his roast beef, eyeing it approvingly. "Camellias have no use. None at all. No fruit. Just flowers, and even they don't last long."

I winced at the thought of the orchard being destroyed. A massacre. I couldn't help but wonder if the Middlebury Pink might be better off in the garden of a Nazi than destroyed.

"Mrs. Dilloway," he said, dabbing the corner of his mouth with a napkin, "I have a great deal of paperwork to attend to. Will you be good enough to bring my dinner to my study? I shall finish in there."

"Yes, your Lordship," she said, reaching for a tray on the side table as he stood up.

Abbott and Nicholas looked wounded, and Katherine stared down at her lap, eyeing something in her hands. "Oh, Father, I wish you wouldn't go," she said, casting a sly glance in my direction. "There's something I wanted to show you. Something that I found in the nursery. It fell out of Miss Lewis's pocket."

"What is it, dear?" her father asked, walking closer to observe her outstretched hand. I squinted, trying to make out the object in her palm, then realized, in a moment of panic, that she held a kumquat. From the conservatory.

"Good gracious!" Lord Livingston exclaimed. "Where did you find this, Miss Lewis?"

Katherine flashed a satisfied smile.

"I . . ."

Mrs. Dilloway intervened. "Mrs. Marden brought home a basket of them from the market. She offered you some at lunch, didn't she, Miss Lewis?"

"Yes," I chimed in. "I tucked some in my pocket for later, and I guess I must have forgotten about them. I'm ever so sorry."

Lord Livingston looked relieved but tired. "Very well," he said. "I'll say good night now."

"Good night, Father," Abbott said, followed by Nicholas. Katherine sulked, but Janie sat up and said, "nigh nigh, Poppy." Her father was already too far gone to hear her.

"Miss Katherine," Mrs. Dilloway said with a frown, "I'll take the kumquat."

Katherine relinquished the exotic fruit and crossed her arms in triumph. "I don't care what you say. I know where you got it."

"That will be all," Mrs. Dilloway scolded. "The boys will have dessert; Janie, too. But you will retire to your room where you will think very carefully about how we welcome our guests at Livingston Manor."

Katherine stood up and walked proudly ahead.

"Please," I said to Mrs. Dilloway. "Don't punish her on my behalf."

Katherine shot me a sharp look. "It doesn't matter," she said, walking toward the stairs. "I don't like Mrs. Marden's old lemon cake anyway."

After the children were asleep, I returned to my room, where I took out a pen and paper to finish my letter home.

Dear Mama and Papa,

I am here in England, and I am fine. But I have a confession: I did not end up at London Conservatory. I have made a detour in the best interest of our family, and I hope you will not be disappointed in me. I've taken a job at Livingston Manor caring for four precocious children. The manor is beautiful and the children are as charming as they are a handful. They recently lost their mother, so it's easy to forgive them for their behavior. The father is cold and unfeeling. He's so different from you, Papa. It breaks my heart to think that the littlest one can't even crawl into his lap the way I did with you as a child. Oh, Papa, Mama, how I miss you so.

Anyway, I must stay here, at least for a while. There's something very important that I must do, and when it is complete, it will mean the end to your financial worries, I am happy to say.

Don't worry about me. I'll be fine here. I have a lovely little room that looks out to the gardens and an orchard composed entirely of camellia trees. There is so much beauty here, and yet it's hardly even acknowledged. I pray that I can help them see it.

Your loving daughter,

Flora

I folded the stationery and then tucked it in an envelope, before climbing into bed. I lay staring up at the stars outside the window, thinking about the children, Lord Livingston, and the mysterious Lady Anna. If only I knew what had happened to her. I tossed and turned for an hour before deciding to put my robe on and go for a walk. A walk would help. And besides, I could check on Janie while I was up.

I tiptoed down the hallway and upstairs, slipping quietly into the main house. It looked so different in the moonlight, which cast shadows that made the paintings look ghostly and the furniture appear ghoulish.

I shivered as I climbed the stairs and walked down the hallway until I came to the girls' bedrooms. I opened each door slowly and peeked inside. Janie slept soundly in her small bed, and Katherine snored in hers next door. Poor things. They didn't deserve to lose their mother.

I told myself I should turn around, go back to my room, but the conservatory on the floor above beckoned. I remembered where Mrs. Dilloway had left the key, under the flap of carpet near the baseboard in the hallway. *Why shouldn't I go in?* She'd ask me to keep an eye on the place, and I had noticed some weeds sprouting up in the orchid pots. I could tend to them. Maybe. Yes, just for a few moments. I'd give the trees a quick drink of water before slipping back down to bed. I found the key and pushed it into the lock, hurriedly stepping into the conservatory and closing the door behind me. I looked up at the moon and stars through the glass roof above and gasped at the stunning sight, like a mural painted by a great artist. No wonder Lady Anna had loved this place.

I walked to the orchids and plucked a weed from a small terra-cotta pot that held a speckled pink and white flower. "There you are, beautiful," I whispered, releasing a patch of clover roots from the bark near the orchid's stem. "Is that better?" In the quiet of the night, I could almost hear the flower sigh.

I walked to the water spigot and filled a green watering can to the brim, then sprinkled the flower and her comrades. I marveled at how the droplets sparkled in the moonlight.

Katherine knew about the kumquats. Did her mother bring her here? I walked to the window that overlooked the front of the house and unhinged the lock, opening the window to let in some night air. I leaned out and noticed a figure standing on the balcony below, gazing out at gardens. *Lord Livingston.* He stood with his elbows propped against the railing, cradling his head in his hands.

I fumbled with the window latch, trying to close it before he noticed me directly above, and as I did, a pebble from the windowsill fell onto the balcony below. I latched the window and shrunk behind the wall before making my way back to the entrance. I shut the door, locked it, then tucked the key under the carpet again.

My heart raced as I tiptoed through the hallway and down the stairs, aware of every creak my feet made on the staircase. I breathed a sigh of relief once I'd made it to the second floor, but when I rounded the corner, I collided with someone. A man, judging by his size. "Excuse me," I said, quickly. "I was just, um, checking on the children." The light was too dim to make out his face, but when he spoke, my arms erupted in goose bumps.

"Flora?"

"Desmond?"

CHAPTER 13

Addison

The next day, my phone buzzed on the bedside table while Rex was in the shower. I didn't recognize the number, so I decided not to answer, for fear that it could be Sean. When I checked my voice mail, however, I was relieved to hear that it was only a business call. A woman in Chelsea inquiring about a new backyard garden for a recently purchased home.

"Did you ever hear from Georgia?" Rex asked from the doorway to the bathroom, towel wrapped around his waist, chest dotted with water droplets.

"No," I said. "I kind of doubt that's going to pan out."

"Well, we'll find another avenue, then," he said. "Maybe she knew someone in town. I thought I'd go to the café today to do some more research; maybe I could ask around."

"Yeah," I said. "That's a good idea."

"Want to come?" Rex asked.

"Nah, I think I'll stay."

"You're going to weed, aren't you?"

"How did you know?"

"You have that look in your eye," he said.

I cracked a smile. "Doesn't it drive you crazy that there are dandelions and clover in the hydrangea beds?"

"No," he said, grinning. "But it drives you crazy. I get it." He pulled me toward him. "You do know that my parents can hire someone to do their weeding, don't you?"

I nodded. "But I *like* weeding."

"You're adorable."

Later that afternoon my phone rang and I answered, cautiously. "Hello?"

"Yes, hello, this is Georgia Hillman." Her voice sounded tired and crackly at the edges. "I got a message to call this number."

"Yes," I said eagerly. "My name is Addison Sinclair. I'm staying in England at a place called Livingston Manor, and I—"

"What did you say?"

"I said, I'm calling from Livingston Manor."

The line went quiet.

"Ms. Hillman," I said, "are you still there?"

"Yes," she finally replied. "I'm here."

"I'm sorry to bother you," I continued, "but I came across some information about a woman who used to work here, a woman by the name of Flora Lewis. Do you happen to know her?"

The woman didn't say anything.

"Ms. Hillman?"

"Yes," she said. "I'm sorry. I haven't heard that name in a very long time."

"Then you know her?"

"I did," she said. "Yes."

"I found a newspaper article with your name in it," I said. "I understand she went missing in England?"

"She did. And I'm sorry to say they never found her."

"Do you have any idea what happened to her?"

"No," she said. "I wish I did. I only knew her for a short time."

"On the ship to England, right?"

"Yes," she said. "She was working with a con man."

"Con man?"

"Yes, and I'm ashamed to say I did too, at one time," she said. "Listen, I'm not proud of that chapter of my life, but I left that life. And I didn't want Flora to get mixed up in it. She was much too good for that."

"I don't understand."

"Mr. Price knew how to get what he wanted," she continued. "He knew how to make people behave like puppets on strings. Flora's family desperately needed the money, and he knew that, so he used it to his advantage."

"So Flora was part of a con operation in England?"

"Yes," she said. "I overheard her talking to Mr. Price, and from what I can remember, she was supposed to locate a rare flower or tree at the manor."

"You don't mean a camellia, do you?"

"Maybe," she said. "Actually, yes, that sounds right."

"What did Mr. Price want with the camellia?"

"Money," she said. "It was probably worth a great deal to someone, and he was hired to get it. He ran a ring of flower thieves. There was no plant or tree he couldn't get his hands on." She sighed to herself. "Well, he died in the 1970s, in a jail cell in Tampa, if that tells you anything about the kind of man he was."

"Do you think Flora finished the job? Do you think she found the camellia?"

"I don't know," she replied. "Part of me thinks she got away, that she slipped off to some faraway place so he wouldn't come looking for her. And he would, if he believed for a minute that she was alive. I like to think of her out there leading the life she always dreamed of. But I'm not so sure. She loved her parents, and as far as I know, they never heard from her again."

"How do you know?"

"I went to see them five years after Flora disappeared," she said. "I had some money, a little, from the last job I did with Mr. Price. What I didn't give back to the family in Sweden we stole from, I intended on giving to Flora's parents to cover their debt. I remembered what she'd told me about how they'd run into hard times. But when I got there, they wouldn't accept any help from me, said that a relative had left them a large sum of money. I was glad to know they were taken care of. But money couldn't replace their daughter. They never knew about her fall from grace, and I'm glad of that."

"Ms. Hillman," I said, "thank you so much for sharing all of this with me. If you think of anything else, anything at all, could you please call me?"

"Yes, of course," she said. "I haven't talked about that time in my life for so long, I'd almost forgotten. My husband, rest his soul, never knew. It's funny how our past comes back around to find us again."

I nodded to myself. "Yes, it is," I said quietly.

After I hung up, I decided to do more exploring in the house. Wednesday was the one day of the week when Mrs. Dilloway went into town. Mrs. Klein had said it was to get her hair done, but if you asked Mrs. Dilloway, she wouldn't admit it. In any case, I knew her absence was the only way I could poke about the house undetected.

Since the first day, when I'd noticed her slipping into a room upstairs, I'd been eager to have a look myself.

After the car pulled out of the driveway, I walked up to the third floor, being sure that no one was following. The only other person at the manor that day that I knew of was John, a village boy Mrs. Dilloway had hired to trim the front hedges. The buzz of the electric trimmer hummed in the distance.

At the top of the stairs, I looked around. Mrs. Dilloway was right, there wasn't anything remarkable about this floor, except perhaps the closer view it provided of the mural on the domed ceiling. I squinted to make out the cherubs fluttering about the garden scene painted above. Up close, I could see the cobwebs that congregated along the edges. I walked toward a door ahead and turned the knob. Locked. I gave the door a push, hoping that the lock might be so old it would give way, but it didn't yield. I sighed, sinking down onto the carpet, tucking my knees against my chest.

I studied the print on the weave, worn and tattered from years of use. Surely my mother-in-law would be removing it soon. "Ghastly," she'd call it. I wondered if there was hardwood below. I peeled back the carpet to find gleaming wood floors, which is when I noticed the glimmer of metal. I leaned in closer, picking up a small brass key. No, it couldn't be. I stood up, quickly inserting it into the old lock. It stuck, but I jiggled it gently, and in an instant, the knob turned. I gasped, pulling the door open.

I took a cautious step inside, marveling at the sight before me. A vast conservatory awaited, or what *once* was a conservatory. Sunlight beamed through the enormous glass roof. I realized that its position at the center of the house precluded its visibility from below. In awe, my heart beating wildly, I lingered in an arbor covered with bright pink bougainvillea, with a trunk so thick, it was larger than my waist. Most of it had died off, but a single healthy vine remained, and it burst with magenta blossoms. I could smell citrus warming in the sunlight, and I immediately noticed the source: an old potted lemon tree in the far corner. *This must have been Lady Anna's.*

I walked along the leaf-strewn pathway to a table that had clearly once showcased dozens of orchids. Now it was an orchid graveyard. Only their brown, shriveled stems remained, but I could imagine how they'd looked in their prime. I smiled when I picked up a tag from one of the pots. *Lady Fiona Bixby. She must have given them her own names.* Perhaps there hadn't been anything sinister going on in the orchard, after all. Lady Anna was clearly a creative spirit, and maybe that played out in her gardens and the names she gave to her flowers and trees.

I sat down on a bench by the window and thought about Flora, the nanny. Had she been here too? Did she love this place as much as Lady Anna? I picked up an old trowel, rusted at the edge. It triggered a memory I wished I could forget. I closed my eyes tightly, trying unsuccessfully to will it away.

Fifteen Years Prior

Jean glanced at the clock on the wall. "Is it already six? I'm late for my meeting." She turned to me. "Honey, there's a can of SpaghettiOs in the cupboard. Can you heat it up for Miles and you?"

"Aren't you forgetting someone?" Sean said, annoyed. "Last I checked, the government sends you a nice fat check on my behalf each month."

She scowled. "And most of it went to fix the wall you scorched last week." She looked at me. "Keep an eye on Miles. I'll be back by eight."

I stared ahead, frozen, as she bustled out the door.

"AA," Sean said. "She never misses a meeting; been sober for a year, at least that's what she wants everyone to believe." He walked to the kitchen and reached above a cabinet, pulling out a bottle of liquor. He unscrewed the cap and took a swig before offering it to me.

I shook my head, frightened.

"Go on, have some," he said. "It'll loosen you up."

"No," I said quickly.

Sean turned to the little boy in front of the TV. "Should we spike his bottle?"

I gasped, shocked he would suggest such a thing.

"I did that once at another home, to this little kid in Queens," he said with a laugh. "It was hilarious."

"That's awful," I said.

"All right, Goody Two-shoes." He took another swig from the bottle, before screwing the cap back on and returning it to the top of the cabinet.

I walked to the living room and sat beside little Miles. He turned to look up at me cautiously.

"I'm Amanda," I said to him.

He smiled shyly and handed me his headless bear.

"I bet we can fix this," I said. "Do you know where the . . . head is?"

The child pointed toward the fire escape near the kitchen. I nodded and walked over to it, peering out the open window. There, near a scraggly potted rosebush, the bear's head lay on the metal grating, facedown. I picked it up, stopping briefly to admire a single blossom, deep orange, the color of a sunset. I touched the rose gently, looking out at the city around me. Horns honked, neon signs flashed. I clutched the railing and froze when I heard movement behind me. I noticed a rusty garden trowel, and I picked it up, instinctively.

"Hey, don't be so scared," Sean said. I felt his hot hand on the small of my back. "What, did you think I was going to push you over the edge?" He reached out to pluck the orange rose. "You like flowers?" he asked. I cringed. Such a waste. "Ouch!" he cried. "This damn thing got me." He held out his hand, displaying a few drops of fresh blood, before dropping the rose and wedging the heel of his boot against the delicate petals.

I shook off the memory, trying so hard to focus on the beauty in front of me and let it outshine the ugliness of the past. I walked over to a potted tree near the arbor, plucking a tiny orange fruit from its branch. I smiled. Kumquats, of course. I took a bite, letting the tart juice enliven my senses, which is when I heard the door opening behind me. And footsteps. I clutched the old trowel and braced myself.

CHAPTER 14

My heart beat wildly in my chest as I stared at the familiar face in the dim light. "What are you doing here?" I asked nervously. I didn't expect to see him again, and there he stood, looking handsome in a gray suit while I stood on the stairs in my nightclothes.

"I live here," Desmond said, smiling up at me.

"What do you mean, you *live* here?"

"This is my home," he said. "Well, my family's home." He shook his head, confused. "But you told me—"

"I'm terribly sorry," I said, cinching my robe tighter around my waist. "I wasn't honest with you." I felt flustered and hot as the words escaped my lips. "There is no job at the London Conservatory. The simple fact of the matter is that I am here as a nanny." I bit my lip. "I understand you'll want me to leave at once." My stomach churned. *How can I explain myself, my lie, without confessing the real reason I'm at the manor?*

"Please," he said, reaching for my hand. "What are you talking about? Leaving? I won't hear of it. You didn't want me to know you were going to be in service. I understand. Everybody has an angle; no harm done."

"An angle?" I said, withdrawing my hand.

"Yes," he replied. "Not one of us is perfect."

"Well if you're implying that I'm—"

"I'm not implying anything." He took a step closer. I took a step back.

"It's funny," he continued. "I worried I'd never see you again, and here you turn up in my home, in your nightgown." He grinned, extending his hand again. "Listen, can we start over? Hello, I'm Desmond Livingston."

I returned his smile, cautiously. "Hi, I'm Flora," I said. "Flora Lewis."

April 15, 1940

"Someone's sleepy?" Mr. Humphrey teased at breakfast the next morning.

"Sorry," I said, trying my best to stifle another yawn. "I'm still having trouble adjusting to European time." I didn't say, of course, that I'd stayed up until after midnight talking to Desmond in the drawing room.

Mr. Humphrey stood up and pulled his napkin from his lap. "Well, I need to be off. Driving his Lordship into town today."

"Oh?" Mrs. Dilloway said. "What is he doing in town?"

The chauffeur looked at me and then back at Mrs. Dilloway. "I don't keep his schedule, ma'am," he said cryptically. "He pays me to do the driving, not the asking."

"Oh, Mr. Humphrey," I said, reaching into my dress pocket, where I pulled out the letter I'd written to my parents. "If there's a chance you'll pass a post office, would you mind taking this in?" I gave him a few coins for postage. "Here, this should cover it."

"Of course," he said, stuffing it into his shirt pocket.

"Thank you."

"How are you getting on here, Miss Lewis?" Mr. Beardsley asked from the head of the table, where he alternately ate breakfast and attended to an open notebook before him.

"Just fine, sir," I said. "It's quite a house."

"It is," he agreed, making a mark in the notebook, without looking up.

"It's just that, sir, I wondered if I could take the children out to the gardens today—after their lessons, of course."

Mr. Beardsley looked up at Mrs. Dilloway, then at me. "The gardens?"

"Yes," I said. "I'd love to see them, and the children seem so cooped up in the house. I'd like to take them on a walk. To the camellia orchard, if I may."

"I wouldn't advise it," Mr. Beardsley said quickly.

"But, sir," I pleaded. "I promise not to keep them out long. Surely his Lordship wouldn't mind a supervised walk?"

"Well," he said, closing his notebook and turning to look at me again, "don't stray too far. The orchard is very large, and when the fog rolls through . . . well, it isn't an ideal place for children."

"We'll be careful," I said. "I promise."

"And be sure you return home by two, when Mr. Humphrey will have his Lordship home," Mr. Beardsley added.

"Yes, sir," I said.

While the children ate breakfast, I watched as Katherine

stabbed her scrambled eggs with calculating precision and a heavy heart. I knew it was going to take much time and patience to understand her secrets, her sadness.

"Children," I said, breaking the morning silence, "after your lessons this morning, how would you like to go out to the gardens with me, to explore?" Desmond had left that morning to attend to business in town, and for whatever reason, he wanted to keep his visit to the house a secret, one I'd promised to keep.

Abbott sat up higher in his chair. "Really? Can we?"

Nicholas made a swinging motion as if he held a sword in his hand. "I'll protect us from the evil spirits."

Abbott elbowed him. "You ninny."

"Me too?" Janie said, attempting to crawl up onto the table. I scooped her into my arms and planted a kiss on her cheek. "You too, Miss Janie."

Katherine looked up at me and smirked. "You do know that Father will dismiss you if he finds out that you suggested such a—"

"What?" I sparred back. "If I suggest that you children get a little fresh air? Rubbish! Children need to be outdoors! I don't see anything wrong with taking a walk to the orchard. Besides, Mrs. Dilloway and Mr. Beardsley gave their permission."

"They did?" Katherine asked.

"Indeed," I said, nestling Janie back in her seat and turning back to Katherine. "So, will you join us?" I smiled when her eyes met mine. "That is, if you're not too busy."

She shrugged.

"All right, then, it's settled," I said, standing up. "Janie and I will spend the rest of the morning in the nursery. We'll meet

you all there at eleven, and we can walk out to the terrace together."

Janie's eyes got heavy at half past nine, and while she dozed
in her bed, I decided to tidy the nursery. First, I realigned the
train tracks, mending the bridge that Nicholas had fussed over
the day before. He'd be glad to see it in working order. I folded
the doll clothes in a neat stack and tucked them into the little
white bureau near the dollhouse. Abbott's comic books got a
proper sorting too; I organized them by type, then walked to
the bookshelf to tuck them away. I climbed up onto the ladder
so I could see the upper shelf. It had looked empty from below,
but upon closer inspection, I noticed a small cedar box pushed
back into the corner of the shelf. I reached up to collect it, marveling at the thick layer of dust that Mrs. Dilloway would have
been embarrassed to know she'd missed. I climbed down the
ladder and knelt down on the floor to inspect the contents of
the box. I lifted the lid. Inside was an envelope addressed to
Desmond in swirly feminine handwriting. I eyed the return
address: Vivien Wainwright. *Who is she?* As much as I wanted to
lift the flap of the envelope and inspect the contents, I willed
myself to set it back and instead retrieved a stack of old photos
bound together with a wrinkled white ribbon. I untied the ribbon and thumbed through the images, at once noticing a photograph of Lord Livingston with an attractive woman at his
side. Her eyes looked away from the camera. *Could this be Lady
Anna?*

When I heard footsteps in the hallway, I quickly tucked the
box back up onto the shelf, just as the children ran through the
doorway. "Hello," I said, a bit flustered.

Katherine approached, followed by Nicholas and Abbott.
"What are you doing?" she asked.

"I was tidying the nursery," I said. "See?" I said quickly. "I found this box on the shelf." I searched the children's faces. "Now," I said, clasping my hands together. "Would you all still like to go out walking with me?"

"Yes!" cried Nicholas. The late morning light from the window illuminated the dark lashes that framed his eyes.

"All right, put your coats on, and let's get your baby sister up."

"A perfect day for exploring," I said, marveling at the sunshine. Birds chirped in the trees all around. "I imagine that you know the property inside and out."

"We used to," Nicholas said, planting his foot in a patch of mud and marveling at the squishy sound his feet made, "before Mum died. Now Father won't allow us out much, except for riding lessons."

Katherine rolled her eyes. "Don't act so tortured," she said. "At least you get to go riding. You're too young to appreciate that."

"Children," I said, "please, let's not spoil this beautiful day."

The boys ran ahead, and Katherine and I walked in silence before I broke the ice.

"I just wanted to say that, well, if you ever want to talk, about anything, I'm here. You must miss your mother, terribly, and, well—"

"You don't know anything about me or Mother," she said dismissively, walking on.

I sighed, eyeing the dark clouds rolling in. Mrs. Dilloway wouldn't be pleased if we got caught in the rain. I pulled Janie's hood over her blond curls and made sure her coat was buttoned. Thankfully, I'd had all the children put on their coats, despite Abbott's protests. I looked up, just as a raven swooped in and landed in a maple tree nearby. The bird pecked at the bark on the branch, then cawed at me as if to say, *Do not walk a step further. Or else.* I shivered. Mama always said that ravens were smarter than given credit for, and cunning. For instance, they knew the precise moment when Papa emptied the rubbish bin in the alley behind the bakery. They would let out a caw of disapproval when there wasn't a stale loaf of pumpernickel, their favorite.

Maybe we should turn back. "Boys," I shouted, "don't run too far ahead!" With Janie on my hip, I couldn't keep pace with the older children.

"We're right here," Abbott called out, running back toward me.

"Boo!" Nicholas said, poking his head out from behind a fir tree.

I felt a raindrop on my wrist. "Looks like storm clouds are moving in," I said. "I think we should continue our adventure tomorrow."

"Aw," Abbott whined, "but we only just left the house." He pointed to the sky. "We're not afraid of a little rain. Besides, there's something we want to show you."

I eyed the clouds skeptically, but the camellia orchard was just ahead, beckoning me. *What would be the harm in walking just a little farther, especially when the Middlebury Pink could be near?* Mr. Price had hoped I could find it and report back before summer's end. I pulled my coat around Janie, tucking her closer to my chest to keep her warm. "All right," I conceded. "But we should turn back soon."

"Goody!" Nicholas squealed.

The wind picked up as we walked down a grassy hillside dotted with purple and light pink wildflowers. "It's a bit overgrown out here," Abbott explained. "Papa would just as well let it all turn to weeds."

"These are not weeds," Katherine interjected. "Can't you see the phlox Mum planted? Look, they're here in the grass."

"Well they look like weeds to me," Abbott said. "I'm twelve years old, and I know a great deal more than you do."

"Now, Abbott," I said, trying to keep the peace, "find what you'd like to show us, and then we must get back, before we're absolutely drenched."

The boy nodded. "All right, it's not much farther now."

Just ahead, I spotted the top of a stone angel, nearly covered in tall grass and thistles. Only the face and the tip of a wing were visible.

"Mummy's statue!" Nicholas cried, running over to the stone angel, which was nearly as tall as he was.

"Be careful, Nicholas," Katherine scolded. "There might be poison flower in the grass."

Abbott appeared disinterested and walked ahead to examine a patch of brambles. I wondered if the stone angel reminded him of his mother. Our eyes met and he looked away quickly.

"What do you mean, Katherine?" I asked.

She pointed to a small bush with sage green leaves and pointed tips. Shoots of purple berrylike flowers sprouted from it. They reminded me of the columbine I'd planted in the pots outside the bakery. "See that?" she said. "It's the poison flower. It can kill you if you touch it. Mummy told me."

I knelt down to have a closer look. "It's hard to believe that something so beautiful could be poisonous," I said.

"Well, it is," Katherine continued. "Mummy wouldn't lie."

"Of course not," I said.

Nicholas tucked his hand back in his pocket and looked up at the angel. "Mummy loved this statue," he said with emotion. "Father had it sent from one of his trips. It arrived on our doorstep all wrapped up in brown paper. She had Mr. Blythe put it here in the garden, near her camellias."

I looked at my wristwatch, the one Papa gave me on my nineteenth birthday. "Goodness," I said, "we haven't seen the camellias yet."

With Abbott as our guide, we made our way down the hill and into a small valley. Fog had rolled in so thick, we were practically enveloped in a cloud. Abbott led us down a row of large camellia trees. I eyed the blossoms. Some were showy, the size of my hand; others were small and fragile, with silken petals. All had bright, waxy emerald leaves. We wandered through the second row, and the third, but so far, no Middlebury Pink.

I reached to touch a blossom and tripped on a protruding root. Holding Janie tight, I lost my footing and lurched left. I held out my left arm to blunt the fall, wincing when I felt a sharp pain on my wrist.

At the same time, Katherine screamed, "Look out, Miss Lewis!"

It was too late. I'd fallen on a rusty rake, left with its prongs pointing upward. I set Janie safely on the ground before inspecting the injury. It was a deep scrape, and blood oozed from my wrist.

Katherine knelt beside me. "Are you all right? Does it hurt?"

"Yes," I said. "I'll need a bandage."

"Here," Abbott said proudly, unbuttoning his coat and tearing a piece of fabric from his shirt. "Use this."

I smiled at the gesture. "Thank you," I said, wrapping the fabric from his white shirt around my wrist. Blood soaked through the first layer, so I asked Abbott to help me wrap it tighter.

"If you'd like to turn back," he said, "I'll understand."

My wrist throbbed, but I rose to my feet, brushing dirt off my dress, and lifted Janie into my arms, being careful not to apply too much pressure to the wound. I could hear Mr. Price whispering in my ear. *This is your chance. This is your opportunity. Take it.* "Let's go on."

"If you're sure," Abbott said.

I nodded. "Just a little farther."

We weaved through the rows of camellia trees—none resembling the Middlebury Pink—and true to his word, a minute later, Abbott stopped. "We're here," he said, his face plastered with a huge grin.

I looked right, then left, and shook my head. "Where? I don't see anything."

"Come closer," he said, pointing ahead, where fog hovered so low, it was difficult to make out the landscape. "You'll see it then."

We walked through an arbor covered in pink climbing roses. I held Janie closer so her arms wouldn't get pricked by a stray thorn. Then, with each step, I began to make out the sight ahead. There was a roof, moss-covered, with an old rusty weather vane standing at attention. A home?

"What is this place?" I asked Abbott, feeling the hair on my arms stand on end.

"The carriage house," he said, in awe, turning to me. "Miss Lewis?"

"Yes, Abbott?"

"Have you ever gotten the feeling that a place could be"—he paused and scratched his head—"well, that a place could be . . . evil?"

Katherine sighed and folded her arms. A few moments later, however, she jumped when a sudden wind gust swept through the valley, causing a window shutter to creak on its hinge.

"See?" Abbott continued, his cheeks pink from the bluster. He spotted a pitchfork resting against the trunk of a nearby maple tree and picked it up. "For protection," he explained.

"Abbott!" I cried. "Please, don't scare your sisters."

Nicholas walked to Abbott's side. "Do you think the evil spirits are here?"

"Maybe," Abbott said, looking right, then left.

Nicholas nodded. "Don't worry," he said. "The camellias will protect us. Mummy said they're special." He looked around the orchard. "It's why she had so many."

Katherine walked ahead, pretending to examine a red blossom on a tree.

Abbott looked at his brother, then swung the pitchfork at a pink camellia blossom. "Well, the trees didn't save Mum when she needed them most," he scoffed.

"Abbott!" I shouted. "Enough." I inspected my wrist again. "Have you seen what you wanted to see?"

"Not yet," he said, eyeing the door of the carriage house as if transfixed by it. "The month before she died, I followed Mum out here. Father was always cross with her back then, so she liked to be alone out in the orchard. I wanted to talk to her. I thought I could cheer her up. But when I walked down here, she was gone. I ran up and down the rows of trees looking for her. Then, I turned around and saw Mummy running out of the carriage house. She was crying."

"Oh, Abbott," I said, placing my hand on his shoulder.

"She probably got a sliver in her hand," Nicholas chimed in. "I always cry when that happens to me."

"That's because you're a sissy," Katherine mocked.

I gave him a reassuring grin. "You are *not* a sissy."

"Well," Abbott continued, "she didn't have a sliver, or any other kind of injury that I could tell; it was that bloody Mr. Blythe."

"Why do you say that?" I asked.

"He was here," he said. "I saw him run after her. He made her cry. I know it."

"Maybe you got the wrong impression," I said, unsure of what Abbott had seen.

He shook his head. "I know what I saw."

He looked at the old building, its roof covered with mounds of soft green pillowy moss. The exterior had weathered to a light gray.

Abbott walked closer and placed his hand on the doorknob, before turning back to face us. "Locked."

"Well, that ends our grand adventure," I said. "Come on now. Enough of this spooky business. Let's head home."

Abbott sighed. "I'm telling you," he said, looking back at the carriage house with an unsettled expression, "there's something queer about this place."

We began walking back, toward the entrance of the

orchard. I placed my hand on Abbott's shoulder, but turned around quickly. A noise. The distinct sound of a door opening and then closing with a thud.

"Run!" Abbott cried, turning to the pathway.

Katherine screamed, and Nicholas dropped the stick he held. Both jetted on ahead, running faster than I could with Janie in my arms.

"Children!" I cried. "Please slow down. You'll get hurt." But it was no use. They didn't stop, so I tucked Janie in closer on my hip and picked up my pace, running down the path lined with camellia trees, without looking back, until I came to the edge of the hillside. From the bottom, it seemed as steep as a mountain, but I charged onward. A thunderclap sounded in the distance and the rain began to fall again, this time with greater force.

"Abbott, Katherine, Nicholas!" I cried. Between the fog and the rain, I could only make out three blurred figures ahead. "Please wait!"

I continued on for what seemed like an eternity, feeling very foolish to have taken the children out in the first place, until finally the house came into view. My heart sank when I saw the scene ahead. Three mud-splattered, rain-soaked children standing under an umbrella beside a stern-faced Lord Livingston, with Mrs. Dilloway at his side.

"I'm ever so sorry," I said, running to them, out of breath. "We went for a walk and got caught in the rain."

"That will be all, Miss Lewis," Lord Livingston barked.

"But Father," Abbott cried, "Miss Lewis is hurt!"

Lord Livingston's eyes flashed with momentary concern. "What happened?"

"Oh, it's nothing," I said. "Just a scratch."

"Children, run up to the bath," Mrs. Dilloway continued. "I'll be up in a minute. Give your wet clothes to Sadie. And hurry, you'll catch cold!"

Katherine and the boys scurried into the house with downcast faces, and Mrs. Dilloway reached for Janie in my arms. "Come here, love," she said. "Poor thing. Soaked to the bone." She looked at Lord Livingston. "I'll give her a bath myself."

I could only imagine how I must have appeared—sopping wet with rouge streaming down my cheeks. The little compact of makeup had been a going-away gift from my friend Pearl. For some silly reason, I'd decided to put some on that morning. "Please, sir," I said. "I really am very sorry, I—"

"Save your sentiments," he said sternly. "You will not take the children to the orchard ever again. Do I make myself clear?"

"Yes, yes, of course," I said, looking down at my waterlogged shoes. *What am I even doing here? And how could I think that finding the camellia would be so easy?* My eyes began to sting, but I willed away the tears.

"Go in and change," he said. "Then, meet me in the drawing room."

I nodded and ran to the back door, peeling off my wet shoes as quickly as I could and then tiptoeing to the door to the servants' staircase, leaving a trail of wet footprints behind me.

Downstairs, I hurried down the long hall to my room, and nearly ran into Mr. Humphrey, the chauffeur. "Sorry," I said. "I'm a little turned around."

"Indeed so," he said. "And I nearly stepped on your foot. Where are your shoes?"

"I left them at the door," I said. "It's terribly muddy out back in the gardens." I glanced down at my wet stockings, which is when I noticed the mud on his boots. "I see you've been caught in the mud too."

"Oh, this? Just stepped in a bit of a puddle in the driveway."

"Well," I said, "I better get changed."

I pulled a towel from the linen pantry and hurried to my room. I pulled the shade closed before I undressed, then dried off. *Was there really someone out there today? Someone in the carriage house? And what did Abbott say about hearing his mother's cries?* I pulled on a fresh pair of stockings and a new dress, then ran a brush through my hair and pinned it back. I took a look at myself in the little mirror above the dresser. I could not let him fire me. Not yet. I needed more time. The Middlebury Pink might bloom soon. I'd find it. I had to.

I smoothed my dress before I walked into the drawing room. Thanks to Mr. Beardsley, my wrist had been washed and bandaged. Lord Livingston sat in a green velvet wingback chair facing the fireplace. The flames, roaring and crackling, reflected in his eyes. "Come in," he said, without looking up.

I walked toward him, feeling the warmth of the fire on my face. I tugged at my hair, still damp from the day's mishaps. "Please allow me to apologize, sir—I mean, your Lordship," I said. I hardly recognized my meek voice.

He continued to stare at the fire for a long moment before turning to me. "Didn't Mrs. Dilloway tell you that I've forbidden the children from going into the gardens?"

I looked down at my hands in my lap. "Why, yes, sir, I mean—"

"Then why did you take them there against my express wishes?"

"My Lord," I said, "I felt sorry for them. Children love to be outdoors. I thought it would be fun."

"Fun?"

"Yes," I said. "And good for their health."

He rose to his feet, running a hand through his dark hair. "I know what's best for my children," he said. "They go into town every Saturday, and the boys have riding lessons during the week. It's not as if we keep them under lock and key, Miss Lewis."

I smiled awkwardly. "That's not what I implied, sir. It's just that, well, I was only trying to cheer them up."

He clasped his hands together. "I'll forgive the incident in the garden today, if you promise never to take the children out there again. Let them play on the terrace if you must, but they must never be permitted to wander into the orchard. It isn't safe. There's an encampment of drifters a few miles from here. You never know who's lurking there." His face softened. "How is your wrist?"

I eyed the bandage, feeling tears well up in my eyes. I missed Mama and Papa. Home. "Fine, thank you," I managed. "But I think it'll be a nasty scar."

He reached toward my wrist, with a momentarily tender expression, before snatching his hand back and glancing at his wristwatch. "The children should be out of their baths now," he said, retreating. "Mrs. Dilloway will be waiting for you to relieve her in the nursery."

"Of course," I said. "I'll go now."

In the nursery, Abbott lay sulking on the sofa. Nicholas played quietly with a toy train and Katherine read a book on the window seat, while Mrs. Dilloway fastened the buttons on Janie's dress.

"Was Father cross with you?" Nicholas asked, with genuine concern in his eyes.

Katherine looked up expectantly.

"Of course not," I said.

"Did he sack you?" Katherine asked.

"Katherine," Mrs. Dilloway scolded.

"He did *not* sack me," I said. "But he has given me strict orders never to take you into the gardens again."

"Blast," Abbott said. "If we could only go back, we might—"

"Abbott, you heard Miss Lewis," Mrs. Dilloway scolded, tying a fresh ribbon in Janie's damp hair, before turning to me. "Miss Lewis, may I have a word with you outside?"

I followed her into the hallway, closing the nursery door behind us. "What is it?"

"You should know that Lord Livingston's estranged son has come home," she said disapprovingly.

"I know," I said.

"You do?"

"Yes," I said. "We, well, we met."

Mrs. Dilloway's eyes widened. "Oh."

"Why did you say 'estranged'?"

"I'm afraid their grievances against each other are so great, I don't know where to begin," she continued. "But he's gone into town for the day, left this morning, before his Lordship saw him. I expect he'll return soon to gather his things. He shan't be staying long." She gave me a decided look. "Besides, he will be moving to the south with his bride after the wedding."

I instantly remembered the letter, the swirly handwriting. *Vivien.* I hoped Mrs. Dilloway didn't see the color in my cheeks. "His *bride*?"

"Yes," she said. "He's marrying a countess. If you ask me, it's the best thing that ever happened to him."

CHAPTER 15

Addison

My breathing hastened as I clutched the trowel in my right hand. "Hello?" I called out, unable to see beyond the bougainvillea. "Who's there?"

A figure pushed through the arbor. "I thought I'd find you here," Mrs. Dilloway said.

"What are you . . . but, I thought you were—"

"Getting my hair done?"

I nodded.

"I came back because I forgot my pocketbook, and I noticed the chandelier swaying. You see, it does that only when someone's moving about the conservatory." She took a step closer, and an icy chill came over me. "When one lives in a home as long as I have, one comes to know the habits of a house. Little quirks that go unnoticed." She stopped in front of the lemon tree. "Hear that?" she asked.

I shook my head.

"The floor creaks right here," she said, pointing to a warped floorboard beneath her right foot. "I had to be careful, always." She pinched a withered leaf from an orchid on the table next to her. "I suppose you'll want to know all about this space," she said, "why it's still here after all these years."

I remained silent.

"I promised Lady Anna," she said. "It only seemed right after . . . what happened to her."

"Mrs. Dilloway, what *did* happen to her?"

She looked to the windows, and a ray of sunshine revealed the glimmer of a tear. Her mouth opened as if she wanted to say something, to let the words flood out. But she quickly pursed her lips. "Come," she said stiffly, motioning toward the door. "I will be late for my appointment."

CHAPTER 16

Flora

April 19, 1940

At breakfast, Sadie looked more tired than usual. She yawned over her bowl of porridge. "I don't have to meet the children in the nursery until ten this morning," I whispered. "They're having their music lessons. Why don't you let me help you with the beds upstairs?"

Sadie's eyes brightened. "Really?"

"Of course," I said. "I'm happy to." I hadn't been able to get Desmond's engagement out of my mind, and I didn't want to run into him downstairs while waiting for the children. I felt silly for caring, and yet, *why hadn't he been honest with me about it?* I thought of the way we'd danced on the ship, the way he'd looked at me that night on the stairs.

The room suddenly fell silent.

I looked up to see Desmond standing in the doorway of the servants' hall. "Top of the morning to you," he said, smiling nervously.

"Desmond," Mr. Beardsley said, rising to his feet. "May we help you?"

"No," he said. "I mean, yes. Well, I— I was hoping to have a word with Miss Lewis, if I may."

Mrs. Dilloway and Mr. Beardsley exchanged glances before I nodded. Together, Desmond and I walked a few paces, until we were out of earshot of the servants' hall.

"You didn't come see me last night," he said, looking hurt. "I was waiting."

"How could I, Desmond?" I asked, looking into his big green eyes. "Mrs. Dilloway told me about your engagement."

"Oh," he said, taking my hands in his. "It's true. I was engaged, but I assure you, I'm not anymore."

I searched his face. "What are you saying?"

"I called it off. I went to see her yesterday." He shook his head to himself. "It was all wrong. I should have known, after . . ." His voice trailed off. "Anyway, marriage should be about love, not about business arrangements."

"Business arrangements?"

"Marrying Vivien might have secured the financial future for the manor, for the family," he explained. "In Father's eyes, I would have been a hero. But I couldn't live with myself. I didn't love her, and I never could."

I searched his face, feeling my heart swell in a way I hadn't expected.

"Now," he said. "When can I see you again?"

"Tonight," I replied.

He kissed my forehead, then turned to the staircase.

"Desmond's certainly taken a liking to you," Sadie said with a smile after breakfast.

I returned her smile, following her up the back staircase until we came to the second floor. We walked along the corridor into the east wing.

"Wait," I said, noticing the closed door on the right. "Whose room is this?"

"The east wing belonged to her Ladyship," Sadie replied, with big eyes. "No one goes up here now—well, except Mrs. Dilloway."

"Why?" I asked, eyeing the door curiously.

Sadie shrugged. "Guilt, probably."

"Guilt?"

Sadie looked pained. "Listen," she said, "we'd better get started on the bedrooms."

"Thanks for your help," Sadie said, fluffing the last pillow.

"Don't mention it," I replied, following her out of the room. She lifted a basket of washing and disappeared down the servants' staircase.

Alone on the second floor, I couldn't stop thinking about the east wing, about Lady Anna. Why did Mrs. Dilloway go into her chambers, and what had Sadie meant when she spoke of her guilt?

I walked back down the corridor, looking over my shoulder twice. When I came to the door, I placed my hand on the knob, expecting it to be locked, but it turned and the latch released easily.

Inside, the air felt thick and sultry as I took a breath. I could smell a musky scent of vanilla and lavender. The drapes had been pulled shut, but as soon as my eyes adjusted to the dim light, I saw a large bed with four intricately carved posts. I walked closer, running my hand along the coverlet. My heart raced as the soft white lace touched my palm. This was *her* room. Her bed. Her linens.

I opened the wardrobe and gazed at the dozens of dresses inside. A white silk evening gown caught my eye, and I lifted its hanger, holding the fabric against me, twirling around like a little girl in a fancy dress shop. The skirt rustled as I hung it back on the rack. I walked to the dressing table, and my cheeks flushed as I regarded myself in the mirror. What would Lady Anna think of me here, in her bedroom—a stranger sifting through her most intimate possessions? In spite of my reticence, I couldn't resist letting my fingers rest on the bulb of the perfume atomizer. A quick squeeze and the yellow cord connected to the stately cut glass decanter flooded the air with a sweet, floral mist. I breathed in the heady scent, and then I heard footsteps in the hallway. *Who's coming? How will I explain myself?* I'd been seduced by my own curiosity and lingered too long. *I have to hide.* I looked ahead, where a dark hallway deeper in the room connected to an interior door, which had been left ajar. I slipped inside what must have been Lady Anna's personal study. Framed botanical sketches hung over a desk and a bookcase.

I took a deep breath and peered through the crack in the door, unsure of whom or what I'd see. A figure walked toward the window and pulled the drapes open. I covered my mouth when I saw Lord Livingston's face in the light. He looked deeply pained, grief-stricken, as he knelt beside Lady Anna's bed. I watched as he hung his head, choking back tears. "I'm so very sorry, my love," he muttered. "So very sorry."

I stood frozen. And then, the creak of the door again. Lord Livingston turned and frowned as Mrs. Dilloway approached.

"Forgive me for interrupting you," she said solicitously. She held a vase of pink flowers. Peonies. "I'll leave you."

Dabbing a handkerchief to his eye, he searched her face. "We were wrong, you know," he said, "terribly wrong."

She looked down at her clasped hands, solemnly. "Yes," she said. "Yes, we were."

My heart raced. *What are they talking about? What could they possibly mean?*

Lord Livingston cast a glance in my direction. "I was just going to . . ." He shook his head, as if he didn't have the emotional energy to continue.

Mrs. Dilloway took a step forward, and he pulled her toward him, burying his face in the crook of her neck. "Please, Edward," she said, looking up. "You don't have to carry this burden alone. Let me—"

He held up his hand, a quick dismissive gesture. In an instant, all trace of their intimate moment evaporated. "No," he said in his usual clipped, businesslike tone. "We mustn't carry on like this." I could see the changed look in Mrs. Dilloway's face too, as she followed his lead. Whatever moment they'd shared, whatever meaning had been exchanged in their eyes had vanished.

After Lord Livingston left the room, Mrs. Dilloway set the vase of peonies on the table near the bed. She paused to smooth the coverlet, before pressing her face against her forearm and weeping. I looked away. It felt wrong to watch her sorrow.

After I heard the door click shut, I exhaled deeply, which is when I noticed a book that appeared to have fallen from the bookcase. It seemed out of place on the floor in the tidy study. I knelt down to pick it up, and eyed the cover with interest. "The Camellias of Livingston Manor; Compiled by Anna Livingston." I tucked it under my arm and hurried out the door, through the bedroom, and out into the hallway.

"What's that in your hand?" Katherine asked suspiciously as I slipped inside the nursery. *How much time has passed?* I glanced at the clock on the wall: a quarter past ten.

"I'm so sorry I'm late, children," I said. "I was helping Sadie with the linens this morning."

Janie ran to my side, where she tugged at the book eagerly as though she'd seen it before. "Flower book," she said, pointing to the cover.

"Where did you find Mummy's book?" Katherine asked, hovering near me.

Cautiously, I revealed the book as I sat on the sofa. "Would you like to look at it with me?" I said, avoiding the question.

Katherine nodded and the boys gathered round as I cracked the spine and thumbed through page after page of beautiful camellias, pressed and glued onto each page, with handwritten notes next to each. On the page that featured the *Camellia reticulata*, a large, salmon-colored flower, she had written: *Edward had this one brought in from China. It's fragile. I've given it the garden's best shade.* On the next page, near the *Camellia sasanqua*, she wrote: *A Christmas gift from Edward and the children. This one will need extra love. It hardly survived the passage from Japan. I will spend the spring nursing it back to health.*

On each page, there were meticulous notes about the care and feeding of the camellias—when she planted them, how often they were watered, fertilized, and pruned. In the right-hand corner of some pages, I noticed an unusual series of numbers.

"What does that mean?" I asked the children.

Nicholas shrugged. "This one was Mummy's favorite," he said, flipping to the last page in the book. I marveled at the pink-tipped white blossoms as my heart began to beat faster. The Middlebury Pink.

I leaned in closer to read Anna's handwriting. "It says here that it's the last remaining variety of this type in the world." I turned to Katherine. "Is it in the orchard with the others?"

"Probably," she said, standing up. "Unless Mr. Blythe moved it. He was always moving things around. He and Mr. Humphrey."

I shook my head. "Mr. Humphrey?"

"He sometimes helps in the orchard," Abbott added, rolling his eyes. "Mummy never liked him skulking. She said he made a mess of her rose garden once."

"Well," I said, "I'm sure he was just trying to be helpful." I turned back to the book, and in the final pages before the Middlebury Pink, Lady Anna had pasted an entry from an old encyclopedia, detailing the story of the camellia's introduction to the New World. I read for a few moments, before turning to the children. "Their seeds were brought by ship from all over Asia and considered very valuable," I said. "According to this book, camellias can live for hundreds of years, which makes them the best secret keepers of all plants and trees."

"Sounds silly to me," Katherine said, feigning disinterest, but I could see that she was captivated. "Trees don't keep secrets."

"Well," I said, "it says that in Victorian times, people used to believe that if you made a wish under a camellia tree, it would come true."

Nicholas grinned. "Sort of like throwing a shilling into a fountain to make a wish?"

"Yes," I said. "Your mother must have been a special person to have loved camellias the way she did."

"Why didn't the trees protect her, then?" Nicholas said. "The day she died?"

Abbott stomped over to the window seat. Of all the children, he seemed most disturbed by his mother's death.

I closed the book, realizing that the memories of their mother might be too much for them to bear. "Let's read something else," I said, setting the book on the side table. I'd have a look again later. Perhaps there was a clue to the Middlebury Pink's location.

"What's that smell?" Abbott asked, pausing to sniff the air.

"I don't know," I said, a bit flustered.

"It smells like Mummy," Nicholas said.

Their mother's perfume.

Katherine huffed. "It's not Mummy's perfume, you ninny," she said, turning her nose to the air. "It's coming from the kitchen. The cook probably burned the roast again."

Nicholas eyed his mother's camellia book before looking at me again. "Miss Lewis, can I ask you a question?"

"Of course," I said.

He sighed. "Our last nanny, Miss Fairfield, said a mean thing about Mummy the day she was dismissed."

"Oh, honey, whatever did she say?"

Nicholas clasped his hands together. "She said, she said . . . that our mother wasn't a real lady."

If I lived at the manor for a decade, I still don't think I'd get used to taking my meals with Mr. Beardsley hovering around the dining room. He served the meals, assisted by Mrs. Dilloway. He'd place rolls on our plates as if we were incapable of reaching for them ourselves. All of it made me long for home, and the quiet, unpretentious meals at the kitchen table in the apartment over the bakery, where Mama and Papa and I would laugh and talk, and dip our bread into Mama's potato soup. And if we wanted another piece or, heaven forbid, more butter, we'd reach for it ourselves. New York seemed a world away.

Mr. Beardsley held a tureen and ladled fish stew into each of our bowls. He eyed me coldly, I thought, as he passed my seat, but then again, I hadn't gotten used to the formality in the house.

"Aw," Nicholas complained. "Not fish stew again!"

I shot him a look before his father scolded him. "What Nicholas meant to say was, 'Thank you, Mr. Beardsley.'"

Lord Livingston nodded at me, and dipped his spoon in his bowl as Mr. Beardsley hovered beside him. "If I may, your Lordship," he said, nervously wiping his brow with a handkerchief. "May I have a word with you?"

Lord Livingston nodded, released his napkin from his neck, and turned to us. "Please excuse me."

A moment later, he returned. Sitting back down at the table, he held out his hand, where a silver coin rested in his palm, and cleared his throat authoritatively. "It has come to my attention that one of the Roman coins from my collection has turned up in . . ." He paused, looking directly at me. "In Miss Lewis's quarters."

My mouth gaped open, and I shook my head in disbelief. "I don't understand," I said quickly. "That can't be."

"I have no other choice but to ask you to leave, Miss Lewis, at once."

"But, sir, but, please, I—"

Lord Livingston held up his hand. "Please, don't make this harder than it is."

My cheeks flushed as I stood up, setting my napkin down on the table. Mrs. Dilloway eyed me with disdain. Janie began to cry. The older children wouldn't look at me.

In the doorway of the dining room, I stopped when I heard the scuff of a chair on the wood floors. "Wait," Abbott said. "Don't go, Miss Lewis."

"Abbott," Lord Livingston said, "I've already made my decision. Do not contradict me, young man."

"But, Father," he said, "Miss Lewis didn't take the coin." He scratched his head nervously. "I did."

Mr. Beardsley exchanged a look of shock with Mrs. Dilloway.

Lord Livingston appeared momentarily astonished. "You did *what*?"

Next, Nicholas rose to stand behind his brother. "I'm to blame too, Father," the younger boy said. "We put it in Miss Lewis's bedroom."

Katherine stood next. "I knew too," she said. "I should never have let them go through with it."

"Children," Lord Livingston said, "why would you do such a beastly thing?"

Abbott looked at Nicholas. "You see," he said nervously, "we didn't like Miss Lewis. Not at first. We thought she'd be like all the other nannies. So we tried to get her sacked." He stopped and smiled at me apologetically. "But then we realized she was different, Father. She wasn't like all the others. But it was too late. We tried to get the coin back, but by the time we went back to her room, it was gone."

"We're awfully sorry, Miss Lewis," Nicholas said.

Lord Livingston slammed his fist on the table. "Abbott, Nicholas, and you, too, Katherine—I've never been more disappointed in my children." He turned to me. "Miss Lewis, please accept my sincere apologies for this . . . misunderstanding."

"Of course, sir," I said quickly. Katherine began cry. "Please, your Lordship, don't punish them. They've been through so much already; it's only natural that they'd—"

"What on earth is this?" Lord Livingston said suddenly, after Ferris trotted in and deposited something in his lap. The dog wagged his tail expectantly, oblivious to the mood in the room. "Beardsley, what has Ferris made off with here?" He held up a mauled piece of fabric, tan in color. "Well, I'll be hanged," he said. "I do believe this is my sock."

A thick silence fell over the dining room. I wasn't sure whether Lord Livingston would storm off to his study or send the boys to their room. Surely one of the two. But then he picked up his napkin and covered his mouth. I detected laughter from behind the napkin. Mr. Beardsley chimed in next, beginning with a chuckle that turned into a roar. The children followed suit, even Katherine.

"I have two very sneaky sons," Lord Livingston said with a wry smile. "But it's most uncanny, Mrs. Dilloway," he continued. "They were telling me earlier how much they'd enjoy helping Sadie wash the dishes tonight. I don't suppose she could use a little help in the kitchen later?"

Mrs. Dilloway looked at me and then at Mr. Beardsley with raised eyebrows. "If you say so," she said. "Miss Lewis, bring them downstairs after dinner."

Abbott and Nicholas smiled through the rest of their

dinner. I knew they didn't care about having to wash dishes, not when they'd seen their father smile for the first time in what was probably a very long time. I smiled too, for now I knew I had earned the children's admiration.

"I hope they weren't too much trouble with the dishes," I said to Sadie in the washroom later that night.

"No," she replied, twisting her long hair into a single braid, "they did their best. Nicholas broke a saucer, but this house has enough saucers to invite the entire country to tea." She paused. "I heard that his Lordship was laughing at dinner."

I nodded, smiling as I recalled the scene.

"This house could use more laughter," she said. "He carries such a burden, you know."

"What do you mean, exactly?"

She tied the end of her braid without looking up. "Lady Anna was a saint, if you ask me," she said. "All those women."

I shook my head. "You're not saying that—"

"That he was unfaithful to his wife?" Sadie shrugged. "That's between him and his maker." She tucked her braid into her nightcap with a sigh. "But, yes, there were many, including—" She shook her head, as if snuffing out the thought. "I mustn't gossip. Well, good night, Miss Lewis. I'd better turn in."

Before I turned my lamp out, there was a knock on my door. "Yes," I said.

Mrs. Dilloway stood in the doorway in her nightgown.

"Come in," I said.

"How can you ever forgive me?" she said.

"Forgive you for what?"

"I don't know what I thought I was doing looking through your things," she said, sitting down in the chair beside my desk. "I worried you were too perfect, and I thought if I found something in your room, I could have a reason to distrust you. Even when I found the coin, I didn't believe you'd taken it, but I—"

"I'm not upset," I said as it dawned on me what she was saying. "I completely understand. You did what you had to do."

She shook her head, dabbing her eyes with a handkerchief. "No," she said. "I was out of line." She looked into my eyes. "I beg your forgiveness, Miss Lewis."

"You don't have to beg for it. I will give it to you freely."

"Thank you," she said, standing up.

"Mrs. Dilloway," I said as she reached for the doorknob. "How long have you loved Lord Livingston?"

She didn't seem the least bit startled by my question. Perhaps the incident tonight had leveled the playing field between us. We'd moved beyond the pecking order of the house to two women—two women facing our own battles, our own loves, our own heartache. "Oh," she said wistfully, "I suppose since the day I arrived at the manor."

I nodded.

"I never meant to hurt anyone," she said. "Especially Lady Anna."

"I know," I assured her. "Please, don't feel that you have to explain yourself."

She took a deep breath. "Miss Lewis," she said, looking at

me with vulnerable eyes. This was the face of a friend. "You see," she continued, "I've come to realize that you can fight a lot of things in life, but you can't help who you love. You can't change who your heart chooses. I'm afraid that very fact will be the greatest tragedy of my life."

I didn't bother to turn on the lamp by my bedside. The light from the moon streamed in through the window with the intensity of a forty-watt bulb. I took out a piece of stationery and an envelope from the desk drawer and sat down to write a letter home:

Dear Mama and Papa,

I miss you terribly, and yet I already worry about leaving the children. I've come to love them, even in this short time. I feel for them, having just lost their mother, and with a father who hardly acknowledges them. Well, perhaps I'm being too hard on him. Perhaps he has a heart after all? Anyway, I fear that without my presence here, they would suffer greatly, especially the littlest one, Janie. She's just two years old, without a parent to show her the love she desperately needs. The ten-year-old girl, Katherine, is my hardest case, though. She misses her mother terribly. And Abbott, the older boy, is deeply troubled. I haven't yet figured out why. Anyway, there's something else: I get the feeling that there is some sort of dark secret surrounding the death of the lady of the house. Don't be frightened for me. I know I'm in no danger here, but there are questions that no one will answer about her death. I'm making it my very own mystery to solve, how about that? Well, please write when you can. It feels very lonely here at times, and I'd love nothing more than a letter from home. I'd ask for you to send bread, but I suppose it would only end up hard and stale by the time it arrived. Instead, I'll imagine Papa's honey whole wheat and dream of home.

Your loving daughter,

Flora

I folded the letter and stuffed it inside an envelope, which I sealed and addressed before setting it on the desk. I'd bring it to Mr. Humphrey to mail in town tomorrow. Then I climbed into bed and thought about Mrs. Dilloway, then Lady Anna and her camellia book. If I was quiet, I could tiptoe up to the nursery without disturbing anyone and bring it back to my room to read.

Once in the nursery, I picked up the book from the table where I'd left it earlier that day. I carried it downstairs to the privacy of my bedroom and I immediately riffled its back pages. But where was the Middlebury Pink? I looked more closely and could see that a page had been torn out. All that remained was its jagged edge.

CHAPTER 17

Addison

Late that sleepless night, I was drawn to the east wing. I entered the darkened bedchamber. A lace-trimmed white coverlet had been pulled taut over the four-poster, and a vase of orange tiger lilies sat on the adjacent bedside table. As my eyes adjusted to the dimness, I noticed a tiny droplet of water on the cherry table. Someone had been here. Perhaps moments ago.

A door creaked behind me.

"What do you think of Lady Anna's room?" Mrs. Dilloway asked from the doorway. A shadow covered her face, so I couldn't make out her expression. "It is just as she left it."

"I'm so sorry for barging in like this," I said, putting down the hand mirror I had found on the dressing table. "I couldn't sleep, so I went for a walk." My words sounded hurried and defensive. "I passed this doorway. It was open. I guess my curiosity got the better of me."

Mrs. Dilloway walked toward the dressing table, gazing at it lovingly. "There has never been anyone like Lady Anna, never before and never since," she said. In the mirror, her eyes flashed with excitement, while her face appeared grief-stricken—a strange mix of exhilaration and pain.

I felt uncomfortable standing so close to her. I wanted to run to the doorway and sprint back to my room, to Rex, but my legs stood frozen. And then I felt Mrs. Dilloway's icy hand on my wrist. "I would like to show you something," she said. "Come with me, please."

Mrs. Dilloway lifted a gold chain from her neck. Two keys dangled from it. She inserted one in the locked door deep inside the room. I peered into the doorway, letting my eyes soak up the scene as Mrs. Dilloway switched on a floor lamp. A gold-trimmed Louis XVI chair sat near the window, by a desk with a book splayed out. The sunlight had long since faded its pages. There were papers scattered about, photographs, a notebook with a pen beside it, as if Lady Anna had only recently finished signing her name on some correspondence, maybe a response to a dinner invitation in London or a formal event at the home of a duke. I imagined her threading her *A* with an elongated dash, curled at the end. Maybe she signed it with a little flower at the corner, as I did. I took a few steps closer, admiring the bookcase near the window. Instead of containing stories, however, the collection was entirely botanical. I pulled a spine from the shelf. *The Care and Feeding of Roses.* Another, larger book, a manual about perennials, featured a sketch of a hydrangea on the cover.

"She was self-taught," Mrs. Dilloway said. "She knew more about plants and flowers than anyone."

I nodded, watching the old woman gaze about the room. She walked closer to me, gesturing toward the upholstered bench by the window. I followed her lead and sat down. I imagined the children running in to see their mother here. The little girl lying on the bench looking out at the gardens while her mother worked, the boys engrossed in comic books. Such happiness. What had destroyed it?

Mrs. Dilloway appeared frail, more so than I'd noticed before. The light from the lamp illuminated the wrinkles on her skin, the tiredness in her eyes. "It's no secret that I am old," she said. "I don't have much time left." She patted her thin white hair. "Ms. Sinclair, the Wednesday appointments are not visits to the beauty parlor. I've been seeing a doctor. I have cancer. I will soon begin treatment, and I will be unable to keep up my duties here."

"Oh, I'm so sorry; I didn't know—"

"I don't want your pity," she snapped. "But I do need your help." She opened the drawer of the desk and pulled out a stack of newspaper clippings. "Before she died, Lady Anna confided in me about a grave matter, something I have been unable to come to terms with all these years."

I scanned the first newspaper clipping. "This is about that missing girl," I said. "Lila Hertzberg."

"Yes," Mrs. Dilloway replied. "And there are others, too."

I flipped to the next clipping. "Jane Ianella," I said, before reading the others. "Ellen Hanover, Doris Wheeler, Beatrice Crane, Lisbeth O'Neely." I shook my head. "All of them abducted."

Mrs. Dilloway nodded, reaching up to a pewter jewelry box on the top shelf of the bookcase. "Lady Anna found this," she said.

I took the box in my hands and opened the lid, where I found a gold bracelet resting on the blue velvet lining. I picked it up and looked at Mrs. Dilloway. "I don't understand. What is this?"

"Read the inscription," she said.

I turned the bracelet over and noticed an engraving on the back. "To Lila, With Love."

"You think it's . . ."

Mrs. Dilloway pointed to the stack of newspaper clippings.

I tugged at my wristwatch. "But Lila was a common name

back then, wasn't it? How could she be so sure that it belonged to *that* Lila?"

Mrs. Dilloway took the bracelet in her hand and turned it over, pointing to the "H" stamped on the clasp. "Because her father was a jeweler," she said. *"Hertzberg* Jewelers."

I gasped. "Where did Lady Anna find the bracelet?"

Mrs. Dilloway paused before answering. "In Lord Livingston's bedroom."

"Did you see Mrs. Dilloway this morning?" Rex asked after breakfast on the terrace.

"Just briefly," I replied. I had yet to mention my midnight encounter to him. "Why?"

"She doesn't look well."

"She needs rest," I said, concerned. "It's time we insist that she take some time off."

Though Mrs. Dilloway didn't agree to a day off, she did come sit beside us on the terrace that afternoon with Mrs. Klein.

We played Thirty-one, and Mrs. Dilloway, at first reluctant, proved to be quite the competitor, winning four games in a row.

Later, while Rex dozed in a chaise longue, Mrs. Klein gazed at the orchard. "When you see a place every day for so many years," she reflected, "you stop noticing how beautiful it is."

"It's lovely," I said, nodding.

"Sometimes I feel sorry for her," she continued.

"For who?"

"For Lady Anna," she said.

Mrs. Dilloway sat up straighter in her chair, but looked away as though she had no interest in joining in the discussion.

"Why?" I asked.

"Well, of course, I never knew her," Mrs. Klein continued, "but I can imagine her plight. A talented gardener who never felt the joy her creation brought to so many is like the cook who never glimpses the smiles of appreciation for her desserts."

"I know exactly what you mean," I said. "The rare tea rose in my New York garden wouldn't have the same appeal without Rex there to enjoy it with me."

Mrs. Klein nodded to herself.

"Maybe she's looking down on it all?" I said after a moment of silence.

"She's probably busy planting flowers in heaven for the angels," she said quietly. Mrs. Dilloway raised her head for a brief moment before quickly turning back to the row of hydrangeas below the terrace. They'd recently come into bloom, and the effect was a stunning wall of blue. Blue hydrangeas only grow in acidic soil, and I wondered if Lady Anna had sprinkled the roots with coffee grounds over the years. It was the only way I could get a client's hydrangeas tinged the perfect shade of periwinkle she'd hoped for.

"Well," I said. "I think I'll go take a nap." I poured a cup of tea, and walked back up to the second-floor bedroom, thinking of Lady Anna with each step. Had she tried to notify someone of what she'd found before she died? Had she confronted Lord Livingston? I couldn't wait to discuss all the details with Rex.

I closed the bedroom door behind me, and immediately heard Rex's cell phone buzzing from his bag. I opened the flap to fish for the phone, but before I could retrieve it, I noticed a manila file folder labeled "Amanda."

CHAPTER 18

In the days Desmond was at the manor, he'd successfully avoided his father, with the help of Mr. Beardsley and Mrs. Dilloway, of course. He wanted to see the children desperately, but we agreed it would be best to keep quiet for now. One word from Katherine or Janie, and Lord Livingston's temper would flare. I wondered about the reason for their falling-out, but I didn't press Desmond for details, and he didn't seem eager to share them.

One morning after breakfast, I met him in the drawing room. He closed the doors behind us and took me in his arms. "I've just received a telegram from my commanding officer," he said. "I'm afraid I have to report to London."

"Oh, Desmond," I cried. "Please tell me everything's all right. Please tell me you won't be in any danger."

"Yes," he said, smoothing a lock of hair away from my face. "At least, I think so."

"How long will you be gone?"

"I don't know."

"But the children, you haven't even seen them yet. What will I tell them?"

"Don't tell them anything," he said quickly. "I don't want to worry them. Besides, I'll be back before you know it." He traced my face with his finger. "Promise me you won't go anywhere?"

"I promise."

He kissed my cheek and then he was gone.

A month passed, and then another. By then, I'd stopped jumping up the moment I heard a car pulling up the manor drive. "Don't worry so much," Mrs. Dilloway said to me one afternoon. "He'll come home again." It was as if she could read my mind.

While I waited, I settled into a comfortable routine with the children. I'd lost sight of the Middlebury Pink, the orchard, until one evening, just after sunset, when a kiss of light remained in the sky, I looked out my bedroom window to the camellias. A shadowy figure weaved in and out of the trees. *Someone's out there.*

"Excuse me, sir," I said, knocking on the door of the butler's pantry, where Mr. Beardsley always went after breakfast. It was less a pantry and more an office, with a closet where the silver was kept. The room adjoined the wine cellar, which always remained locked.

"Yes, Miss Lewis," Mr. Beardsley said, looking up at me from his desk. His very demeanor commanded respect.

"I'm sorry to interrupt, sir," I said. The children were still having breakfast, and I had another fifteen minutes before I'd meet them in the nursery. "I wanted to mention something to you. Something I saw."

"Oh? What did you see, Miss Lewis?"

"Last night," I said, "before I went to sleep, I saw from my window a man—in the orchard, sir."

"A man?"

"Yes," I replied. "It seemed strange. Who would be walking out there so late?"

"Strange, indeed," he said. "I'll ask Mr. Humphrey to go have a look this afternoon."

Later that morning, I ran into Mrs. Dilloway and Sadie just outside the nursery. "Is everything all right, Miss Lewis?" Sadie asked. "You look tired."

"Yes," I said. "I'm fine."

"You've been working so hard since you arrived," she continued. "Why don't you . . ." Sadie looked at Mrs. Dilloway and then back at me.

"What is it, Sadie?"

"Well," she continued. "I don't mean to overstep my bounds, but it's just that, well, Mrs. Dilloway, Miss Lewis hasn't had a day off since she arrived."

Mrs. Dilloway's stiff expression softened momentarily. "Yes," she said. "You're right, Sadie. Miss Lewis, if you'd like to have a day to yourself, you may."

Sadie smiled victoriously as I turned toward the children in the nursery. Nicholas, who'd been listening to our exchange, made a sour face behind Mrs. Dilloway's back.

"I can take care of the children while you're out," Sadie said, indicating the doorway. "Why don't you go into town, have a look around? You haven't done anything but chase after children and mend clothes since you arrived." She turned to Mrs. Dilloway. "And she could ride in with Lord Livingston and return this afternoon."

Mrs. Dilloway hesitated. "But, I don't—"

"He wouldn't mind," Sadie added. "Miss Fairfield used to have every Saturday off, and he'd let her ride along into town with him."

Mrs. Dilloway nodded. "All right," she said, a bit reluctantly. She eyed her watch and smiled. "You have just enough time to run down to your room to fetch your handbag."

"Well," I said, "as long as you don't think Lord Livingston would mind."

"Oh, before I forget," Mrs. Dilloway said, reaching into her pocket and pulling out a letter, "*this* came for you."

"For me?" I examined the envelope, expecting something from Mama and Papa, but I didn't recognize the handwriting or the return address in London. "Thank you," I said, turning to the stairs.

Inside my bedroom, I closed the door behind me, tore open the envelope, and held the letter in my hands.

Don't get too cozy there, Miss Lewis. You have a job to do. Complete your assignment or I'll pay a visit to your father, and it won't be a cordial one.—Philip

I closed my eyes tightly, crumpling the letter in my clenched fist.

Mr. Humphrey had his head in the trunk of the car when I approached the driveway. "Oh, hello, Miss Lewis," he said, flashing a startled smile. He threw two dirt-stained work gloves inside the trunk, then slammed it shut, before holding the side door open for me. I slid into the backseat and placed my black purse on the floor near my feet, where I immediately noticed a glint of metal that had caught the sunlight. I hovered for a closer look. "Mr. Humphrey, I think I've found something—"

"Ah, yes," he said, swooping in to collect what looked like a silver necklace from the floor of the car. "There it is. I thought I'd lost it. It's a gift for my mum. Purchased it in town yesterday." I watched as he opened the glove compartment and tucked it inside, looking behind him when he heard the crunch of gravel in the distance.

I tugged at my gloves nervously. I should have worn my black hat instead of this blue one that clashed with my handbag. What did it matter? Whom did I expect to run into in town? I leaned back in the seat, but sat up again when I saw Mr. Humphrey straighten his stance.

"Miss Lewis is here, my lord," he said. "She'll be joining us today in town."

"Very good," Lord Livingston said, poking his head into the car. "Hello, Miss Lewis."

"Hello," I replied.

He sat beside me in his freshly pressed gray pin-striped suit, the one I'd seen Mrs. Dilloway ironing late last night. I'd watched her for a moment, noticing how she had ironed the pleats on the breast of the suit with such care, going over them again and again until she'd made a perfect crease.

Lord Livingston didn't keep a personal valet, so the extra duties fell to Mrs. Dilloway, but she didn't mind. I folded my hands three different ways, then turned to look out the window.

"I trust the children are minding you, Miss Lewis?"

"Yes, thank you," I said, shifting my attention to the view through the windshield.

"And your room, is it satisfactory?"

"It's very nice."

He paused a long while, then turned to me. "Miss Lewis," he continued. "What I want to say . . . what I mean to tell you . . ." His gaze pierced my cheek. "I'm quite satisfied with your work with the children. I want you to know that I'm glad you're here."

"Oh," I said, a little taken aback by his words. "Thank you."

"If you don't mind my asking, Miss Lewis," he continued, "how did you end up as a nanny? I suppose what I mean is that it seems that you ought to be married to some nice young chap in America by now."

My cheeks burned red. "I suppose it's a rather long story," I said.

He nodded as if he understood. "Well, I'm glad you could come into town today. Did you have any special plans?"

I shook my head. "No, not anything special," I said. "I just thought I'd poke around the shops, sir—I mean, Lord Livingston, sir . . . I mean . . ." *Why does he make me so tongue-tied?* I was perfectly capable of talking to any of the well-to-do who came into the bakery at home. One time the governor stopped in, and I waited on him myself.

From my pocket I pulled out a letter I'd written my parents. "And I'll drop by the post office to mail this letter home."

He plucked the letter from my hand. "No need to waste your precious day off standing in line at the post office," he said. "Have Humphrey take it in for you."

He leaned over the seat. "Humphrey, you'll see to it that Miss Lewis's letter is delivered, won't you?"

The chauffeur eyed his master through the rearview mirror. "Yes, my Lord," he replied.

"Thank you," I said.

He pointed out the window at the rolling hills tinged with purple heather. "I've traveled the world, Miss Lewis, but nothing is as beautiful as these moors."

I nodded. "I'd love to paint that scene," I said, pointing out to the windswept meadow.

"Oh, you're interested in art?"

"Well, yes," I replied. "Botanical art."

"Would you really paint that scene, just as it is?"

"Well, I suppose," I said. "I'd need the right supplies. A proper easel, a canvas, some paints. I brought only my sketchbook to England."

"Ah, simplicity," he said. "Your sketches must be lovely."

A few minutes later, Mr. Humphrey pulled the car into town. He stopped at the train station first.

"Well," Lord Livingston said, "I'm off to London for a few days."

"Have a good trip," I said.

Before he stepped out of the car, a pretty woman, about my age, waved from the sidewalk. Her cream-colored dress clung to her body, accentuating her figure. She approached the car, smiling as though she and Lord Livingston might be old friends. He rolled down the window, regarding her somewhat coldly.

"Hello, Theresa," he said. Mr. Humphrey watched the exchange in the rearview mirror.

"Will you be coming in today, Lord Livingston?" she asked, grinning, until she noticed me. "Oh, I'm so sorry," she continued. "I didn't know you had a guest with you."

Lord Livingston turned to me reluctantly. "Miss Lewis, this is Theresa Mueller," he said. "Theresa works at the restaurant down the street."

"I'll be going now," she said, turning to the sidewalk before casting a final glance his way.

"I'm sorry about that," he said.

Mr. Humphrey cleared his throat. "His Lordship is a bit of a celebrity in town," he added.

"Well, it's getting late," Lord Livingston said. "I'll miss my train." He reached for his bag, then paused to look at me again. "Miss Lewis," he said before he stepped out onto the sidewalk, "I meant to say . . ." He searched my eyes. "You see"—he rubbed his forehead—"I'm quite sorry I was so hard on you about that matter of the coin."

"It's all right," I said.

His face relaxed. "Well, I hope you can forgive me."

I nodded.

He stepped out of the car, and Mr. Humphrey, who had already run around to open his door, bid him farewell. "Have a good trip, my Lord."

"Thank you, Humphrey," he said, casting a glance back toward the sidewalk where Miss Mueller had stood. "See to it that Miss Lewis is taken care of today."

"Yes, sir," he said.

Mrs. Dilloway knocked at my door later that evening. "How was your time?"

"Fine, thank you," I said, recalling my day in the village. I'd wandered down to the square and bought a bag of peanuts before planting myself on a bench and watching children play in the fountain. Then I ordered a cup of tea at the café, slipped into an upholstered chair, and finally finished *The Years*. "I'd go say good night to the children, but I take it they're already asleep."

"They are," she said, walking into my room and shutting the door behind her. "Do you mind if we talk privately for a moment?"

"Of course not," I said. "What is it?" My eyes narrowed. "Is everything all right? Janie hasn't caught a cold, has she? She had a bit of the sniffles yesterday and I worried—"

"Janie's fine," she said. "You're so good with them. Too good, perhaps. That's what I want to talk to you about."

"I don't understand."

"Miss Lewis," she said, "nannies like you don't stay forever. You can't. You have a whole life ahead of you. Marriage. Children of your own, even."

"Well, someday, but—"

"But you're not staying forever, are you?"

"No," I said.

"Exactly my point. I'm just thinking of the children, that's all. I'm thinking of how they'll take the news if it turns out that your intentions are . . ." She paused as if to search for the right word. "*Different* than intended."

The hair on my arm stood on end. Was she hinting at something? "I'm sorry, I'm not sure what you mean."

"All I'm saying is if you decide to leave, for whatever reason, give them time to get used to the idea," she explained. "Their mother left just like that, and then a stream of nannies came in and out of this house. I can't bear to see them lose you so suddenly after what they've been through."

I nodded. "You love them, don't you, Mrs. Dilloway?"

"I suppose I do," she said, glancing at the clock on the wall. "Well, it's getting late, nearly half past nine. I promised Mrs. Marden that I'd put the steaks in the marinade before bed. She likes them to baste a full twelve hours before lunch." She smiled briefly before turning to the hallway. "Good night, Miss Lewis."

"Good night," I said.

After she left, I thought about the lonely life Mrs. Dilloway had chosen. I rested my head on my pillow and sighed. She was right, though. Someone had to look after those poor children. Abbott was on the verge of manhood, and yet he was so fragile and sensitive. I wished his father would pay him more attention. And Nicholas, sweet Nicholas, with his handsome face, that raven-colored hair and cheeky smile—the only thing he ever wanted was to be noticed. Katherine's troubles seemed deeper than I could understand, and I wished I knew how to help her. Janie was too young to remember her mother, and that fact alone may have spelled her from the heartache the older children carried—burdens so great you could see their grief sometimes hovering in their eyes and their distant expressions. And Desmond. *Desmond.* Would he return? When?

Their father was such a complicated man. He'd seemed so stern and calculating when I first arrived, but today he warmed to me in a way I hadn't expected. How could I get him to show that warmth to his children? How could I make him see how much they needed him? I yawned, reaching for the extra wool blanket at the foot of the bed. Nights were chilly in this big house.

Mrs. Dilloway was right. I wouldn't be here forever, but I'd make the most of the time I had. I thought of the letter from Mr.

Price. There wasn't much time now. I'd need to find the camellia, or else.

During the month that Lord Livingston was in London, the entire house seemed to let out a sigh of relief. Even the grandfather clock in the foyer seemed less solemn in its movement, as if time had gone on holiday. I didn't worry when the children's game of hopscotch spilled into the rose garden or when Janie knocked a bowl of pea soup on the rug. We all had more breathing room.

Every night before bed, I visited the conservatory on the third floor. It was nice not to worry about tripping over a flowerpot and disturbing Lord Livingston on the floor below. I still had to be inconspicuous, though, so I worked by lamplight.

I had come to love the space, and I could see why Lady Anna had too. The orchids were positively glorious. She'd tagged each flower with its proper botanical name, but I favored the pet names she'd given each bloom. For instance, a stunning pink *Cattleya* was named "Lady Catalina." And a yellow *Oncidium*, which to me looked like a flock of ladies in fluffy party dresses, was called "Lady Aralia of the Bayou."

The night before Lord Livingston was to return from London, I went up to the conservatory to water the flowers, knowing it might be a few days before I could get back again. After the children were in bed, I tiptoed up the stairs the way I always did, slipping inside using the key under the flap of carpet. I gave the orchids a good drink, then refilled the watering can at the spigot and walked over to the plants by the east window. A bit of water soaked the hem of my nightgown as I emptied the can over the trunk of the lemon tree. I looked out at the night sky, remembering how I'd seen Lord Livingston on the terrace in his robe. I blushed at the thought. He'd been looking out at the camellia orchard that night. Was he thinking about the children? About Anna? Was he thinking about his regrets?

I poured the last few drops of water onto a palm in a terracotta urn, and reached for the lantern, when something outside caught my eye. I looked carefully into the night, and then I saw what looked like a faint glow in the orchard. A lantern? It moved right a few paces, then went out.

I hurried to the door, looking both ways before venturing into the hallway, then locked it behind me. I heard a sniffling sound.

I looked down to see a figure huddled in a ball. I recognized the pink nightgown immediately. "Katherine?"

She sat against the wall, knees tucked against her chest, and looked up at me with tear-streaked cheeks.

I knelt down beside her. "Katherine, what's the matter, dear?"

"I followed you," she said. "I wanted to know why you came up here every night."

"Oh," I said, setting down the lantern.

"Mother never let me go in there," she said, pointing to the door. "She'd spend hours inside. All I wanted was to see her flowers. I just wanted to see them."

"Oh, Katherine," I said, stroking her dark hair.

"Never mind," she said, standing up and composing herself. "It's silly of me to go on like this."

"It's not," I said, standing next to her. "We may never understand why your mother didn't let you join her in the conservatory, and I'm sure she had her reasons." I sighed, remembering Mrs. Dilloway's warnings. *What good does this place do all locked up when it could bring joy to this little girl who misses her mother so desperately?* "You know, Katherine," I continued, "I think you should see it now."

Her eyes widened. "You do?"

"Yes," I said. "But you mustn't tell your brothers or Janie."

She nodded eagerly. "I won't tell."

"Good," I said. "It will be our secret." I inserted the key in the door again. "Come on."

Katherine followed me inside, mouth gaping as she took in the sight. "It's, it's . . . so beautiful," she marveled as we passed the citrus trees. "Mummy used to bring us kumquats." She paused, then looked at me with an embarrassed smile. "I'm sorry, Miss Lewis. I've been terrible to you."

"It's all right," I said, kneeling down to look into her eyes. "You didn't know me then." I plucked a kumquat from the tree and popped it in her mouth. "And now you do."

I touched her arm tenderly. "Honey, may I ask you about these marks? What happened?"

She pulled back her arm instinctively, then took a deep breath, relaxing. "Do you promise not to tell?"

I nodded.

She pulled her sleeve up slowly, turning over her small forearm to reveal skin littered with wounds—some scarred, some fresh, others scabbed. I winced.

"Oh, Katherine!" I cried. "Please tell me who did this to you."

She looked down at her feet. "I did."

I placed my hand over my mouth. "I don't understand."

"I should have made Mummy happier," she said, beginning to cry. "If I had been a better daughter, she wouldn't have been so unhappy."

"No, no, Katherine," I said, wrapping my arms around her. "That's not true at all. Her unhappiness didn't have anything to do with you. I promise you that."

She buried her face against my shoulder.

"You must stop hurting yourself," I said. "Please tell me that you will."

"I'm so ashamed," she cried.

"You have nothing to be ashamed of, dear," I said, taking her hands in mine. "Your mother wouldn't want you to feel this way." I looked into her eyes. "I bet she's looking down on you now, wanting to see you smile again."

"Do you really think so?"

I nodded.

"And you don't think she'd be cross about me being here with you?" Her dark hair fell all around her face, and I tucked a lock behind her ear.

I didn't know the answer, of course. Not really. The more I learned about Lady Anna, the more mysterious she seemed. I wanted to believe that she had loved her children and wanted the best for them. But it didn't matter what the truth was, not anymore. All that mattered then was what Katherine needed to believe.

"Of course she wouldn't be cross, dear," I said. "In fact, I think she was waiting until you turned ten to show you this place. Ten's a very important age, you know."

"It is?"

"Indeed."

She held her head up a little higher and skipped over to the window to get a closer look at the palm. "Is this the one from the King of Thailand?"

"The King of Thailand?"

"Yes," she said. "I remember Papa talking about it."

"Perhaps," I said. The conservatory was full of treasures. But I wanted Katherine to have one of her very own. She deserved that. While she admired the kumquat tree, I walked over to the orchids and found one with a blank tag. Its bright purple blossoms appeared almost blue in the moonlight streaming through the glass roof. I picked up a pencil on the table, scrawled out "Lady Katherine of the Moors," and wedged the tag into the flowerpot.

"Katherine," I said. "You must see this."

She ran over beside me. "What is it?"

"It's one of your mother's orchids. Its botanical name is *Dendrobium*, but look, she's written something else on it."

She leaned in to read the tag, and then looked up at me with astonishment. "She named it Katherine," she said. "After me."

"See?" I said, grinning. "She named the most beautiful orchid after you. I bet she couldn't wait to show you that."

Katherine tucked her arm around my waist and gave me a squeeze. "Thank you, Miss Lewis. Thank you ever so much for letting me come in here with you."

"You're welcome," I said.

I glanced out the window and saw the light flicker in the orchard again.

"Come on," I whispered to Katherine. "Let's get you back to bed."

CHAPTER 19

Addison

Rex appeared in the foyer, holding the mail in one hand and a vase of flowers in the other. He'd spent the early part of the morning at the café, working on his research. "Look what was waiting for you on the doorstep."

He set the mail down on the entryway table and handed me the orange roses. "You must have a secret admirer," he said, grinning.

I opened the little envelope with trembling hands. On the card was one word: "Remember?"

"Who sent those?" he asked.

"Ah . . . my friend Kelly," I said, thinking fast.

Rex scratched his head. "Kelly? From college?"

"Yeah," I said. "She, um, she wanted to wish us an early happy anniversary."

Rex nodded. "Wow, that was nice of her to remember." He eyed the arrangement for a moment, curiously.

"How is your research going?" I asked as I set the flowers on the table next to the mail.

"Fine," he said, rubbing his forehead. "I can't help but think that this story is missing a crucial element—"

"I may have an idea for you," I said. "I couldn't sleep last night, so I went walking. And, well, Mrs. Dilloway showed me Lady Anna's study. Rex, I think something very dark happened here long ago."

"Really? Like what?"

"I'm not sure just yet," I said. "I think I'll head into town this afternoon to see if I can dig anything up."

"Good idea," he said. "I wish I could join you, but one trip into town is enough for today. Besides, I'm meeting with the foreman at noon."

"Foreman?"

"Yes," he said. "The man my father's hired to do the renovation."

I knew changes were in store, but I hated to think of them changing anything major about the manor. "They're not doing anything dramatic, are they?"

"I'm not sure," he said. "But it's not my decision. My parents have already made their plans. I just have to sign off on some final details."

I thought of the conservatory. Was it scheduled to be destroyed? Would they turn it into a media room? Would the bougainvillea be toppled to make room for a flat-screen TV?

My heart pounded. "Rex?"

"Addison?" he said, his eyes meeting mine.

I searched his face, so loving, so honest and strong. He was my rock, my peace, the only family I'd ever known. So why couldn't I say what was in my heart? The conservatory, Mrs. Dilloway, the arrangement of orange roses that symbolized the terror of my past. I opened my mouth, but no words came out.

"You OK, honey?" Rex asked, kissing the spot between my neck and my right shoulder. He set his bag down by the stairs, and a few files slipped out, including the one labeled "Amanda."

He quickly knelt down to tuck the files back into his bag before facing me again. I thought I detected distance in his eyes then, just a flash, a hint that just as he didn't know everything about me, maybe I didn't know everything about him.

I forced a smile. "Of course I am."

Rex looked at me curiously from the stairs. "Be careful driving into town, OK?"

I nodded as I passed the vase of orange flowers, their petals the color of a bright, hot flame.

On the road into town, I swerved left, then right, narrowly missing an oncoming car. The honk of the horn bellowed behind me as the car passed. Despite my frequent visits to England with Rex, I could never get used to driving on the opposite side of the road.

I pulled into a parking spot in town, rethinking my plans for the day. What did I think I'd find here? I eyed the storefronts along the cobblestone road. The post office. A cobbler. Gretchen's Café. Milton's Pub. I watched as a policeman swung his baton around his wrist before walking into a brick building with a red door. I hastened my pace and approached.

"Can I help you, miss?" a middle-aged woman with John Lennon–style glasses asked from behind a desk. She wore her hair in a ponytail, and her blunt-cut bangs formed a perfectly straight line across her forehead.

"Yes," I said, feeling my chest tighten. "I'm doing a little research, and I wondered if you could point me in the right direction."

"Oh, you're an American," she said warmly. "Welcome to Clivebrook."

"Thank you," I said.

"What brings you to these parts?"

"My husband's family recently purchased Livingston Manor," I said. "We're spending the summer here."

"Ah," she said. "So you're part of the Sinclair family."

"Yes," I said. "I'm Addison Sinclair."

"Pleased to meet you," she said, extending her hand. "I'm Maeve." She passed a file folder to an officer who had appeared by her desk, then turned back to me. "It'll be good to see people smiling up at the old house again," she continued, "after all the sadness there." She shook her head to herself. "Some folks in town think the place is cursed."

I nodded. "That's why I'm here. I understand that some young women went missing from town in the 1930s and '40s."

"Indeed," she said, pointing to a placard on the wall near the door. "Their names are all up there."

"So they were never found?"

She shook her head slowly. "Such a dark time in our history. Of course, I'm too young to remember any of that, but my mum still talks about it as if Clivebrook's very own Jack the Ripper is still out there."

"Goodness," I said. "Do you think he could be?"

"Oh, heavens no, dear," she said. "If he was, he'd be pushing ninety." She shook her head. "No, the crime spree stopped in 1940. My hunch is that he died then. But we may never know."

I pulled out my notebook and wrote down the date. I'd ask Mrs. Dilloway about it later. "Do you know much about Lord Edward Livingston?"

"Just that he died in the 1960s," she said. "He was deeply private. No one knew much about him, just the rumors. I remember he came into town once when I was a girl, and I was out there by the fountain playing jacks and one of the boys shouted at him.

Called him a murderer. I felt sorry for him." The woman sighed. "He didn't look like the type of person who would kill his wife. Much too debonair for a crime like that, if you ask me."

I nodded. "Anything else you can think of? Anyone else who may have worked at the manor over the years who struck you as off?"

"Well, there's that housekeeper," she smirked. "What's her name, Mrs.—"

"Dilloway?"

"Yes," she said. "She gives me the creeps, that one. To live in that old house for seventy years—she has to be hiding something."

"She cared a great deal about Lady Anna Livingston," I said. "It's why she's stayed all these years, to look out for her gardens."

"Is that what she told you?"

"Yes," I said. "I have to believe that it's true."

"Then why would she have filed a motion to have the autopsy report of Lady Anna sealed?"

"What?" I steadied myself on the edge of the desk.

"Sit down," she said. "I'll go see if I can pull the file."

A moment later, Maeve returned with an envelope. "If you can believe it," she said, "the judge favored her request. The documents are sealed, but you can see the motion right here." She pointed to a photocopied page. "Look," she said. "There's her signature at the bottom."

I wandered along the street for the next hour, trying to make sense of everything Mrs. Dilloway had said. If she had loved Lady Anna so much, if she had wanted to protect her, why would she want to conceal the truth about her death?

I walked along the sidewalk, until I came to a little park at the edge of town. Children played near a small garden. I listened to their laughter and watched as two little girls glided through the air on their swings. Happy. Carefree.

Fifteen Years Prior

"Manda!" the little boy cried.

I rubbed my eyes as I jumped up from the couch. How long had I been asleep? Aunt Jean, on a bender, had asked me to watch Miles. She was due back yesterday, but hadn't returned. I ran to the bedroom, but he wasn't lying on the cot beside Jean's bed. The crumpled Big Bird blanket lay on the wood floor.

"Manda!" he cried again. This time, I ran to the window, peering out over the fire escape to the alley below, where some benevolent resident of the apartment had years ago installed an aluminum swing set. I gasped. Sean. He was swinging him too high. Miles's little hands held on to the rusty chains for dear life. "Stop!" I screamed from the open window. "Sean, he's going to fall off!"

I sunk my feet into my shoes and grabbed my jacket, wincing as the sleeve rubbed the spot on my wrist where Sean had put out a cigarette against my flesh the night before. Miles screamed in the distance. "I'm coming, Miles!" I shouted as I began climbing down the fire escape, scolding myself for oversleeping. Sean could torture me, but I would not let him hurt that little boy.

Once on the street, I turned a sharp corner into the alley, where the old rickety swing set swayed as if it might topple over and take little Miles with it.

"Manda!" he cried. "Help me!"

"Stop it, Sean!" I cried.

"Make me," he said, smirking.

"Please!" I shouted. "He's going to fall."

I hated Aunt Jean for leaving us alone with this monster. I looked at Miles, barely three, his little legs flailing in the air. A few more moments and he would fall. He didn't have the strength to hold on. He was slipping.

"Look, he's going to wet his pants again," Sean said, laughing. "Let's see how long it takes."

"Stop it!" I cried, trying to pull him back.

"That will come at a price," he said, shoving me. "You know what I like."

"You're disgusting," I said, shuddering and then clenching my teeth. "I won't let you touch me."

The next moments played out as if in slow motion. Sean's hand making contact with Miles's back. The little boy's final cry. The look of sadness, fear, defeat as his small body drifted through the air, his blond hair flapping in the breeze. And then his head hit the cement. He lay there, eyes open, blood trickling from his nose. The face of a child who had never known love.

I ran to him, cradling his head in my arms. "Miles," I cried. "Honey, no, no, please don't die. I'm here. I'm here. I won't let him hurt you again. I promise." He lay there, lifeless. I rested my head on his still body before turning to Sean with rage. "You killed him!" Tears streamed down my face. "How could you do this?"

He smirked and folded his arms across his chest. "I didn't do anything."

"You pushed him," I said. "You knew he was too little to hold on!" Blood covered my hand as I touched his cheek. "I'm going to the police."

Sean took a step closer, unfolding his arms. For the first time, he looked frightened. "No, you won't," he said.

"I will," I replied, gritting my teeth. "You won't get away with this."

He laughed. "No, you have it wrong. *You* won't get away with this."

"What are you talking about?"

"Murder," he said. "Jean put you in charge of Miles. You were his babysitter. And now you have blood on your hands. Quite literally."

I looked down at my hands, covered in the boy's fresh blood. "No," I said. "You're wrong. They'll hear the truth and they'll—"

"But who will they believe, is the question." He smiled, pointing up to the sixth-floor window that had been left open. "I'll tell them he annoyed you, and that you pushed him."

"They won't believe you," I said. "You're a liar."

"They will believe me. I promise you that."

My hands trembled. Could he be right?

Sean placed his hand on my waist. "Here's what you're going to do," he said. "You're going to walk upstairs and get a trash bag."

"No," I whimpered.

"Yes," he said. "What's the name of that stupid garden you volunteer at in the Bronx?"

"The Botanical Garden," I said under my breath.

He nodded. "Do you have a key?"

"Yes, but I—"

"Good," he said. "Tonight, after dark, we'll bury him there. No one will know. It's the perfect cover-up."

I looked out at the street through my tears. The world looked foggy, gray, lonely. "But what about Jean?" I sobbed. "What about Miles's caseworker?"

"We'll tell them he ran away," Sean said, grinning. A thin

mustache grew above his upper lip. "Foster kids always run away. No one will care."

"No," I said. "I won't do it."

He clenched his hand around my wrist, sending a jolt of pain up my forearm. In that moment, all I wanted was to make him stop, to make it all stop, to end the pain, the sadness. "Please!" I cried. "You're hurting me."

"Go upstairs, Amanda," he said methodically. "Get the trash bag."

My body quivered as I stood up. Did I have any other choice?

"Hurry," Sean said from behind me. He'd wrapped Miles's body in three layers of black plastic, then stuffed him into an old duffel bag he'd found in Jean's closet. "Faster!" he barked

I numbly walked toward the entrance of the Botanical Garden. My hands felt clumsy and tired as I inserted the key into the lock. Before this day, the gardens had been my private sanctuary, a place where Sean couldn't hurt me. I volunteered twice a week, watering plants, sweeping up leaves. When my shifts were over, I hated going home. Jean was rarely there anymore. But I returned for Miles. Sometimes I brought him with me to the gardens. He loved it. I remembered the day he'd climbed the oak tree by the knot garden. I remembered the way he'd smiled. And now he would be buried here. Tears welled in my eyes.

"Are you sure no one's here?" Sean whispered.

I nodded as we pushed past the doors. The evening gardeners left at nine. As we walked ahead, I eyed the fire alarm on the wall. I could reach out and sound the alarm. Then what? Sean would run, and I'd be left here with the body of the little boy. How would

I explain myself? And what if Sean was right—what if no one believed me? It didn't matter now. Nothing would bring Miles back.

Sean lifted a shovel from a rack on the wall, then pointed to the gardens in the distance. "We'll bury him out there," he said. "Come on."

I followed him through the doors and out to the rose garden. The soil in the center had recently been tilled. No one would ever suspect that the ground had been disturbed. Sean dropped the duffel bag onto the ground with a careless thud, and I watched as he plunged the shovel into the earth. Sweat beaded up on his forehead, trickling down to his thin dark mustache. I looked away in disgust, resting my eyes on an orange rosebush a few feet away. Miles's life had been a sad one. He'd seen so little beauty in the world. At least now he'd be surrounded by it. Sean wiped the sweat from his brow before heaving the duffel bag into the makeshift grave. The roses swayed in the night breeze. They'd watch over the little boy. Roses were maternal like that.

As Sean began to scoop dirt into the hole, I stopped him. "Wait," I said, reaching into the pocket of my coat to pull out Miles's beloved bear, the one whose head I'd painstakingly sewn back on. I held the matted stuffed animal against my cheek before nestling it beside the boy in his final resting place.

I rubbed my arms to blunt the chill. The wind had picked up. When had the children left the playground? I stood up, gathering my bag, which is when I noticed him, standing there leaning against the maple tree. He took a long drag of his cigarette before dropping it to the ground, smashing it with his boot.

"Hello, Amanda," he said, grinning.

I froze. The familiar terror returned. He looked the same. Just as I'd imagined. Longish, greasy brown hair. Thick eyebrows. The stubble on his chin.

"Did you get my flowers?" he asked.

"Leave me alone, Sean," I said, making a fist, looking around for someone, anyone. The park was empty. "I told you, I don't have the kind of money you want."

"Oh, Amanda, you always were the smart one," he said, walking closer. "So clever. Here's the thing," he said, now inches from my face. I could smell his unwashed hair, the sourness of his skin. "I had a lot of time to think about you while I was locked away. Ten years I spent in prison."

"That wasn't my fault," I said. "You raped a girl." I shook my head. "I read the story in the newspaper. She was only thirteen, you bastard."

He smiled at me as though I amused him. "Do you remember Miles? Do you remember how he cried for help?"

I shook my head. "You're sick."

Sean chuckled to himself. "You could have stopped me."

"I tried."

"Not hard enough," he said, still grinning. "And you know what? You're right. It's not money I really want. I have plenty of it from my last job. The cops couldn't get to my offshore account." He nodded to himself. "You see, my dear"—he traced the outline of my face with his finger—"what I really want is *you*."

I spat in his face, and he reached up to wipe the smear with his sleeve before reaching for my wrist, pulling my watch lower on my arm. "It's still there," he said. His touch made me feel nauseated. "What do you think that husband of yours will think when he learns that you killed a boy?"

"Don't touch me!" I screamed.

In the distance, two people turned toward us, a man and woman. "Help me, please!" I shouted.

"Shut up, Amanda," Sean warned.

The man ran toward us. "Let the lady go," he said. His companion stood in the distance. She had a bobbed haircut and wore sunglasses. I thought she looked familiar, but in that adrenaline-filled moment, I couldn't be sure.

Smirking, Sean shrank back and ran toward the pathway that led back to the main street. "This isn't over, Amanda!" he shouted.

"Let's go to the police," the man said. "You'll want to file a report."

"Back already?" Maeve, the woman in the police station, asked. "Solved the Clivebrook Killer case?" Her expression changed to concern when she noticed the tears in my eyes. "Everything all right, miss?"

"She's been assaulted," the man said. "We found her just in time."

"Come," Maeve said, standing.

A female officer directed me to a chair in a room in the back. "Please, sit down," she said. "My name is Lucy."

She handed me a Styrofoam cup of water. I set it on the table, then bit the edge of my fingernail, tasting fresh blood.

"How long have you done that?" she said, indicating my hand. Instinctively, I tucked my fingers inward, covering my ragged nails.

"It's a bad habit I've been trying to break for years."

"People do that when they feel trapped, frightened," she said. "I know. I've been doing this job a long time."

I opened my hands and looked at them with new eyes.

"It's OK," she said.

A tear spilled out onto my cheek, and when she asked me my story, I didn't hold back. I told her everything—about the abuse, Miles, the burns on my wrist, the threatening letters and calls, the promise to divulge my true identity to my husband, the past I'd tried so hard to hide and to move on from. When I'd gotten it all out, I felt lighter, somehow.

"Don't blame yourself, miss," Lucy said. "You were fifteen. You were only a child then. Anyone in your position would have done what you did. The important thing is that you tried to help the boy."

I nodded.

"If you'll wait right here, I'll go call our counterpart in America and have them run this Sean character's name," she said. "I'll see what they have on him."

I nodded. A half hour later, she returned with a handful of pages fresh from the fax machine. She handed me one with a photo of his mug shot. "It's him, all right," she said. "Wanted in three states, for theft, rape, child endangerment, and other crimes. If we find him, and with your testimony, we'll get him back to America, back behind bars where he belongs."

"Thank you," I said.

"Where's your car?" she asked.

"Down the street."

She nodded. "It's dark. I'll have an officer escort you home. For safety."

"Thanks," I said.

"Thank *you*, Amanda," she continued. "For your bravery."

I shook my head. "It's Addison. I'm no longer that girl."

—————

I had planned to tell Rex about the incident in the park when I got home to the manor, but when I walked into the bedroom and saw his face, I couldn't. If I told him about that, I'd have to tell him everything. I wasn't yet ready to shatter his image of me, the one I'd so carefully crafted over the years.

After Rex had fallen asleep, I tiptoed downstairs to make sure all the doors were locked. I stopped in the drawing room when I noticed a few tubes of rolled-up paper in the corner by the windows. Were they the blueprints? I walked over and unrolled them, spreading them out on the floor in front of me. I was happy to see that much of the house would remain the same. A new kitchen would be going in on the first floor. The entryway would get a refresh, with new columns. Fine. The nursery, Anna's study, the third floor with the conservatory, at least according to these drawings, appeared to be untouched. I flipped to the next page, with a detailed drawing of the property and gardens. Would the orchard be spared? It appeared so, but then I turned to the final page in the stack, and I could hardly believe my eyes. Could it be? Would Rex really have kept this from me? I remembered the way he'd acted when he got the phone call the other day, the way he spoke with secrecy. I shook my head, then started at the page, illustrated with crudely sketched plans for what appeared to be a golf course. A handwritten note in the margin read, "Overgrown orchard will be demolished this summer." In the corner were my husband's initials, RLS.

CHAPTER 20

August 1, 1940

The atmosphere in the house changed the morning Lord Livingston was due back from London. Table linens were pressed with greater diligence. The silver received a second polish. Even the children seemed on edge. Janie clung to me all morning, refusing to nap, and the tutor said that Nicholas was quite distracted during his arithmetic lessons.

We knew when he would arrive, because Mr. Humphrey had gone to pick him up at the train station. It was a fifteen-minute drive into the village and back, so I let the children stand in the driveway to wait for him at half past ten. Janie squealed when the boys spotted the car in the distance, motoring up the winding road toward the house. She began walking toward the vehicle, but I scooped her in my arms.

Katherine patted her braid. I'd twisted it into a bun and pinned it up, surprised at how grown-up she looked. "Do you think Father will notice that I'm wearing my hair up now?" she asked.

"Yes," I said. "I'm sure he will, dear. He will think you are most beautiful."

"I hope he brought us presents from London," Nicholas said, grinning.

Abbott turned to us. "Do you think he got the model airplane I told him about? The one in the Harrods catalog?"

I hoped, for the children's sake, that their father was as excited to see them as they were him, but when the car pulled up to the driveway, he stepped out without so much as a smile.

"Welcome home, Father!" Nicholas cried.

Lord Livingston walked up the steps to the house and nodded at us. "Hello, children," he said without emotion, before handing his hat and coat to Mr. Beardsley. "Bring my tea up to my study at once," he said. "There's an urgent matter that needs my attention."

He hurried into the house and the door closed swiftly behind him. It hadn't felt cold outside when we first stepped outside, but the wind had changed. Janie shivered and Katherine rubbed her arms. Nicholas stuck out his lower lip. "Come, children," I said. "We'll see your father later."

Abbott kicked a pebble and it flew out to the driveway, where it ricocheted off the hubcap near Mr. Humphrey.

"Abbott!" I cried. "Apologize to Mr. Humphrey at once!"

"I won't!" he shouted, running off to the terrace.

Mr. Humphrey knelt down and immediately began shining the hubcap with his handkerchief. He muttered something under his breath.

"I'm sorry," I said to the chauffeur. "I'll speak to him about it."

"It won't do any good," he said, scowling. "I told you that boy's the devil."

We didn't see Lord Livingston again until lunch, and by then the children had spent the morning sulking. But when they arrived at the table a present waited at each of their seats. The parcels were wrapped in blue paper and tied with twine. Katherine let out a scream of joy when she saw hers, tearing open the paper immediately to find a porcelain doll with a dress made of pink silk. Janie received a set of children's books, and Nicholas a train. My heart fluttered a little when Abbott opened his box. But by the look on his face, I knew the gift wasn't a model airplane. His face stiffened. "Thank you, Father," he said, holding up a pair of riding boots. "I will enjoy these."

Lord Livingston sat at the head of the table and smiled. "There's something for you, too, Miss Lewis," he said, indicating a box wrapped in pink paper near the corner of the table.

"Oh," I said, surprised. "How kind of you, but truly, you didn't have to get me anything."

He smiled. All traces of his foul mood from earlier that afternoon had vanished. "I wanted to. Go on, open it."

Katherine nodded with anticipation. "Yes, please do!"

I pulled the box in front of me, carefully untied the ribbon, then tore the wrapping, lifting the box free and opening the lid. Inside were three small canvases, a smock, a set of acrylic paints, and five paintbrushes."

"I've asked Mr. Humphrey to bring the easel to your room," he said. His eyes sparkled. "I hope you'll be pleased."

"Yes," I said, finding my voice. "I don't know how to thank you."

"You don't have to," he said. "Just enjoy it."

I nodded. "Oh, I will. I promise."

Nicholas looked at me curiously. "Miss Lewis, we didn't know you were an artist."

"Well, I'm not, really," I said. "But I do enjoy painting flowers and nature."

"Mummy did too," Katherine said, smiling at me proudly.

Lord Livingston cleared his throat uncomfortably. "Well, I was hoping you might paint something for us, a scene to add to the manor's collection, perhaps?"

"Oh, I hardly think anything I'd paint would be worthy."

"I beg to differ," he said, nodding to Mr. Beardsley, who ladled soup into the bowl in front of him.

The children ate their lunch happily, and afterward, I excused them to the nursery to play with their gifts. When Mrs. Dilloway and Mr. Beardsley had left, I also got up to leave. But Lord Livingston cleared his throat.

"Will you wait just a moment, Miss Lewis?"

I stopped in the doorway. "Yes, of course."

"Thank you," he said.

"For what?"

"For making me see."

I shook my head. "I don't understand."

He sighed. "I've been so lost in my grief that I didn't see that the children needed me." He rubbed his forehead nervously. "When I came home today, the way you had them out there waiting for me, well, it touched me. I didn't realize it right away, though. In any case, I do realize I've been a loathsome father of late."

"You haven't been *loathsome*," I said. "Your children love you a great deal."

"Well," he said, "I have some making up to do."

I nodded. "You might start with Abbott. He seems to have gotten it into his head that he needs a model airplane."

"Oh?"

"Yes," I said. "Even better if his father would fly a model airplane *with* him."

His eyes drifted to the floor as if he'd just realized that everything he thought he knew about his son was as insignificant as yesterday's newspaper. "I'll . . ." He paused, looking up at me with a troubled expression. "I'll give it some thought."

"Well," I added, indicating the box of art supplies. "Thank you again, for the gifts. I had better go check on the children."

After I tucked the children into their beds, I tidied the nursery and yawned as I walked down the stairs. It had been a long day, and I was anxious for sleep, but I'd promised Janie I'd mend her doll's dress. She'd left it on the sofa in the drawing room. I'd just need to retrieve it before finding Mrs. Dilloway to see about getting the right color pink thread to match the rose-colored fabric.

I hurried into the drawing room, scanning the sofa for Janie's doll. *That's funny, she only just left it here.*

"Looking for this?"

I jumped, turning around quickly to see Lord Livingston holding up the little blond-haired doll.

"Oh, yes," I said, taking a deep breath.

"I'm sorry, I didn't mean to frighten you," he said, walking toward me and placing the doll in my hands.

"You found Agnes," I said, smiling.

"Agnes?"

"Yes, well, Aggie," I continued.

"Yes," he said, turning to the radio on the side table. "Now if I can just get a signal on this bloody thing."

I knew finicky radios well. The one in the bakery was always dusted with flour, but I never failed to make it produce a signal. I couldn't knead without a tune. "Would you like me to have a look?" I asked, walking toward the table. "I have a special touch with these contraptions."

"Thank you," he said. "If you don't mind."

I turned the dial gingerly, and listened as it wavered in and out of frequency, sending out garbled sounds and high-pitched noises. "It's the antenna," I said, reaching to the back. I pulled the wire toward the window, and a moment later a male voice drifted through the speakers, as clear as if he were standing right in front of us.

"Quite good," Lord Livingston said.

I looked back at the door. "Well, I'd better be going."

"Stay if you like," he said, gesturing toward the sofa. "I mean, if you'd like to hear an update on the war."

"I'm afraid I find it all terribly depressing," I said.

He looked away awkwardly, then stiffened. "Right, yes," he said.

A series of drumbeats sounded from the radio speakers. "Hitler and his army are advancing. What does this mean for England, for the world?"

My eyes remained fixed on the radio. All I could think of was Desmond. "Well," I said, sitting down without thinking, "maybe I'll stay. For just a minute."

As it had in the car, it felt strange to sit so close to Lord Livingston, especially in the dimly lit room. But war was on the horizon, and the severity of the situation broke down emotional barriers. I clenched my fists at the sound of gunfire through the speakers, and listened intently: "As Hitler and his men sweep through Eastern Europe, more boys have been called up to protect the homefront," the broadcaster went on, giving detailed reports about the status of the war. We listened for twenty minutes, until the broadcaster finished with, "We can only hope and pray that our home is spared from the atrocities of war. God save England, and God save the Queen!"

Lord Livingston stood and turned the dial until the garbled sound gave way to soft music, like the type you'd hear in a club back home. He sat down again beside me.

"Do you think it's true, what they're saying?" I asked. "Do you think war will come to England?"

"None of us wants to believe it, of course," he said. "But we have to prepare for it."

I nodded.

"We still have time," he said. "One of my business associates in London, high-ranking in the Royal Air Force, ensures that nothing is imminent while they're ramping up their defenses."

A soft, melodic song began to play. I recognized it immediately. Louis Armstrong. *All of me, why not take all of me?* I looked down when I felt Lord Livingston's eyes on me.

"Do you miss home?"

"I do," I said, studying my hands in my lap. In that moment, my heart ached for Mama and Papa, for the bakery, for the bustling streets of New York, so far from the threat of Hitler, from this strange family and their problems. "I love it here, I do; it's just that I didn't anticipate the world changing while I was gone." I wiped a tear from my cheek.

"Here," he said, handing me a handkerchief from the pocket of his jacket.

"Thank you," I said, dabbing my eyes.

I turned around when I heard footsteps behind us. Mrs. Dilloway stood in the doorway. "Pardon my intrusion," she said stiffly.

Following Lord Livingston's lead, I stood up quickly.

"Katherine's had a nightmare," she said. "You ought to go up and check on her." Though she was speaking to me, she looked through me. Her eyes—tired, pained—fixed straight ahead, directly at Lord Livingston. I felt awkward standing there, out of place.

"Of course," I said, my voice cutting the silence like a knife. I hurried past Mrs. Dilloway into the foyer as the door closed behind me, muffling the murmur of their voices.

Upstairs, Katherine sat at the edge of her bed with her knees pulled up to her chest. "I dreamed that Mother had gone into the village with Mr. Humphrey, and, and . . ." She sobbed into her hands. "And that he crashed the car." She continued to sob. "Mr. Beardsley tried to save her, but he couldn't."

"My dear Katherine," I said lovingly, stroking her hair.

She frowned. "Father's already forgotten about Mother, hasn't he?"

"Of course not," I said quickly.

"He has!" she cried, her eyes welling up with tears once again. "He has, and I hate it!"

Before I retired to the servants' quarters I stopped in the conservatory. Without a lantern, the space was fairly dark.

The moon, partially hidden behind a cloud, provided only a glimmer of light, enough for me to water the plants. Though Mrs. Dilloway had warned me about bats, I jumped when one screeched and flew over the glass roof.

I stood looking out the window. The edge of the palm branch tickled my cheek. What had Katherine said? That it had been a gift to Anna from the King of Thailand? I couldn't compete for the children's affection with a woman who'd possessed such unparalleled charm it had summoned gifts from kings, nor should I. I was there for a reason, I reminded myself. The Middlebury Pink.

I peered through the window to Lord Livingston's terrace below. Music played softly, and I paused to listen to the romantic melody. Under the cover of darkness, I watched as two shadows were cast across the terrace in the moonlight.

The next morning after breakfast, Mr. Humphrey announced that he was taking Lord Livingston to the train station.

"Oh, he's leaving so soon?" Sadie asked, glancing at Mrs. Dilloway, who appeared more tired than usual this morning.

"All I know is that he had urgent business in the city," the chauffeur said. "He asked me to have him there by ten and no later."

Mrs. Dilloway's eyes met mine before she turned back to her breakfast.

Mrs. Marden shrugged. "If you ask me, it's just as well. One less mouth to feed around here."

Mr. Beardsley frowned. "Mrs. Marden, I won't have you speaking of Lord Livingston in that manner. You'd all do well to know that the reason his Lordship is spending so much time in London has everything to do with our livelihoods at the manor."

"What do you mean?" Mrs. Marden asked.

"Before you speak ill of him," Mr. Beardsley continued, "remember that he works very hard for this house, for all of us."

"Mr. Beardsley," I said, "has anyone heard from Desmond?"

"I'm afraid not," he replied.

Mr. Humphrey stood up abruptly. "Well, I better be going." He looked at Mrs. Marden. "I'll pick up the groceries when I'm in town. And I can make a trip to the post office if anyone has a letter to be sent." I handed him an envelope addressed to Mama and Papa, then turned to Mr. Beardsley. "You haven't gotten any mail for me yet, have you?"

"I'm sorry, I haven't," he said. "Were you expecting something?"

"Oh, no," I said, both relieved to have not heard from Mr. Price again and worried that I hadn't received anything from Mama and Papa.

"I just realized," Sadie said, turning to Mrs. Dilloway, "what day it is."

"What day?" I asked curiously.

"Her Ladyship's birthday," Sadie continued wistfully. "Remember the way his Lordship would surprise her at breakfast, the way he'd—"

I heard the sound of porcelain shattering beneath the table. "Well, look at me," said Mrs. Dilloway.

Sadie rushed to her side, picking up shards of white china and setting them in a pile on the table. "Don't you worry," Mrs. Dilloway said, holding out her hand. "I can manage." She turned to Mr. Beardsley. "Please see that it's deducted from my paycheck."

Mrs. Marden shrugged. "Why all the fuss over a bloody teacup? I'd give a kitchen full of teacups for a decent apple." She looked at Mrs. Dilloway. "Did you see the ones that came in this morning?" she asked disdainfully. "They're all craggy and worm-eaten. I don't know how I can be expected to turn out a proper tart with substandard ingredients."

Sadie pushed the newspaper toward her. "We should get used to it," she said. "I overheard Mr. Beardsley talking to his Lordship in the foyer yesterday, and, well, I wasn't meant to hear it, but his Lordship said he's in some kind of financial pickle."

"Well," Mrs. Marden huffed. "I wouldn't be surprised, with the way he spends money. Did you see the shipment of cigars that came in from South America yesterday?"

"Not a good time to be having money troubles, if you ask me," Sadie replied. "I don't want to be out of a job in the middle of a war. It says right here that the Germans are advancing. Before we know it, they'll be on our doorstep asking us to cook them bacon and eggs."

"Stuff and nonsense," Mrs. Marden said, standing and tightening her apron around her ample waist. "I'll believe it when I see the whites of their eyes. For now, I suppose there's no sense fretting about any of this."

My parents had concerns about war in Europe when I left, but no one could believe that things could escalate to this level and that we might actually be in real danger. I reached for the newspaper and scanned the front page. Surely it was wrong. It had to be wrong.

Later, when I greeted the children, Mrs. Dilloway handed Abbott a box wrapped in brown paper, tied with a white ribbon. "Your father asked me to give this to you," she said, giving me a knowing look.

"For me?" Abbott cried.

Mrs. Dilloway nodded, handing it to him. A moment later, he'd torn open the wrapping and was gazing at his very own model airplane.

"Thank you," Mrs. Dilloway whispered to me.

CHAPTER 21

Addison

"**A**re you sure you don't want to go with me?" Rex asked, tucking a lock of hair behind my ear. I considered the idea of accompanying him to London, where he'd made plans to see an old friend. After the incident in town, I didn't want to be alone, but I was getting closer to solving the mystery at the manor, so I didn't want to leave. And I couldn't take any chances with Sean lurking.

"No," I said. "I think I'll stay here and go through the camellia book again. "I feel like there's something we must have missed in the orchard. Some clue."

"All right," he said. "I'll be back tomorrow, and then we can lay it all out together. The more we learn, the more I realize that there's a novel brewing here."

He slung his bag over his shoulder, and I remembered the file marked "Amanda" inside. I hadn't asked him about it.

"I'm going to miss you," he said, kissing my cheek.

"Have fun with Kevin."

Rex smiled at me curiously. "You don't get it, do you?"

"Get what?" I asked.

"I have the most fun when I'm with *you*."

I smiled up at him, grateful for this man whose love for me was so genuine. But would he feel the same if he knew the truth about my past?

"That's my cab," he said as a car pulled up outside.

"Careful," I said, kissing him good-bye.

"Remember which side of the road to drive on if you take the car out."

I rolled my eyes playfully.

"I'll call you from the hotel," he said.

I watched as the cab drove away toward town, then I locked the door, instantly regretting my decision to stay behind. I listened as the antique clock ticked furtively on the wall. I made a fist, determined to ignore the fear I felt. No, I wouldn't let Sean make me crazy. I'd be fine. Even if the police hadn't found him, they were patrolling the area regularly, and I had the station's number on speed dial.

Upstairs, I pulled out the letter from Nicholas Livingston, and dialed his number.

"Yes, hello," I said. "This is Addison Sinclair. My in-laws recently purchased the manor. They're traveling in Asia now, so when I saw your letter arrive, I took the liberty of opening it on their behalf."

"Yes, of course," he replied. "Hello, Addison." He cleared his throat. "There's a matter I'd like to discuss with you in person, if I may. Are you available tomorrow?"

"Yes," I said. "I'll be here."

"Good. I could catch the nine a.m. train and arrive by lunchtime."

"That would be fine," I said. "Mr. Livingston, it's just that, well, I thought, considering the circumstances of the sale, that the family, er, that you, had no interest in returning to the manor again."

"It's true," he said quickly. "Especially after . . . well, we can discuss this all tomorrow, Ms. Sinclair."

That night, I heard a knock on my bedroom door shortly after I'd laid my head on the pillow. "Ms. Sinclair, are you awake?"

I slipped my arms into the robe draped over the chair near the bed and cinched the tie around my waist. Mrs. Klein stood, breathless, outside the door. "I'm so sorry to bother you, ma'am, but it's Mrs. Dilloway. She fainted. Knocked her head on the counter. I've called for an ambulance."

I followed her downstairs to the kitchen. Mrs. Dilloway sat on the floor, leaning against a cabinet. Her eyes looked drowsy. I fell to my knees beside her. "Are you all right?"

She muttered something unintelligible. I squeezed her hand and turned to Mrs. Klein. "How long before the ambulance arrives?"

She looked out the window. Headlights flashed in the night. "I think I see it pulling in now."

Mrs. Klein ran to the door and directed the paramedics to the kitchen. Mrs. Dilloway turned to me before they wheeled her out on a stretcher. "Please . . . the letter . . ."

I shook my head, squeezing her hand. "Save your strength."

"It looks like she's had a stroke," one of the paramedics said. "Loss of speech is a sign."

"I'll go with you to the hospital," I said.

"It's late," Mrs. Klein said. "You stay. Rest. I've been working for Mrs. Dilloway for twenty years. I'll go. Better she sees a familiar face if she's disoriented."

I nodded. "But do call me when you have an update."

I drew the curtains on the first floor after they left. It felt odd to be in the house alone. Just one soul in a home that could house hundreds. Or maybe there were hundreds of souls here with me. Souls that had long since passed. Souls that were watching, waiting. I shivered as I walked up the stairs to the bedroom. Lord Livingston had slept there. With Anna. And others?

The air felt cold suddenly, so I went to the closet to find another blanket, which is when I noticed a wooden box wedged into a corner on the top shelf. I reached to pull it down, knocking over a stack of blankets above my head. I carried the box back to the bed, opening the lid slowly. Inside was a crumpled piece of paper, folded into a square. I knew what it was almost before I opened it. The page from Anna's camellia book. The Middlebury Pink. The pressed flower was gone, but all the notations were there. Lord Livingston had taken it. Why? And why had he saved it?

I walked to the window, looking out at the orchard under a veil of darkness. The Middlebury Pink was out there, I knew it. And— my eyes widened—so was someone else. A flashlight shone through the orchard, moving about through a row and then down the next. I slunk back behind the curtain, racing to the bedside to retrieve my cell phone.

"Hello, yes, this is Addison Sinclair, from Livingston Manor," I said to the dispatcher. "I think there's an intruder in the orchard. Could you send an officer over?"

CHAPTER 22

Flora

September 18, 1940

Summer left with little fanfare and no word from Desmond. Lord Livingston spent the majority of it in London, holed up in his flat there. He told Mr. Beardsley that business had detained him, but I worried it was something else, something serious. On a rainy Tuesday morning, he phoned from London, and I overheard Mr. Beardsley speaking to him in the drawing room.

"Your Lordship," Mr. Beardsley said into the phone, "it's so good to hear from you. . . . Yes, yes, the children are fine. . . . Yes, Miss Lewis too. . . . Oh? I'm very sorry to hear that. . . . Is there anything that can be done? . . . Very well, yes, of course. . . . Oh, is that so? . . . Lord Desmond, sir? You don't say. . . . Well, it's just that I had no idea, my Lord. None of us did. . . . Yes, yes of course."

"Excuse me, sir," I said from the doorway once Mr. Beardsley had hung up the phone.

"Yes," Mr. Beardsley replied, straightening his jacket. "That was Lord Livingston. He phoned from London to check on the children. His Lordship expects to stay in the city another two weeks before returning home for the remainder of the fall."

"Good," I said. "The children miss him terribly."

He nodded.

I hesitated before saying, "I wonder if I may ask you a question?"

"Yes, what is it, Miss Lewis?"

"When you were on the phone just now, you mentioned Desmond. Is everything all right?"

Mr. Beardsley pulled a handkerchief from his jacket pocket and pressed it against his forehead, as if to soak up phantom perspiration. "Nothing for you to worry about, Miss Lewis," he said, tucking the cloth back into his pocket.

"Of course," I said. An awkward silence fell over us. "I understand."

"Well, if you'll excuse me."

"Yes, sir," I said, watching him walk to the stairs.

Oh, Desmond. Please come home.

"Storm's coming," Mrs. Marden said as she whipped cream by hand in the kitchen. Mr. Beardsley had offered to buy her a modern mixer, one with a proper stand and a mechanical whisk, but she refused. "It would be like cheating," she said. "I'm a cook. They pay me to whisk, and I'll whisk."

"I can't bear to part with summer," Sadie said, looking out at the garden longingly from the kitchen window.

Mrs. Marden plunged a finger into the white bowl in front of her and held it up, examining the peaks that the cream made. She shook her head, dissatisfied, and continued whisking.

"What does it matter if the weather changes," she said, "when you don't have a beau to picnic with?"

Sadie poured a cup of tea and set it on the saucer in front of me, ignoring the grouchy cook. "I suppose you'll be wanting to get back to America soon."

"Yes," I said. "But I spoke to Mr. Beardsley about it yesterday. They've closed down passenger routes in the Atlantic, at least for now." I sighed, sitting down in the chair Mrs. Marden used when peeling vegetables.

Sadie patted my back. "I bet you miss your folks terribly."

"I do." I sighed. "I just wish they'd write to me. I can't understand why they haven't. It's been five months."

"You sure you're using the right return address, and all?" Sadie asked.

"Yes," I said. "I've checked it many times."

She shrugged. "Maybe they're just busy."

"No," I said. "I'm worried that something's wrong." *What if Mr. Price's men reached them? What if . . . ?*

Mrs. Marden handed me a sack of potatoes and a peeler. "I'll make you a deal," she said, her smile revealing her crooked tooth. "If you help me peel these, I'll tell you about the time I saw Lord Livingston without a stitch of clothes on."

Sadie howled with laughter. "You don't want to miss this one," she said.

I smiled. "Well, the children will be busy with their lessons for another half hour. I suppose I could peel a few of these."

A week passed, and then another. The leaves began to fall from the old maple tree in the orchard, dancing in the wind as if to remind us of the uncertainty all around. War hovered over England like a dark storm cloud, and we all prayed it would pass like a mild thunderstorm, with more bark than bite.

One morning in early October, I agreed to let the children listen to the radio after breakfast. When the broadcast finished, I stood up. "All right, children, Mr. Beardsley's having the drawing room repainted this morning, so it's time to go up to the nursery."

As the children headed upstairs, the front door slammed, and Mr. Humphrey hurried toward us. "I'm just back from the village," he said, out of breath. He held out a rain-speckled newspaper. "Look!"

The headline blared: GERMAN BOMBERS STRIKE LONDON; CASUALTIES.

"Dear Lord!" Mrs. Dilloway cried. She fanned her face.

"What about Lord Livingston?" I said. "Has anyone heard from him?"

"Not yet," Mr. Humphrey said. "I've already been in to see Mr. Beardsley. He's telephoning London as we speak."

We rushed to the butler's pantry, where Mr. Beardsley sat at his desk.

"Any news from his Lordship?" Mrs. Dilloway asked. Her voice quivered in a way I hadn't known it could.

"I'm afraid not," he said. "The phone lines are down. We'll just have to wait." He reached below his desk and pulled out a decanter. "And pray."

Mr. Beardsley stood guard at the telephone, awaiting news from London. Since the painters had come in that morning,

Mrs. Dilloway asked me to check in on their progress. I wondered how the fresh color would look on the walls. The latest thinking was emerald green, which I quite liked.

"Excuse me," I said to a man in the drawing room. He sat in Lord Livingston's chair, with his back to me and his feet kicked up on the ottoman. *How irritating.* Mr. Beardsley was right. Workers were getting lazier these days. You hired them to do a job and they expected an easy chair and a smorgasbord. "Remove your feet from the furniture at once," I said.

The man spun around in the chair. *Desmond.*

"Top of the morning to you," he said, rising to his feet.

"Desmond!" I cried, running to him. He wrapped his arms around me and held me close.

"I've missed you so," he said into my ear.

I stepped back to look at him. "Why didn't you write? Why didn't you call?"

"I couldn't," he said. "I was deployed. Our mission ended up taking a lot longer than anyone anticipated. Communication was forbidden."

"Well," I said, "I guess I could forgive you for that."

"Come here," he said, pulling me close again. "I can't tell you how much I missed you."

CHAPTER 23

Addison

"We did a full sweep of the property and didn't find any-one," the officer said on the doorstep. "You sure about what you saw?"

I nodded. "I thought I was. I'm sorry to waste your time." I couldn't imagine the same special attention from the NYPD.

"No time wasted," he said. "If you'd like, I can sit out front for a while, until sunup if it makes you feel better."

I exhaled deeply. "Yes, it would. Thank you."

I took comfort knowing that the officer's car was parked outside the manor, and yet I didn't sleep, knowing that Sean was near. I could feel his presence, the darkness that lingered.

"You going to be all right here for a bit, miss?" the officer asked the next morning. He yawned. "If you'd like, I can get someone on the day shift to check in on you later."

"It's kind of you to suggest," I said, noticing the dark shadows under his eyes. "But don't worry. My husband will be back from London today."

"Well," he said, "just the same, lock the doors."

"Thank you," I said, latching the deadbolt behind him.

I walked over to my purse on the entryway table. Maeve, from the police station, had handed me an envelope the night Sean attacked me, but I'd been too worn out to open it. "Just something I found," she'd said. "For your *other* investigation."

I opened the envelope and pulled out the pages inside, photocopies of a 1942 deposition given by a waitress at a café in town regarding the disappearance of her friend and coworker Theresa Mueller. The sticky note on top of the pages read, *Another missing girl from the '40s. Maybe there's a connection? Good luck to you!*

I opened the camellia book and thumbed through each page to see if the date of disappearance, June 25, 1940, matched any of the numbers in the book. It didn't. I sat down on the stairs. Maybe my hunch was completely off base. The missing girls may not have been connected to one another, or to Lady Anna.

I scanned the deposition, almost giving up, until I noticed the name Lord Livingston on the bottom of the second page:

OFFICER RANKINS: You said that Miss Mueller waited on Lord Livingston the day of her disappearance.

SUE GILMORE: Yes, sir. He missed his train that day, and he came in for lunch. I remember because Theresa asked me to cover for her while she ran to the back to touch up her lipstick.

OFFICER RANKINS: Did you get the feeling that the two of them, Miss Mueller and Lord Livingston, knew each other outside of the café?

SUE GILMORE: I know she wanted that to be the case, but I'm not sure if they were ever sociable, if you know what I mean. Theresa did say that she wished she could go with

him to London. She was always a bit forward like that, saying things that weren't quite appropriate.

OFFICER RANKINS: Did he ask her to go to London
with him?

SUE GILMORE: Not that I'm aware of, sir. She left early that
day. Complained of a headache. For all I know, she may have
gone with him. She didn't say.

I looked up. So there *was* a connection. But why wasn't there a
notation in the book? Why hadn't the date of her disappearance
been recorded? I bit my lip, and then realized. Of course. Theresa
Mueller's disappearance came *after* Lady Anna's death. She wasn't
there to add it to her record, to strengthen her case. Had she suspected her husband? Someone else? Did someone want to silence
her when they realized she had gotten too close to the truth?

I tucked the pages back in the envelope and moved my operation to the table in the drawing room, where Rex had left the blueprints for the manor. I pulled a small pad of sticky notes from the
drawer and wrote down the six numeric codes listed in the camellia
book that appeared to contain dates, cross-checking them with the
dates the girls had been abducted. My heart raced as I worked. On
the blueprint that showed the existing layout of the orchard, I
matched each sticky note with the codes listed in the book.

I took a step back, gasping when I saw the circular pattern on
the map. *Dear Lord, what if those poor women are buried out there?*

CHAPTER 24

Flora

October 6, 1940

Mr. Beardsley appeared in the doorway of the servants' hall shortly after lunch, out of breath. He held up a telegram. "This just came. From London. Lord Livingston is safe and well. He'll be back by tomorrow."

We all cheered, and for the first time since the news had broken of the blitz, the color returned to Mrs. Dilloway's cheeks. It was the best news we could have received, of course, but much had changed since Lord Livingston left. The axis of the earth had shifted, and with it, Livingston Manor.

"And Miss Lewis has informed me that Desmond's returned," Mrs. Dilloway added.

"What will his Lordship say?" Sadie asked as she folded kitchen towels into neat stacks.

"Well," Mrs. Dilloway continued, "he'll have to accept Lord Desmond. After all, he is his son."

Mr. Beardsley cleared his throat. "I will speak to his Lordship when he arrives. For now, I think it's best that Desmond not take up residence in his old bedroom. Better have him stay in a guest room—Lord Livingston is less likely to encounter him there."

"Yes," Mrs. Dilloway said, walking to the hallway. "Miss Lewis, come along. The children are waiting for you in the nursery."

Halfway up the stairs, Sadie caught up to us. "Mrs. Dilloway, you're wanted on the telephone."

"Can it wait?"

"No, ma'am," Sadie said. "It's the grocer. There's been a problem with the order."

"Can't Mrs. Marden handle it?" Mrs. Dilloway asked.

Sadie shook her head. "He refuses to speak to her after the egg incident."

Mrs. Dilloway smiled knowingly. "All right, I'll take the call." She sighed. "Is there any part of this house that can run properly without my involvement?" She looked at me. "Miss Lewis, go on up without me and get Desmond settled. I'll meet you upstairs in a moment."

Heading toward the stairs to the second floor, I walked through the foyer, but stopped suddenly when I saw a man standing near the front door carrying a large, empty duffel bag. When he turned around, I froze.

"Mr. Price!" I said. "What are you doing here?" I eyed the duffel bag in his hands. "Why do you have that bag?"

"Oh, this?" he said, smiling. "It's funny you ask." He fingered a gold-plated table lamp. "You never know what one might find in these old manors. All kinds of treasures."

"Leave the Livingstons alone," I pleaded.

"Let me remind you, Miss Lewis," he said. "That kind of attitude will do nothing for your parents." He took his hat off and stared at me, amused. "No point in talking about such unsavory things, when I only came to pay my employee a visit."

He walked toward me in a slow and calculated manner. "You see, I've made several attempts to reach you by mail."

"But I, I—" I faltered. "I only got one. I promise." I looked both ways, fearful that someone might be listening.

"Don't lie, young lady," he said, now a few inches from me. "It's very unbecoming."

I heard footsteps on the stairway, and I panicked. "Please, let's not talk here. Someone might hear us."

"And learn that you aren't who you say you are?" he said. "My, my, have you actually taken a liking to this job? Do you fancy yourself as the doting nanny now?"

I took his arm and led him quickly into the sitting room by the front door. With the door closed behind me, I sighed. "Please, you must go."

"Not until I know where the camellia is," he said. "I take it you've found it by now."

"That's just the thing," I tried to explain. "I haven't. I need more time."

"More time? Miss Lewis, you've been here for months— either the camellia is here or it isn't here. I'm beginning to think you've had it unearthed yourself." He stepped closer to me. "But you wouldn't do that to me, now, would you?"

"Give me a few more months," I begged. "I just need more time in the orchard. It's nearly impossible to identify the trees when they're not in bloom."

He nodded. "All right. But if you haven't found the camellia by the end of November, I'll have my men go have another chat with your father."

"I knew it was you," I said, making a fist. "Please, leave him out of this, I beg of you."

"That's up to you, Miss Lewis," he said, grinning. "Now, my dear," he said, holding out his hand. "My card, in case you've misplaced the last one. He turned to the door. "Call me when you've found the camellia. And next time, I won't be so patient."

I waited until I heard the door click shut before I ventured back out into the foyer, which was, thankfully, empty.

I took a moment to collect myself before walking toward the drawing room.

"Oh, there you are," Mrs. Dilloway said, appearing on the first-floor landing.

"Sorry," I replied. "I was just showing a . . . solicitor to the door."

We walked into the drawing room together, and Desmond jumped up from a chair and lifted her by her waist. "Mrs. Dilloway!" he cried, twirling her around.

Her pursed lips melted into a smile. She touched a badge on his uniform. "The army suits you."

He stiffened and stood at attention, staging a faux salute. "Second lieutenant."

Her eyes clouded with worry. "I suppose you're going to join the fight?"

"Yes, ma'am," he said with a proud smile. "I've just returned from my first mission, and my unit ships out again, this time to the south, in about a month." His eyes met mine and looked away. "I thought I'd spend my last few weeks here—that is, if it's not an imposition."

"Nonsense," Mrs. Dilloway said. "I'm glad you came home. We all are."

"And my father?" he said.

"I can't say. You parted on poor terms. Only time will tell. In any case, he's in London now."

Desmond's mouth fell open.

"He's safe," Mrs. Dilloway assured him. "We received a telegram this afternoon. The house in London was just a few blocks from where the city was hit hardest. But he was lucky."

"Good," Desmond said, relieved. "When will he be home?"

"Tomorrow," she said.

"I'd like to see the children, if I may."

Mrs. Dilloway nodded. "Miss Lewis can take you up to see them now."

"Let's surprise them," Desmond said to me with a glimmer of mischief in his eyes.

"OK," I whispered as we got closer to the nursery door. I could hear Abbott whining about something and Nicholas making fire truck noises.

Desmond leaned in closer to me and whispered, "Go in and tell them that their tutors are here."

"They'll have a conniption," I said, grinning. "Lessons on a Saturday!"

"Then," he continued, "I'll wait behind the door and surprise them."

I nodded, walking toward the door.

Inside the nursery, Abbott lay on the floor with his legs against the toy chest. He tossed the comic book he'd been reading onto the floor. "Why must life be so boring?"

Katherine and Janie sat beside the dollhouse while Nicholas pretended to push a toy fire truck toward the little building, drawing screams of annoyance from the girls.

"Children," I said, "I'm sorry to inform you that we will be having lessons today."

"Lessons?" Abbott cried. "But it's Saturday. That's . . . illegal!"

I grinned coyly. "I assure you that it's *not* illegal."

"Poppycock," Janie said with a grin.

"Miss Janie," I replied, unable to contain my laughter. "Where on earth did you learn the word *poppycock*?"

"Nicholas," Katherine said, smiling.

"All right, all of you," I said. "I've even hired a special Saturday tutor just for the occasion. In fact, he's right outside."

Katherine groaned. "I think I may die."

"I am *quite* certain that you will not die."

"Who is the tutor?" Nicholas asked. "Not that stuffy old codger with the mustache."

"Mr. Worthington is not a stuffy old codger," I said. "He's a very nice man." I lifted Janie to her feet, and Katherine followed. "Come," I continued. "Let's go meet him."

With long faces, the children plodded along single file into the hallway, just as Desmond jumped from behind the door. "Surprise!" he said.

"Desmond?" Nicholas cried, grinning from ear to ear.

"Desmond!" Katherine squealed. She ran to his side and wrapped her arms around her eldest brother.

Janie clapped her hands, though I don't think she recognized him.

Desmond knelt down beside Janie. "Last time I saw you, you were only a baby," he said. "Look how you've grown!" She beamed. He then looked up at Abbott, who frowned over crossed arms.

"What's the matter, Abbott?" I asked.

He didn't take his eyes off of Desmond. "It isn't right!" he shouted. "You can't just come back here as if nothing happened at all!"

Desmond's face looked ashen.

"It isn't fair!" Abbott shouted before he pushed past us and ran to his room.

"You stay with the children," I said. "I'll go to him."

I ran down the hallway to Abbott's bedroom. The door was locked. "Abbott," I said, "please open the door, honey. Please talk to me about how you're feeling."

"Leave me alone!" he shouted. "Please, leave me alone!"

"All right," I said. "But I'll be back to check on you."

Desmond and the children spent the afternoon in the drawing room, where Janie and Katherine took turns dancing a waltz with him. Each of them squealed with delight as he whisked them around the room. Nicholas clapped his hands and played along.

Desmond manned the gramophone. "I picked this one up from a record store in the city," he said, fumbling with the spindle. "Glenn Miller. He's a big deal in America. Do you know of him?"

"Yes," I said, remembering the bands at the Cabana Club at home in the Bronx. I'd wanted to be brave enough to dance with the boys who asked me, but I'd always found a reason to say no. That night with Desmond on the ship was the first time I'd ever danced with anyone.

"All right," he said. "Then you'll know 'Moonlight Serenade.'" He reached for my hand.

Katherine grinned as Desmond wrapped his right arm around my waist. I clutched his shoulder as our hands clasped together.

"Pretty song, isn't it?"

"It is," I agreed, happy to be in his arms again.

I don't know how long the song lasted, but it felt like an eternity. I lost myself in the music and in his embrace, as he whisked me softly around the room.

"Excuse me," Mrs. Dilloway said from the doorway. "I'm sorry to interrupt. Miss Lewis, may I have a word with you?"

I stepped away from Desmond and hurried toward the hallway. Mrs. Dilloway closed the door to the drawing room.

"I'm sorry," I said. "I guess I got carried away."

"I'm not here to scold you," Mrs. Dilloway replied. "Heaven knows I'm the least qualified to speak on matters of love." She let out an exhausted sigh. "It's Abbott," she continued. "I went to check on him a moment ago and he has a terrible fever. I'm calling a doctor."

Abbott refused dinner that evening. I worried about him. At twelve, he was somewhere between boy and man. I hated seeing him so upset. *Why did the sight of Desmond affect him so?* The doctor had visited late in the afternoon, and declared that Abbott had contracted a rare form of viral meningitis. He'd need rest, and time.

Despite the weight of Abbott's illness, Katherine and Nicholas chattered away at Desmond during dinner. "Do you have a real gun?" Nicholas inquired.

"Yes," Desmond said, "I do have a gun."

"Do you have it here?" he continued. "Can we see it?"

"Now, I don't think Miss Lewis would have me speaking about firearms at the table," he said, casting a smile my way. "It isn't proper."

Sadie added a log to the fireplace in the dining room, then turned and curtsied for Desmond.

"Sadie," he said. "Nice to see you again."

"You too," she said, looking flustered in the way she always did when one of Livingstons noticed her.

Mr. Beardsley shook his head, then offered Desmond a dinner roll. But before the butler could use the tongs to set it on his plate, Desmond plucked one from the basket and tossed it in the air, catching it behind his back. Nicholas watched him with eyes the size of hard-boiled eggs.

"Say," said Desmond, "who wants to go out stargazing tonight? Just like old times."

Nicholas leapt to his feet. "I do! I do!"

"Me too!" Katherine added.

I shook my head. "I hate to be an old meanie, but the children need a bath and then they're off to bed."

"Aww," Nicholas whined, plopping dejectedly back onto his chair.

Katherine crossed her arms.

"I'll be here for a whole month, so we'll have lots to do," Desmond said with a grin.

Nicholas stood up. "May I be excused, Miss Lewis?"

"Yes," I said, eyeing his plate. "But you've hardly touched your dinner."

He shrugged. "If Abbott can't eat, I won't either. I'm doing it for him."

"That's an awfully creative way of getting out of eating your peas," I said, then turned to Desmond. "Will you stay here with the children while I go up to check on Abbott?"

"Of course," he said.

Nicholas's show of solidarity for his brother faded as soon

as Mrs. Dilloway brought out cake. "I'll have an extra large slice," he said, before turning to Desmond and asking eagerly, "Do you also have a sword?"

I placed my hand on Abbott's forehead. "You're burning up." I wrung out a washcloth and set the cool compress on his forehead. He shivered in his bed, mumbling something under his breath. "You poor thing; it's a bad fever." I smoothed his hair. "It will pass, dear. We'll get you through this."

On the way out, I met Mr. Beardsley in the hallway.

"How is he?" he asked.

"Not well, I'm afraid."

"He's a strong boy, Abbott," he reassured me. "I think he needs a good night's sleep more than anything. Dr. Engstrom will be back to check on him first thing tomorrow."

Before he turned to the stairs, Mr. Beardsley smiled at me. "Thank you," he said.

"Thank you for what?"

"For caring for the children the way you do."

"I'm not doing anything special," I said.

"But you are. And her Ladyship would be grateful."

After Abbott had drifted off to sleep, I helped the others into bed and tiptoed downstairs, carrying a basket of the children's laundry with me. A pair of Nicholas's trousers fell to the floor, and when I reached to pick them up, Desmond swooped in. "I'll get that," he said.

He handed the garment to me with a grin. "They work you pretty hard around here, don't they?"

"I don't mind," I said, half-grinning.

"Let's go steal another piece of Mrs. Marden's cake from the kitchen," he said, flashing a mischievous grin.

I shook my head. "You know what Mrs. Marden does to intruders found skulking about her kitchen."

He smiled. "Why else would I ask you to be my accomplice?"

"Sneaky," I said with a smile.

Desmond wiped a few stray cake crumbs from his mouth and walked toward the butler's pantry. "None of it's changed since the day I came to live here. Beardsley's desk, the linen closet"—he looked up at the lightbulb that dangled from a wire in the hall—"everything."

My eyes narrowed. "Oh, I always assumed you were born here, that your family had always lived here."

"Well, I . . . it's a long story," he said.

We walked together to my bedroom door. "Say," Desmond said, looking at the back door, "it's a beautiful night. Let's go look at the stars."

I smiled, remembering how we'd gazed at the stars when we first met. "Like that night on the ship?" I asked.

"Precisely," he replied. "I'd imagine they still have quite a lot to say." He held the back door open for me, and together we walked outside. "Look," he said, pointing ahead. "Not a cloud in the sky."

"I don't think I've ever been out here this late," I said, marveling at the moon overhead. "Honestly, the place is a bit spooky in the dark."

"Don't worry," he said with a grin. "I won't keep you out past your bedtime." He reached for my hand. "You're cold," he said, blowing warm air into my hand.

"It's a bit chillier than it looked."

"I'll just run around to the front and grab my coat for you."

I smiled, remembering the way he'd draped his coat over my shoulders on our first night together. It felt like a lifetime ago.

A moment later, he was back by my side, holding out his coat for me to slip my arms into. It was heavy and thick, and I was glad for its warmth as we walked beyond the terrace.

"I used to love coming out here at night," he said, gazing out at the gardens. We wound through what was left of the rose garden, passing a pink bloom that grew despite neglect, and looked out over the grassy hillside that led down to the orchard. He pointed to a stone bench ahead, and we sat together.

"Desmond, what happened between you and your father?"

"It's complicated," he said. He didn't look much like Lord Livingston, not really. I imagined he must take after Lady Anna.

"You know what I used to like to do, when I was a boy?"

"What?"

"I would come out here with Mum, and we'd lie in the grass and gaze up at the clouds looking for pictures. Once I saw a steam engine, as plain as day."

"You were close, you and your mother, weren't you?"

"We were," he said.

I hesitated before speaking again. "How did she die?" I only knew what Sadie had told me.

Desmond sighed.

"If it's too hard to talk about, I understand. I just—"

"No," he said, raising his eyes to look at the orchard. He remained quiet for a few moments before speaking again. "She and Father had a terrible fight," he began. "There was always a lot of fighting. He wanted her to be someone she wasn't, to keep her in this house, like a little bird on display in a golden cage. But she couldn't be confined that way. She wanted to be free." He threw a pebble down the hillside. "One day, I found her on the terrace crying. I asked her what was the matter and she said she was thinking about going away for a while. She asked me if I'd take her to the train station. Of course I tried to talk her out of it. But she insisted. Said she wanted to go home to Charleston by herself, and that she'd be back after she cleared her head."

"So you drove her there, then? To the train station?"

"No," he said, looking at his lap briefly. "Father overheard our conversation from the upper deck. He stormed down in a terrible rage, blaming me for meddling in his business. Blaming me for everything, actually."

"I don't understand," I said. "How could he be so accusing?"

"We've never seen eye to eye," he said, "and I've come to realize that we may never."

He leaned forward, resting his elbows on his knees. "Anyway, Father was terribly angry. I'd never seen him like that before. Mum came unglued. They shouted at each other. Father stormed out. After that, Mum called Mr. Blythe up from the rose garden and invited him to join her for tea on the terrace. She did it to spite Father, knowing he could see them from his study. Mr. Blythe loved Mum. Everyone knew that. It used to irritate Abbott. He hated Mr. Blythe."

"He did?"

Desmond nodded. "Anyway, Mr. Blythe joined Mum for tea. Afterward Mum walked down to the orchard, alone."

"Did your father go out looking for her later?"

"No," he said. "I don't think he thought anything of it. Arguments were commonplace for them, and Mum always found solitude in the orchard." He folded and then unfolded his hands. "But Mum didn't come up for dinner, and I began to worry, so I decided to go talk to her, encourage her to come back home. It was getting dark, and she never liked the orchard at night. I walked down the hill and just past the meadow, at the edge of the orchard, I found her, lying in the grass."

"What happened to her?"

"Her heart had stopped before I found her," he said, his voice faltering a little. "I keep wondering how things would be different today if I'd only gone after her sooner. If Father hadn't shouted at her the way he did, if he hadn't driven her away . . ."

"Oh, Desmond," I said, "how terrible for you."

"It was," he said. "I carried her up to the house. Fortunately, the children were asleep, so they didn't see her in that state."

"Do you know why she collapsed?"

"No one knows for sure," he said. "And believe me, we all took it hard. Mrs. Dilloway, especially, and Abbott. He was so protective of Mum. For a time, every one of us was a suspect. But in the end, the doctor concluded that she died of natural causes. She was born with a weak heart. But Father blames me for her death. And I suppose, in a way, I blame him."

"But of course neither of you is to blame," I said.

Desmond shook his head.

"You don't mean that he . . . ?"

"No," he said. "No, he didn't kill her, if that's what you mean. I think she died of unhappiness."

I shivered at the thought.

"I suppose we'll never know, though," he said. "I'm ready to move forward with my life now, ready to put it all behind me. Whether my father played a part in her death or not, I can't hate him forever. Hate is like cancer; it corrodes the heart. I've decided to forgive him for the past. It's why I came home again, why I want to see him this time. The war's given me an eerie sense about leaving without mending fences with him."

"I'm sure your father will appreciate what you have to say."

"I hope," he said with a sigh. "I just wish we could have saved her. I've turned the story over in my mind a hundred times, and I still can't make any sense of it. I miss her so much." He looked up at the big star that sparkled overhead. "You know, I've thought an awful lot about this, and I think that people are much like those stars up there. Some burn faintly for millions of years, barely visible to us on earth. They're there, but you'd hardly know it. They blend in, like a speck on a canvas. But others blaze with such intensity, they light up the sky. You can't help but notice them, marvel at them. Those are the ones that never last long. They can't. They use up all their energy quickly. Mum was one of those."

"That's beautiful," I said.

Desmond continued to stare up at the sky.

"Do you think you'll come back home," I asked, "after the war?"

He looked thoughtful for a moment. "I don't know. When I was a boy, Mum would take me out here and we'd talk about life and where I might end up when I became a man. She told me never to stop searching until I find my true north."

"Your true north?"

"She wasn't talking about a direction, in the longitudinal sense, but rather finding my way, my place in life, the intersection of life and love. My truth." He paused, turning to me. "The day I stepped off the ship in Liverpool," he said, "I made a promise to myself."

I looked up at him curiously, with a shy smile, and waited for him to finish.

"I promised that if I ever saw you again, I'd make sure I never let you out of my sight."

His words surprised me, and yet they were heartfelt. I knew, because I felt that way too. I searched his face. "What are you saying?"

"I mean that after the war, after all of this is behind us, I want to spend every day of my life with you, Flora Lewis."

My mouth fell open. "Do you really mean that?"

"With all my heart," he said, kissing me tenderly.

I hardly knew him, of course. But I knew I loved him, perhaps from the moment I'd first seen him.

"Make me the happiest man," he said, "and promise me you'll wait for me. Promise me you'll be here after the war."

My mind swirled with flashes of Mama and Papa, Mr. Price, the children, but everything paled when I looked into Desmond's eyes. "I promise."

I looked to the left when a figure suddenly appeared in the distance, trudging up the hill from the orchard. Desmond rose, moving in front of me protectively. "There's an encampment of gypsies a few miles to the east of here," he said in a hushed voice. "Sometimes we get drifters."

"Yes," I said, "your father told me."

It was difficult to make out the figure ahead, but his shadow loomed large. "Who's there?" Desmond shouted.

The figure, a man, stopped to look at us, then walked a little closer, until the light from the house illuminated his face.

I gasped. "Mr. Humphrey?"

"Miss Lewis," he said, tipping his cap. He held a shovel in one hand and a burlap sack in the other. "Good evening, Lord Desmond."

"Hello, Humphrey," Desmond replied curtly. "What were you doing in the orchard at this hour?"

Mr. Humphrey fidgeted for a long moment. "I was just checking on the carriage house, sir," he said. "I thought I saw a light down there a day ago and wanted to be sure we didn't have anyone setting up shop."

"Very well," Desmond said. "And did you find everything to be in good order?"

"Yes, my Lord."

Desmond eyed the burlap sack Mr. Humphrey held. "What's in the sack, Humphrey?"

"Oh, this, my Lord? It's nothing. Just, er, thought I might bring Mrs. Marden some potatoes if I found some."

"Potatoes?"

"Yes, my Lord. There are wild potatoes that grow down there."

"All right, Humphrey, don't let us keep you, then," Desmond said.

"Goodnight, Miss Lewis," Mr. Humphrey said before continuing on toward the house.

Desmond turned to me. "I don't like him," he whispered. "Never have."

"He means well," I said.

"Just the same, I don't trust him."

Desmond stood up and looked toward the driveway. "A car," he said. "Who's here?"

We watched as Lord Livingston stepped out into the driveway. "He must have taken an earlier train," I said. "Mr. Beardsley wasn't expecting him until tomorrow. I sure hope everything's all right." I stood and took a step toward the house, but Desmond reached for my hand.

"I can't," he said. "I can't see him. Not yet. I'm not ready."

"Then what are you going to do? We can't exactly *hide* you this time, now that the children have seen you."

"That's exactly what I was going to ask you to do," he said. "Just until tomorrow. The children are in bed, and Father's always in a better mood once he's had a good night's sleep. I'd rather meet him then than surprise him tonight when he's tired and been through God knows what sort of ordeal in London."

"You have a point."

"Take me through the basement," he said. "I can't stay on the second floor. I can't risk running into him tonight. Believe me, you don't want to see Father's temper."

"Wait," I said. "I have an idea. Come with me."

We tiptoed into the basement through the back door, careful not to wake Mr. Beardsley as we passed his bedroom. His snoring rattled the plaster. At the linen closet, I slowly opened the door. It creaked, and I cringed at the sound. "Here," I whispered, handing him a blanket and extra pillow. "We'll go up the back staircase."

The rear staircase was primarily used by Sadie, who transported the linens and laundry to and from the basement. We opened the door to the third floor, and I looked both ways before stepping into the hallway. "Where are you taking me?" Desmond whispered.

"You'll see," I replied with a grin.

I knelt down to the floorboard and lifted the flap of carpeting to reveal the key. I slipped it into the lock. Desmond followed me inside. "What is this?"

"You mean you've never been up here?"

"No," he said. "The door's always been locked. I assumed it was attic space." He walked inside, marveling at the pink bougainvillea trained around the arbor. He breathed in the scent of the citrus trees. "This was Mum's, wasn't it?"

"Yes."

He walked to the orchid table. "Everywhere she went, there was beauty. I'm surprised Father hasn't gutted this place."

"Mrs. Dilloway saved it. She kept it just as your mother left it. I come up here to water the plants and look after them. I brought Katherine up here too. She liked that." I plucked a browned leaf from one of the dendrobiums and turned back to Desmond. "Stay here tonight. There are a few sacks of peat moss over there by the window; they'd make a fine mattress. And the sunrise ought to be spectacular."

Desmond set the blanket and pillow down on a burlap sack of peat. "Yes," he said, soaking up his mother's presence, "it will be perfect."

He walked to the edge of the conservatory and opened a window. The hinges squeaked.

"Shhh," I said. "Your father will hear."

Desmond kept his ear pressed to the window. "Listen, do you hear that?"

Soft music filtered through the open window. "I'll See You in My Dreams," he said.

I smiled. "I beg your pardon?"

"That song," he said. "I know it. Django Reinhardt." He walked toward me intently and took my hands in his. "Dance with me."

The music had to be coming from Lord Livingston's suite below, but I didn't care. My body flowed with Desmond's effortlessly, naturally. We fit. I pressed my cheek against his, and when the song ended, he pulled me closer than he ever had before and pressed his lips against mine.

The next morning, I sat up quickly, disoriented. I had dreamed that I met Lady Anna in the camellia orchard. She said she needed my help, to save the camellia she loved most, the Middlebury Pink. A headless man loomed in the distance, with a torch in hand and a black spider on his lapel, and we raced to save the tree before he burned it. Anna was lovelier than I could have imagined, and I had felt ordinary and plain in her presence.

I dressed quickly and went upstairs to check on Abbott, thinking of his mother.

I approached Abbott's bedroom and knocked. "It's Miss Lewis," I said. "How are you feeling this morning?"

"Come in," he called out.

I set a tray of toast and tea on the table near his bed, while he sat up and stretched.

"Better," he said.

I held my hand to his forehead. "Your fever is gone. I'm so relieved."

"How long will Desmond stay here with us?"

"Well, I suppose as long as he'd like to. It's his home too, Abbott."

The boy turned to face the wall.

"I wish you'd tell me why you're so upset with Desmond," I said.

"I don't want to talk about it!" he cried, sinking back and covering his head with his pillow.

"All right," I said. "You rest today, but we must work this out. You two are brothers, after all."

Downstairs, Sadie waved at me from the kitchen. "Mr. Beardsley's looking for you," she said. "He needs us in the servants' hall."

"What's going on?"

"I don't know," she said. "But I think it's something big."

I was eager to bring Desmond a pot of tea and pastry in the conservatory, so I hoped Mr. Beardsley would impart the news quickly. And painlessly.

"What do you think he's going to say?" Sadie whispered.

"I have no idea," I replied.

"How's Abbott?"

"Better, thankfully."

"I'll look in on him this morning while you're with the children," she said.

"Thanks," I whispered.

Mr. Beardsley and Mrs. Marden walked into the room together, exchanging a glance, before she sat down beside him near the head of the table.

Mr. Beardsley stared ahead. "It has come to my attention that some of the crystal and silver has gone missing."

Sadie gasped.

"These are heirlooms that belong to this house," he continued, looking at each one of us carefully. "And I will stop at nothing to see that they are returned. Do I make myself clear?"

We all nodded.

After breakfast, Sadie and I followed Mrs. Marden into the kitchen. "Strange about those things going missing," Sadie said. "What do you think's going on? You don't suppose we have a real, live thief in the house, do you?"

I prayed that I didn't look guilty. I wouldn't dream of stealing from the Livingstons, and yet, my intentions weren't far removed.

"It's a shame," Mrs. Marden added. "Lord only knows who could be involved."

"Don't look at me!" Sadie exclaimed, grimacing.

Mrs. Marden lowered her voice. "There's a shifty-looking milkman who comes round on Sundays and Wednesdays. Always tries to poke around the kitchen and talk all friendly-like before he heads back to the village. Once I ran down to the stockroom for a mere minute and when I returned he was helpin' himself to bread and butter!"

I smiled. "I didn't realize that milkmen were such a shifty lot."

"The worst kind," she said.

"Oh, by the way, I was going to ask you—do you happen to know much about potatoes?"

"Do I know much about potatoes?" she parroted back. "That's like asking a doctor if he knows much about medicine!

Girl, I can fry, bake, poach, and roast potatoes. I can whip them and mash them and puree them. Do I know about potatoes? Hmph!"

I smiled. "No, no," I said. "I didn't mean preparations. I was wondering about the way they *grow*. Do you have to plant them from seed?"

"Well they don't grow magically, child," she said with a laugh.

"So they don't grow wild, then?"

"No chance of that," she replied. "Least not around these parts, with such tough, stubborn soil. I'm surprised her Lady-ship got anything to grow out here. Besides, potatoes aren't easy. Got to plant the little devils, and even then, they some-times grow all shriveled-like." She stirred her soup pot. "Say, why do you ask?"

"It's nothing," I said. "Just curious, that's all."

"Americans!" she muttered to herself as I tucked a scone into my pocket and headed to the back staircase.

"Desmond?" I whispered as I slipped into the conservatory.

He sat up groggily. "Top of the morning to you," he said with a yawn.

I smiled to myself. Someday, I hoped I'd hear him say those words each and every morning.

He stretched and looked up at the glass roof of the conser-vatory, where daylight had just begun to show. "Wow, what time is it?"

"Half past seven," I said. "How'd you sleep?"

He rubbed his eyes. "Fine. You know, if I was an

enterprising man, I'd go into business making mattresses out of peat moss. I think that was the best night's sleep I've had in a good while."

"I'm glad to hear it," I said. I handed him the scone from my pocket. "I smuggled this up for you. I wanted to bring tea, but I lost my nerve. I couldn't exactly say that I was bringing it for the children."

"Awfully kind of you," he said, taking a bite. "Here I am, a stowaway in my own house."

I sat down beside him, blushing a little as I thought of the night before. "Speaking of the children," I said, collecting myself, "I meant to ask you about Abbott."

"Yes?" he said.

"What happened between the two of you? Why does he have such hard feelings?"

"Oh, I wouldn't worry about him," he said. "He'll come around. I'm sure he's just being moody. Everyone's moody at the age of twelve."

I shook my head. "He's not usually that way. Your visit set him off. I wish I knew why."

Desmond stood up and brushed the crumbs off his uniform, before polishing off the rest of the scone. "Any chance a tired soldier can get a hot breakfast?"

"Mr. Beardsley always serves breakfast at eight sharp."

"Good old Beardsley," he said with a smile. "Always the same, day after day. But wouldn't you like to see him lighten up a little?"

"Well, I—"

"Schedules and traditions, traditions and schedules." He shook his head. "It's not for me."

I searched his face. "You're a different sort of person, aren't you? You're not like them."

"I'm not," he said.

A noise emanated from beyond the window, which had been left propped open. Desmond and I exchanged a cautious glance.

"Probably your father on the terrace," I said. "He sometimes reads the newspaper there before coming down for breakfast." I paused for a moment. "Are you ready to see him?"

"Ready as I'll ever be."

We walked to the door, but before I opened it, I turned back to Desmond. "About Abbott," I said. "Could you try to talk to him?"

"I'll certainly try," he replied. "But I have one bridge to cross first, and I'm not sure it's going to be easy."

"Come on," I said. "I'll go with you."

CHAPTER 25

Addison

W as Sean here in the foyer? I searched the first floor, then tiptoed to the front door, peering out the side window. I
breathed a sigh of relief at the absence of a car parked in the driveway. No one; my ears were playing tricks on me. I took a step back
from the window, then paused when I heard a car approaching. A
taxi.

An older man, in his sixties, stepped out of the car, which is
when I remembered Nicholas Livingston's visit.

"Hello," I said, walking outside, grateful for his presence.

"Addison," he said. "Pleased to meet you. I'm Nicholas Livingston." He looked up at the old manor quietly, as if the sight had
momentarily stunned him. "It's just as I remembered it."

I suppose the manor would always be untouched by time. Years
could pass. Mortar could crumble. Stone could crack in jagged
lines. But it would, more or less, remain the same.

He eyed a pair of wood pigeons pecking at one of the house's
cornices. "All these years," he said. "I didn't think the old house
would have this effect on me. The bird calls still sound as lonely as
I felt back then."

"You might be interested to know that the place will be changing a bit soon," I said. "My in-laws have a remodel in store." I looked out to the gardens, still wondering how Rex could sign off on what appeared to be the demolition of the camellia orchard to make way for a golf course. "Well, at least as far as the house is concerned."

Behind him, the cab driver stood staring at the stone lions near the entryway. His body language indicated that he wouldn't step a foot farther. I wondered if he shared the belief of the woman in town that the house was cursed. "Thanks," Nicholas said, tucking a bill into his hand. He drove off quickly, in good-riddance fashion.

"That's what I wanted to talk to you about," he said, looking around him as if the trees might have ears. "Is there a place we can go to talk . . . privately?"

I nodded, leading him inside the house. "The last time I was inside the manor, I was thirteen," he said, standing in the foyer. "I never came home after boarding school. I went straight to university."

"I don't understand," I said. "Why would you stay away so long?"

His hair had grayed with age. The baby cheeks depicted in the photographs now looked distinguished. And yet, unlike Lord Livingston in the photos I'd seen, the edges of his face appeared gentler, softer. Together, we walked to the parlor and sat on the sofa near the side windows that looked out to the orchard. "There were too many sad memories here," he said. "And after Katherine married and Abbott's condition worsened, I guess there wasn't much for me here anymore. Everything changed."

"What do you mean about Abbott's *condition*?"

He nodded gravely. "Abbott came down with a fever in 1940. The doctors said it was meningitis. It seemed that he made a full recovery, but the fever weakened his heart. He was never the same.

And as he got older, he worsened. By the time I went to university, he was bedridden."

"How terrible," I said. "So your father looked after him?"

"No," he said. "Father died in 1963. Mrs. Dilloway cared for him after that, until his death last year."

"I'm so sorry," I said. "I didn't know."

"I tried to visit Abbott so many times, but Mrs. Dilloway claimed that the family's presence wouldn't be good for his nerves."

"I don't understand."

"I didn't either," he said. "So one day, late in the 1970s, when my daughter was ten, my wife and I made a visit. We thought it was only right for Abbott to finally meet his niece. Mrs. Dilloway wasn't here when we arrived, and we found Abbott sitting out on the terrace in a wheelchair. He looked terrible, like a hollowed-out version of himself. I'll never forget his face, so thin and pale. He appeared much older than his years." He retrieved a handkerchief from his shirt pocket. "He didn't recognize me, not at first. But then his face formed a smile, and he"—Nicholas paused to dab his eyes—"he said, I'll never forget it, he said, 'Brother?'"

"We talked for a while," Nicholas continued. "He told me something that I haven't been able to get out of my head. Of course, I'm not sure how much of it was the illness talking, but . . ."

"What did he say?"

Nicholas looked over his shoulder. "He said that Mum was murdered."

"But he was only a young boy then," I said. "How could he have known?"

"To be honest," Nicholas said, "I thought his illness had softened his mind. And yet, he kept saying that someone was responsible and they'd have to pay. He said that over and over again."

"Who was that someone?"

"Well, I don't know, exactly, but I felt compelled to look into the matter further," he said. "I hired an attorney. I tried to get the case reopened, to get Mother's autopsy report analyzed by a specialist, but the housekeeper, Mrs. Dilloway, had it sealed."

"I know," I said. "I checked the records myself. But do you have any idea why she would do that?"

"At the time, her petition stated that she was protecting my mother's dignity. She claimed that some of the village men had been needlessly looking at the autopsy photos of her nude body." Nicholas shuddered. "But I don't think that was the case at all. The only obvious reason is that she wanted to hide something," he said. "When Katherine told me about the way she loved Father, I began to wonder if there was more to the story than any of us could ever know."

I gasped. "She loved him?"

Nicholas sighed. "Yes. Of course, we didn't know it at the time, but according to Katherine, Mrs. Dilloway loved him even when Mum was alive."

"Well, think what you will about her," I said, "but she's in the hospital now. She had a stroke last night."

"Oh," he said, a little stunned. "I'm sorry to hear that." He rose and walked to the window, running his hand along the sill. "I wanted to come here once more to see if I missed something. For Mother. Your family will be making changes here, as you've indicated, and before that happens, I want to be certain."

"I'm sure my in-laws won't mind if you want to have a look around," I said.

"Thank you," he said. "I didn't know if they'd be happy with my little investigation, which is why I hired a pair of private investigators."

"Private investigators?"

"I hope you'll forgive me," he said. "It wasn't you they were spying on. I only wanted to know what the plans were for the property and poke about the orchard, to see if they could find anything of interest in the carriage house."

"So that's who was down there that day," I muttered.

I followed him to the windows looking out to the garden. "Then I don't have to tell you about the golf course, since you already know."

He looked momentarily confused, but then his eyes met the view from the windows leading out to the terrace. "The orchard!" he cried. "Mum would be so happy that it's just as she left it. Well, a bit overgrown now, but still grand."

"Yes," I said. "Mr. Livingston, there's something I'd like to show you. In the drawing room."

I handed him the file of news clippings about the women who had gone missing, then I showed him the map of the gardens that I'd annotated with the sticky notes.

"What is this?" he asked.

I picked up his mother's camellia book, opening it to the Petelo camellia. "Have you seen this before?"

His eyes got misty. "Yes," he said. "I remember the day that Flora found it."

"Your nanny?"

"Yes," he said, turning to the file of news clippings. "When she disappeared, we feared the worst. She dropped off the face of the earth, it seemed. Didn't even say good-bye to us." He studied the page in the book, lost in thought. "Mum loved her camellias. I can still see her out there, walking through the orchard, humming quietly to herself. It reminded her of her beloved Charleston."

"Mr. Livingston," I said, "I believe your mother may have been trying to solve a mystery before her death." I pointed to the numeric code at the top right corner of the page. "I've traced these numbers to the dates the women went missing. I think your mother had a hunch that something very dark was happening right here at the manor. Can you remember anything? Any small detail that might help shed light on what may have happened to these women?"

"Well," he said, "my investigators did find something down in the orchard."

We walked outside, where a couple stood by a blue car in the driveway. The woman, with bobbed blond hair, took off her sunglasses and smiled.

"You," I said. "You were the ones who saved me in the park."

"Yes," the man said. "I'm James and this is Mira. We work for Mr. Livingston. It was purely a coincidence that we ran into you in town. We recognized you, from the day down by the carriage house. I'm sorry about that. We didn't mean to frighten you."

"It's all right," I said. "I'm just glad it was you and not . . ."

"I remembered your face," he continued. "So when I noticed that man walking behind you in the park, we followed too."

"I'm so glad you did," I said.

"Did they catch him?"

"No," I replied. "But they will. I know they will."

I pointed at the blue convertible in the driveway, remembering the mysterious woman who had stopped to talk to Rex on the day we arrived. "You were here," I said, looking at her curiously. "You spoke to my husband. He said you were a courier."

"Oh that," she said. "Yes."

Nicholas Livingston pointed to the orchard. "We'll explain everything."

I nodded, turning to the camellias in the distance. "OK, let's head down there before the rain rolls in."

"Your mother kept quite a garden," I said to Nicholas. "I'm a garden designer, and I can tell you, I've never seen anything like it."

"Yes," he said, "she was very proud of her collection. There are some rare varieties here. At least, there used to be."

I pulled out the page torn from the camellia book. "This one," I said. "It's called a Middlebury Pink. Do you know it?"

Nicholas took the page in his hand. "I remember it," he said. "It only bloomed once, after Mother's death." He shook his head. "She never even got to see its flowers."

"Where is it?" I said, pointing to the place in the garden where, according to the numeric code, it should have been. All that remained was a sunken spot in the soil.

His eyes lit up as if he'd been struck with a sudden memory. "Over here," he said, pointing to the carriage house. "If it's the one I'm remembering, I believe Father had it moved. After Mother's death, he had reason to believe that someone was trying to steal it. Flower thieves. He had it moved back here, behind the carriage house." We walked behind the old outbuilding, but where the tree might have stood, only a stump remained, and an old one at that.

"Such a shame," I said, sinking down onto the mossy ground, heavy with disappointment.

James motioned to Nicholas from the side of the carriage house. "Would you like to see what we found?"

I followed them to the door. "It's locked," I said, tugging at the rusty lock.

James smiled. "My specialty. Just give me a second." In a

moment, he had pried the padlock from the latch on the door, and he pushed it open.

Mira and I followed the men inside.

"Looks like an old garden shed," I said.

Mira and James exchanged glances. "See that little door?" James said.

I nodded.

James opened the door to reveal a small room. A few shovels and rakes lay against the wall, where a crude message appeared to have been hand-painted in dark ink. I walked closer, peering into the little room, and read the words: "For the flowers shall be anointed with her blood, and spring forth beauty."

"What is this?"

Mira looked at James again. "Miss Sinclair," she said turning to look at me, "we think it was painted in blood."

"We're filing a police report," James said in the driveway after we'd walked back to the house. "I think there's sufficient evidence to relaunch an investigation into Lady Anna Livingston's death." He clutched the files I'd given him, with the map of the gardens. "And with your help, Addison, I think we may have something solid."

"Keep in touch," I said as he and Mira climbed into the car.

"We will," she said, as they drove off.

"Well," Nicholas said. "I ought to think about heading back too. My wife doesn't like that I'm here. The old place gives her the creeps."

"It can have that effect," I said, smiling.

He retrieved his cell phone from his jacket and arranged a pickup from the cab company.

"What became of your other sibling?" I said. "Your sister? Did she stay away from the manor too?"

"After Father's death, Katherine and Janie never returned," he said, "perhaps for the same reasons I didn't come back. Katherine married a banker in London, started a family of her own. Janie moved to Switzerland."

"So there were four of you, then?"

He looked off into the distance before his eyes met mine again. "There was another," he said. "Desmond."

"Desmond?"

"Our eldest brother," he said. "He disappeared in the war. Sadly, they never found him."

"I'm sorry," I said.

"Well, Ms. Sinclair," he said as a cab pulled up in front of the manor, "it has been a pleasure. I'll keep you informed of our progress with the investigation. The police will likely be by to take your statement and look around."

"That's fine," I said. "I'll let my in-laws know." I watched the cab motor away before stopping along the walkway to admire the peonies, growing in profusion in a garden bed. Their blooms were so lush, so heavy, they bent forward onto the gravel pathway as if to kiss the ground. I knelt down to prop them up. "Poor things," I said. "Someone needs to stake you." I stood up. "I'll just go see if I can find some twine in the house."

I looked up to the steps, and I almost didn't see him there; he blended into the gray of the stone. But when I did, my heart stopped.

"Hello again, Amanda," he said.

CHAPTER 26

Flora

Desmond waited in the foyer as I slipped into the dining room, taking my usual place at the table beside Janie. Lord Livingston immediately stood up and set his napkin down. "Miss Lewis," he said, smiling cheerfully. "It's so very good to see you again."

"You as well," I replied.

He'd been gone for two months, but I felt as if years had passed. He was visibly thinner, and more gray had appeared along his hairline.

"We're all so glad you're home safe," I said.

"Thank you," he replied.

Mr. Beardsley refilled the children's water glasses and cast a nervous glance toward the foyer. Mrs. Dilloway nodded at Desmond to signal it was time.

"Forgive me for the interruption, your Lordship," Mr. Beardsley said cautiously, "but there's someone here to see you."

Lord Livingston set his napkin on the table. "Oh? I didn't hear anyone come in."

Mr. Beardsley looked toward the foyer and nodded at Desmond, who slowly walked into the dining room.

"Hello, Father," he said, stopping at the head of the table.

Katherine cheered. "Can you believe it, Father? Desmond's come home!"

"I see," Lord Livingston said, looking away.

An icy silence fell over the dining room. Thankfully, Janie tapped her fork on her plate and squealed.

"Aren't you happy, Father?" Katherine asked nervously.

Lord Livingston stood up and faced Desmond. "I will speak to you privately."

They walked out to the foyer, and Mr. Beardsley followed, closing the door behind them.

I tried to distract the children from the shouting we all could hear. A few minutes later, Desmond stormed out the front door, slamming it behind him. Lord Livingston returned to the dining room smoothing his hair, which appeared unusually disheveled. He took a deep breath before addressing us. "I've asked him to pack his things and leave at once."

"But, Father," Nicholas said, clearly devastated.

Katherine began to cry.

"He can't stay here," he said coldly, as if speaking of a stranger instead of his own flesh and blood.

"But why, Father?" Katherine cried. "Why must you be so cruel?"

"I've made my decision," he said, turning to Mr. Beardsley.

"Your Lordship," Mrs. Dilloway said boldly, "I beg you to reconsider." She reduced her voice to a hush. "For her Ladyship's sake."

"Yes," Mr. Beardsley added. "He's family. You can't turn away family."

Lord Livingston threw his napkin on the table and rose. "Why yes, old chap," he said, "you can." He looked at all of us. "Is there anything else you're keeping from me?"

Mrs. Dilloway nodded. "You may like to know that Abbott has been ill," she said cautiously. "He had a high fever. The doctors said it was a bout of meningitis, but he's making a good recovery."

"May I go see him?" he asked, his eyes flooded with emotion.

"He's sleeping now," Mrs. Dilloway said. "You might attend to your *other* son first."

"Father!" Katherine cried. "Please, can't you let Desmond stay? Won't you make an exception? England is at war!"

He slammed his fist on table, rattling the water glasses. "I'm well aware of the state of the war."

Katherine began to sob; Janie too. Nicholas's face went white.

I stood up and lifted Janie into my arms. "There, there," I said, patting her back softly. I could no longer keep quiet. My heart raced as I turned to Lord Livingston. I didn't care anymore about the Middlebury Pink, the delicate family issues. I cared about the children. "You may know what's best for the manor," I said, "but you certainly don't know what's best for your children." I turned to them and extended my hand. "Katherine, Nicholas, come with me."

Only once the children were settled in with their tutors did I pause to consider the degree to which my confronting Lord Livingston had compromised my position in the house. I peered through the window glass, but I couldn't bear to look at my reflection.

Out my bedroom window, I watched the way the sunlight filtered through the clouds onto the camellia trees, making their emerald leaves sparkle. I went to the closet and retrieved the easel that Lord Livingston had bought for me, then reached for the box of art supplies underneath the bed.

I placed the tubes of paint on the palette and selected a small canvas. I prepared the palette with an assortment of colors, then closed my eyes, remembering the way the moors had looked when I rode into town with Lord Livingston. He'd been so different on that drive into the village before he left for London. Had that been the side of him that Lady Anna had fallen in love with? I dipped my brush into the black paint and then mixed in some white until I'd created the right shade of gray, then touched the brush to the canvas. I loved the feeling of the paintbrush in my hand. He'd been kind to buy me the art supplies, but I remembered how he'd behaved in the dining room and at other times before that. *How could he be so cruel, so unfeeling?*

Once I'd painted the clouds, I moved on to the hills, mixing a sage green color for the grass and then dotting the foreground with a bit of lavender to simulate the heather. I stepped back from the canvas and frowned. It needed something else. But what? I looked out the window to the orchard.

The Middlebury Pink. *Who took the page from Lady Anna's book? Lord Livingston?* I dabbed my brush into the brown paint and created the structure of the tree. Next I dotted the branches with its heart-shaped leaves and large, white, saucer-size blossoms with pink tips. I stepped back again to have a look at my work.

"You've captured it beautifully."

I turned around, startled. Lord Livingston stood in the doorway.

"It was my wife's favorite camellia," he said. "The Middlebury Pink. It took me a great deal of time and energy to locate it. She'd seen it in an old botanical book and wanted it more than anything in the world. The same variety had once grown at Buckingham Palace, you know." He looked lost in thought. "She was like that, Anna. She could become absolutely consumed by something. But nothing captured her attention like the camellias. I hired a gardener to search the country. After a year, we almost gave up. Its existence seemed only a fable. Botanists who devoted their careers to studying rare flowers scoured the country for the variety. But no one could find it. I couldn't fail her. I wouldn't. Then, a man in the village said he believed the Middlebury Pink was here on the property of Livingston Manor. Of course I didn't believe him at first, but then we found it, near the carriage house. A botanist identified it, which wasn't easy to do when it wasn't in bloom." He shook his head. "It had spent the last century undetected right under our noses. I kept the secret to myself and then surprised her with it on Christmas morning." He rubbed his forehead. "That wretched tree never bloomed for her, though. She always said it would bloom when it sensed peace, and a rightness with the world." He kept his eyes on the canvas, and smiled. "Yes, you've captured it perfectly, Miss Lewis," he said, wiping away a tear. "It's a wonder that you have such an interest in botany."

He sat on the bed, looking out to the orchard. "There are many things I regret in life," he said. "But there's so much I regret about Anna."

"Please," I said. "We all make mistakes. You mustn't blame yourself."

He shook his head. "But I should," he said. "And now I must pay." He collected himself and stood beside me. "I'm sorry I bothered you." He turned to the door.

"Please wait," I said. "What about Desmond? Surely whatever disagreement you had isn't worth losing your son forever."

Lord Livingston sighed noncommittally. "I can't promise reconciliation," he said, "but I have asked him to stay."

"And how did he answer?"

"He's giving it some thought."

"Good," I said. "He'll be shipping out soon, for the war, and I know you'll be glad you had the time you did with him."

His eyes met mine. "I suppose we all will."

At breakfast the next morning in the servants' hall, Mr. Beardsley turned away from his notebook and stood up abruptly. "Miss Lewis," he said. "May I have a word with you?"

"Of course, sir," I replied, following him to the butler's pantry.

"Have a seat," he said, closing the door.

"I've been going over the logbooks," he began, "and I've come across something that may be a coincidence. Forgive me for asking, but the gentleman who paid you a visit recently— what is his relationship to you?"

My palms felt moist. *Mr. Price.* "I didn't know that you—"

"Mrs. Dilloway told me of his visit," he said. "We keep record of everyone who comes to the manor. It's a tradition."

"Oh," I said, shaken. *She must have been the one who let him in.*

"Miss Lewis," he continued. "I didn't realize it until this morning, but the day the silver and crystal went missing was the day your visitor came to the manor. Surely you can understand my concern."

I nodded.

"Who was he, Miss Lewis? Please."

I rubbed my forehead.

"Miss Lewis," Mr. Beardsley said again. "Are you in some kind of trouble? Because if you are, let us help you."

I stared up into his big, kind face. I had deceived these people, and I was ashamed of myself. Deeply ashamed. "Yes," I said. "I am. But I can take care of myself. I wouldn't dream of burdening you or anyone at the manor. Forgive me for the intrusion. If it turns out that the man did steal those things from you, I will take personal responsibility for it."

"But, Miss Lewis," he said. "There's no way you could cover the costs. They'd cost you four years' wages, at least."

"So be it," I said. "If my presence brought a thief into Livingston Manor, then I will pay the price."

"That's very honorable of you," he said. "But let's be clear. No one is calling you a thief."

At the table, I stirred one teaspoon of brown sugar instead of two into my porridge, since Mrs. Marden had warned us of war-related food shortages. We were lucky to still have sugar, she said.

"What was that about?" Sadie whispered to me. "Did he catch the thief?"

I shook my head.

"I think old Beardsley probably misplaced the silver," she

said. "Last month he turned the house upside down to find a missing shoehorn, and sure enough, it was on his desk."

"I doubt it's Mr. Beardsley's doing," I said. "He knows every ladle in the kitchen."

She drizzled a bit more cream on her porridge. "I hate to think that there's a thief among us."

"Watch it there, missy," Mrs. Marden warned. "We have to make that stretch; Mr. Beardsley hasn't had his coffee yet. You know he likes cream."

Sadie set the pitcher down. "Yes, ma'am."

"We're all going to have to get used to living without the little luxuries we're accustomed to, now that the war's heating up," Mrs. Dilloway said.

"Indeed so," Mrs. Marden added. "I spoke to another cook in town yesterday, and she said she couldn't even get flour. Molasses was entirely out of the question. Fortunate for us, his Lordship has a supplier in London, but I hear that we won't be able to count on that route for long. Everything's being rationed, and it doesn't matter who you are or who you know. The pickings are slim."

Sadie leaned in to me. "No wonder someone's stealin'," she whispered.

I remembered seeing Mr. Humphrey late the other night. The incident struck me as strange, especially after talking to Mrs. Marden about potatoes. "Sadie," I whispered, "does Mr. Humphrey have any business being in the orchard?"

She scratched her head. "The orchard? Why would he be in the orchard? He's the chauffeur."

"Exactly," I said.

CHAPTER 27

Addison

Sean took a step toward me, smiling in a way that made my hair stand on end. "Did you think I forgot about you?"

I have to get out of here.

He continued to smile. "Cat got your tongue?"

I inched backward.

"Actually," he said, "don't talk. I'll do the talking. You see, prison time is thinking time." He was close now, too close. "Time to think about what I'd say to you if I saw you again. What I'd do." He clutched my wrist. "My, you're pretty. I watched you getting dressed this morning." He nodded. "And, I mean, damn, girl. You're a ten, Amanda. An eleven. But you ought to consider getting some shades in the bedroom there. You never know who could be watching you."

I looked away from his face, that awful, twisted smile.

"Have you told him yet?" he said, keeping a tight grasp on my wrist. "Have you told him what you've done?"

At once, I was fifteen again. Scared. Trapped. I hated that he could reduce me to this level.

"I asked you a question, Amanda," he said, his eyes narrowing, his mouth forming an angry snarl.

I heard a car on the road. I prayed that it would turn toward the manor. *Please, God. Please, let it be Rex.* He'd called that morning and promised to be back sometime in the afternoon. The engine noise grew louder, closer, until the car passed. My heart sank.

Then, I remembered the keys in my pocket, the ones Rex had left with me. There was one to the front door and another for the car. If I could break free, if I was fast, I could get to the old Rolls-Royce in the driveway. Parked in front of the fountain in the circle drive, it wasn't far. But could I get there?

"Amanda!" he said again, this time more insistent.

He let go of my wrist, moving his hand to my waist, which is when I broke away. "Don't call me that!" I screamed, running to the car. Just a few more paces. I heard his feet dig into the gravel, as if in slow motion. I pried open the door and leapt inside. He reached the driver's side door just as I pushed the latch. I leaned to the other side to lock it too. My hands trembled as I fumbled with the key. It slipped out of my hand just as I felt a sudden impact beside me. Sean had bashed the window with an urn. The glass shattered into a jagged pattern, revealing a hole the size of a baseball. Like an animal that knows its prey is near, he reached his hand through the hole, tugging at the shards. Blood dripped from the window and he cursed me, pulling his hand back. I jammed the key in the ignition and revved the engine, peeling out of the driveway so fast, gravel sprayed into the air.

I saw him in the rearview mirror, running after me, shouting. I gunned the engine.

I wished I had my cell phone to dial Rex, the police. It was only a ten-mile drive into town. I blinked hard, feeling the sting of fresh tears. I recognized a song on the radio, playing faintly through the car's old speakers: *Good day, sunshine. Good day, sunshine.* The lyrics seemed to mock me. There was nothing about this day that was good or ever could be. Tears blurred my vision, and as I reached to wipe them away, I started to lose control of the car. I'd forgotten about the steep curves on this part of the road. I grasped the steering wheel as the car lurched left. I heard the gritty crush of metal on metal as the car pushed past a flimsy guardrail, catapulting over the hillside.

No, no, please God, no no no . . .

Tall grass and canopy trees hurtled by, and the car hit the hillside with a violent thud and was swallowed whole by the dark forest floor. Warm blood trickled from my nose and left an acrid, metallic taste in my mouth. A bird chirped in the distance, its song pure and sweet—the antithesis of the fear I felt. *No, this isn't happening.* I tried to lift my legs from the seat, but they wouldn't budge. Pain shot through my limbs with the intensity of a freight train. *No, I can't die like this. Alone. So far away from home.* Would Sean find me here? Would Rex? My eyes blinked like a camera shutter clicking through the frames of my life, except the images were mismatched and haphazard: a ragged-looking doll with a rose-colored dress; crocheted white baby mittens, slightly unraveled; a row of tulips, vibrant red; Rex's smile; a rusty weather vane whirling in the wind.

My eyelids fluttered, fighting to remain open, but when they closed, the welcoming image that waited beckoned me to stay, promising to give me the comfort, the peace I longed for.

The camellias.

I could see them, seemingly endless rows of big, bushy green trees with waxy leaves and showy flowers the size of saucers. Pinks, reds—bursting into bloom, as if they'd been painted by the Queen of Hearts.

November began with a rare snowfall. The children, of course, were delighted, running out after dinner to build a snowman right in the drive. Fortunately, I'd taken their winter coats out of storage and had them cleaned.

Desmond had joined his father in town for some business earlier that day. They hadn't yet returned. I'd noticed how they left in cheerful accord. "It's good to see them getting along," Mrs. Dilloway had commented while clearing the breakfast dishes.

The children couldn't get enough of the snowflakes, so I decided to let them play a bit longer before bedtime. Just this once. I slipped into my coat and joined them on the terrace. Janie and Katherine stuck out their tongues, collecting flakes in their mouths, while Abbott and Nicholas were engaged in a serious snowball fight. As the wind picked up, I worried the frigid air would be too hard on Abbott; he hadn't fully recovered from his illness. "Just a few more minutes," I said, "and then let's go in for some hot tea. I don't want you children to get frostbite."

Nicholas suddenly stopped and pointed toward the sky. "What's that, Miss Lewis?" he asked.

I looked up, but I didn't see anything in particular, just darkness. "What did you see?" I said.

"There," he said, pointing at a low-flying plane in the distance. Its lights shone through the darkness.

My heart began to race. "Children!" I screamed. "Inside, now!"

I led them into the basement through the servants' entrance.

"Dear Lord!" Mrs. Dilloway cried. "Do you think it's a . . . ?"

"I don't know," Mr. Beardsley said. "But we must dim the lights, just in case." He flipped a switch on the wall and the house went dark.

Janie leaned against me, and I could feel her body trembling. "It's all right, sweetie," I said. "Everything's going to be fine."

"Are we going to die?" Katherine asked.

"Of course not, honey," I said, though I hoped she didn't hear the quiver in my voice.

I heard a sniffling sound behind me. I turned around, and in the darkness I could just make out Abbott wiping his eyes. "Father and Desmond are out there," he said. "What if, what if they—"

"Don't fret, dear Abbott," I said. "Your father and Desmond will make it home soon; I'm certain of it."

Abbott buried his head in his hands, then looked up again tearfully. "Desmond will be leaving for war soon, I suppose."

"Yes, I suppose," I said wistfully. In the past weeks, Abbott had warmed to his elder brother, and I was glad of it.

"I'm ashamed of the way I treated Desmond," he said, "when he came home."

"Why did you act that way, Abbott?"

He took a deep breath before saying, "I overheard Father speaking to Beardsley in his study after Mum died. They were discussing the business of the estate. He said that Desmond wasn't his real son, and that he'd cheat *me* out of inheriting the manor someday."

"I don't understand," I said. "How can he not be his son? He's—"

Mrs. Dilloway cleared her throat. "Perhaps we might talk about something else, shall we?"

"Yes," I said quickly.

Before bed that night, I knocked on Mrs. Dilloway's bedroom door. "Pardon me," I said in the doorway. "May I come in?"

She invited me to sit in the threadbare blue chair while she sat on the bed.

"What Abbott said about Desmond today," I said, "is it true?"

Her eyes would neither confirm nor deny. They only looked lost in memories. "Lord Livingston met her Ladyship in London at a society ball," she said. "She was visiting from America, and he fell for her the moment he laid eyes on her. Some say it was her fortune he loved, but that was never the case. He loved her. Madly and deeply. But he didn't know her past."

"Her past?"

"She had a son," she said. "In America."

"Desmond."

"Yes," she replied. "Lady Anna was only a girl of fifteen when he was born. Just a few years older than our own Katherine. The father was a farmhand at the family's home in Charleston. She wanted to run off with him, but her parents wouldn't hear of it. They sent him away, and after the baby was born, they put her on a ship to attend an exclusive school for girls in London. She never forgave her parents for taking Desmond from her."

"And Lord Livingston didn't know when he married her?"

"No," Mrs. Dilloway replied. "It tarnished his view of her when he learned of it. He couldn't look at her the same way after that, especially after Desmond came to live at the manor. His presence fueled his Lordship's paranoia. He was irreparably hurt, and Lady Anna only sunk deeper into her own sadness. She spent much of her time in her gardens after that. And he, well . . . there were many women."

"And Desmond?"

"He'd been in America all those years, and I don't think he was more than nine years old when he came to live here. By the way Lady Anna told it, she loved him at first sight. But Lord Livingston never warmed to Desmond, even after Anna begged him to."

"And what about you?" I asked. "How did you bear to live here, given the way you felt for—"

"I've almost given my notice a hundred times," she said. "There were moments when it felt too difficult to bear." She sighed. "But I decided to stay, to devote myself to Lady Anna. It was my penance, my punishment. I promised her I'd look out for her gardens, always, and I'm bound to that."

"Did she ever know about you and . . . ?"

Mrs. Dilloway looked grieved. "I don't know," she said. "But if she did, I pray that she's forgiven me." She shook her head, her face deeply distressed. "Women had been going missing in town," she said. "And, I think she had her suspicions."

"What did she think happened, exactly?"

"A few of the girls that Lord Livingston had"—she cleared her throat—"*entertained*, well, they vanished."

"And Lady Anna thought that he had something to do with it?"

"She didn't know what to believe," she said. "Nor did I."

I sat down, feeling weak. "Why didn't you go to the police?"

She gave me a queer look. "You must not understand, Miss Lewis," she said. "A servant never betrays her master, no matter what the stakes."

CHAPTER 29

Addison

Darkness engulfed me like a trench coat two sizes too big. I squinted, trying to make out the scene. *Where am I?* Crickets chirped in the distance. The clouds had parted to reveal a stream of moonlight that filtered through the trees, just enough to illuminate the spiderweb pattern of the cracked windshield and the spot where my head had made impact earlier. *The accident.* I touched my hand to my face and felt fresh blood. I shivered. *How long have I been here? Hours? Days?* I tried to lift my legs but they still wouldn't move, and then I felt a burning sensation in my feet, followed by a deep pain in my stomach. *My God, I'm pinned!*

I swallowed hard, and winced at the dry ache in my throat. I noticed a water bottle on the floor near my feet, and I inched my fingers closer. *Almost there, just a little farther.* I thought of the Pilates classes my friend Emma was always dragging me to. *Stretch, Addison.* Finally, my fingertips reached the mouth of the bottle. I grasped it with trembling fingers and brought it up, then twisted the cap off and held it to my lips. A few drops of water trickled into my mouth before I lost hold of the bottle and it fell to the floor, rolling under the seat, past my reach.

The moon disappeared behind a cloud again, and a thunderclap sounded overhead. "Dear God!" I cried. "If you can hear me, please, please don't let me die like this. Please bring me back to Rex." I let out a sob. "Please, God, give me a sign that everything will be all right."

When I opened my eyes, a ray of moonlight shone on the tree branch that had earlier impaled the windshield—a camellia, just a common variety, light pink, with an unremarkable yellow stamen. I'd seen hundreds of them over the years. But that night, I had never laid eyes on a thing of such beauty. Thunder, this time louder, filled the countryside anew, and I watched as a single pink petal fell into my lap. I listened as raindrops began to fall on the roof of the car. At first they made polite pecking noises overhead, and then they grew louder, faster, falling in an angry torrent. I closed my eyes tightly, thinking of Anna, Flora, letting the sound lull me to sleep.

CHAPTER 30

November 5, 1940

"What's America like?" Nicholas asked me at dinner.

I felt a pang of homesickness as I recalled the way New York looked from the bakery's window, thinking about Papa standing behind the counter and Mama fussing with the dinner rolls in the window display. "It's a wonderful place," I said.

"Will you take us there someday?" he asked.

I gave him a squeeze. "Maybe someday," I said. "Now, run along upstairs with your sister. I'll be up to meet you in the nursery."

I carried their plates to the kitchen, and nearly ran into Mr. Humphrey, who was dropping a sack into the rubbish bin.

I brushed against the side of his coat. "Pardon me," I said, as an envelope fell from his pocket.

He scrambled to pick it up, but recognizing the handwriting immediately, I grabbed it first: one of my letters to Mama and Papa. It had been torn at the edge. "Mr. Humphrey," I said, startled. "I don't understand. This should have been mailed weeks ago. Why do you—"

"I'm ever so sorry, miss," he said. "I didn't want you to find out, but now I have no choice but to tell you. Lord Livingston asked me to keep them."

I shook my head. "Why?"

He shrugged apologetically. "He asked me to keep them all. He read this one in the car on his ride back in from London."

"It's despicable," I said, scowling.

"You have every right to be angry."

"Well," I said, collecting myself, "I'm glad to know his true colors."

"The telephone's right here," Mr. Beardsley said, pointing to a table in the butler's pantry. He smiled apologetically as if he knew all that had happened. "If Lord Livingston has a problem with it, I'll have the cost deducted from my paycheck."

"You're too kind," I said before dialing the operator and asking her to connect me with the dry cleaner next to my parents' bakery. Eli could get a message to them.

"Eli!" I cried. "It's Flora. Flora Lewis. . . . Yes, listen, Eli, I'm calling from England. . . . Yes, England. . . . Yes, I'm fine. . . . I need you to go get my mother. Can you do that?"

I put my hand over the receiver. "He's going to get her! I can't believe I've waited so long."

A moment later, my mother picked up the phone. "Flora?" Her voice was like medicine for my soul. My knees weakened, and Mr. Beardsley pulled his chair out for me.

"Mama!" I cried. "It's so good to hear your voice."

"Oh, Flora," she said. The line crackled, reminding me that we were separated by an ocean. "We've been so worried."

"Oh, Mama, I have so much to tell you," I said. "I don't know where to begin."

"Where are you?" I could hear her muffled sniffles. "Are you safe?"

"Yes, yes, I'm safe. I took a job as a nanny caring for three children in the English countryside."

"Why didn't you write?"

"I did," I said. "But the letters, well"—I looked at Mr. Beardsley—"the letters were never sent. But please know that I have thought of you every day. I just assumed you were too busy at the bakery to write."

"Oh, honey," she said. "When you left, I was so frightened for you. But I hoped you were making an adventure for yourself. Your father believed you would. I'm more thickheaded."

"How is Papa?" I asked.

"I'm so sorry," she said. "Your father's taken ill."

"Mama, what is it?"

"His lungs. They've weakened, probably from breathing in flour for so many years. The doctor says that with rest, he might recover." She began to weep. "Oh, Flora. I pray he will."

"Oh, Mama!" I cried. "I'll come home. I'll do anything I can to get home."

"But how will you, honey? The war's shut down all ship passage."

"I'll find a way. I have to."

The next morning, Mrs. Dilloway looked after the children in the nursery while I went up to Lord Livingston's study. "Oh, Flora," he said as he looked up from his desk, a bit surprised. "So nice to see you this morning."

"I know about the letters," I said quickly, getting right to the point.

He looked down at his desk.

"How could you?" I continued. "And now I learn that my father is sick. He may be dying, and I didn't even know it!"

"Well, then I shall turn the tables," he countered. "How could *you*?"

I sat down in the chair in front of his desk. "You know?"

"I do," he said.

"For how long?"

"I've known for some time now," he said. "Of course, I only became suspicious after you found Anna's book. And then my man in London traced you to a con man by the name of Philip Price." He leaned back in his chair, grinning at me as if this amused him very much. "I wanted to see if you could go through with it. I wanted to see if you had it in you." He reached into a desk drawer and withdrew a folded square of paper. He placed it on the desk and unfolded it so I could see it. "Were you looking for this?"

It was the missing page from Lady Anna's book.

"I decided a long time ago that I could never betray you or the children," I said. My chin quivered.

Lord Livingston smiled coldly. "But you thought about it, didn't you?" He crumpled the page and tossed it in the wastebasket below his desk.

"No," I said. "That's not true at all. I fell in love with them; I fell in love with all of you. And Desmond."

"And what will he think of you now," he said, reaching into his desk again, "after he finds out the hideous truth about you?"

My heart beat faster. "And what about the truth about *you*?" I countered. "All those women, and the ones who disappeared?"

When I saw the look on his face, I wished I could retract the statement.

He shook his head. "I don't know what you mean," he said, turning to his desk drawer, where he pulled out my letters to Mama and Papa. Months' worth of information, tied up in twine. My cheeks burned as I reached for the stack of letters, before running out the door.

"Wait, Flora," he called after me.

I ran to the foyer.

I ran past the driveway and down the hillside, without knowing my destination. And then I saw the orchard. It was snowing again, but I didn't care. With each step I took, I distanced myself from the sadness of the house. I couldn't bear it anymore. Had Anna felt such sorrow when she escaped into her beloved orchard? I gazed out at the camellias. They looked like confections dusted with powdered sugar.

I continued on the path, turning toward the old carriage house. I ran to the door, pulling it open. It wasn't locked this time. Inside, the hooks along the walls held rope, a saw, garden shears, and other tools. A large burlap sack lay on the ground near a small interior door in the far wall. I opened the door and looked inside, gasping when I saw a cryptic message painted in deep red on the shiplap of the back wall: "For the flowers shall be anointed with her blood, and spring forth beauty."

I heard the crack of a branch outside. My breathing hastened, sending out puffs of fog into the frigid air. *I have to get out of here.* I opened the door slowly, stepping outside, and I noticed a second set of footprints in the snow. Fresh footprints. I looked right, then left, and decided to follow them. "Who's there?" I called out. My words immediately evaporated into the snowy air.

Behind the south side of the carriage house, I spotted a camellia I hadn't noticed before. And just under a lower branch, a speck of pink caught my eye. I walked closer. And, there, dangling on a dainty branch, a flower emerged. It was just a small blossom, but stunning nonetheless, white with pink tips. I gasped. The Middlebury Pink.

"A snow flower." The deep voice reverberated in the air behind me.

I spun around to find Desmond.

"It's why she loved camellias so much," he said. "They bloom when nothing else does."

"What are you doing down here?" I asked, a little frightened.

He took off his coat and wrapped it around me, as he always did, before turning me to face him. I looked up at his face, so strong and sure, a face I could look at for a lifetime and never grow tired of, and yet, could I trust him? He took my hands in his. "Your fingers are like ice," he said, rubbing my hands briskly between his, just like the night he told me he loved me, except everything felt different now.

"I'm going home," I said.

"I don't understand," he said, obviously wounded. "Why?"

"My father is ill. He needs me. I don't know if I'll be able to board a ship, given the war, but I'm certainly going to try."

Desmond turned away from me. "You know you'll break my heart if you go," he said. "Break it into a thousand pieces."

"I don't want to."

He turned back to face me. "What can I do to convince you to stay?"

"I'm sorry, Desmond," I said, "I have to go." As deeply as I cared for him, I was weary, too weary. And frightened.

He reached into his pocket. "I want you to have something." He opened my hand and let a cool silver chain fall into my palm.

"What is this?" I asked.

"A very special necklace. It was my mother's."

I held it up, taking a closer look at the locket attached to the chain. A flower that looked like a camellia had been engraved on the front. There was no doubt it was the necklace Mrs. Dilloway had described, the one she believed sheltered a precious item inside.

"Desmond," I said, shaking my head, "where did you find this? Mrs. Dilloway said—"

Desmond smiled to himself. "Mum never took it off. It was her mother's. It's quite an antique. Pure silver. They don't make them like that anymore."

I tugged on the clasp of the locket, but it was jammed.

"Let me put it on you," he said. "She would have loved for you to wear it."

I shivered as his cold hands touched my neck. My heart beat faster as he fastened the clasp. *How did he get it?*

"Take it off," Lord Livingston said, appearing from behind us. "That necklace belonged to my wife."

"But I, I—" I stammered.

"Mum would have wanted Flora to have it, Father," Desmond said.

Lord Livingston's eyes narrowed. "What do you know

about what your mother wanted? You were just a spoiled child. You were purely a burden to her."

I hated hearing such ugly words.

Desmond took a step toward his father, fist drawn. "How dare you!"

Anger churned in Lord Livingston's eyes. I looked away. "You convinced your mother that she didn't love me," he said. "You planted the seed in her heart."

"I didn't have to plant the seed," Desmond countered. "It was already there."

Lord Livingston lunged at him, and the two fell to the snowy ground. I hovered over them, pleading for them to stop. The older man's eyes swelled with deep sorrow, madness, even. He leapt to his feet, stumbling to the carriage house. When the door wouldn't open, he kicked it down, pushing his way inside. A moment later, he returned holding an ax.

"No!" I screamed. "What are you doing?"

He walked toward us, but his gaze was fixed on something behind us. The camellia. I gasped. *The Middlebury Pink.*

"I should have destroyed this tree a long time ago," he said. I hardly recognized his voice, rough with urgent desperation. "She had too much time to think about life down here. Too much time to grow apart from me." He wielded the ax over his head. "Step aside!" he shouted.

Desmond and I moved out of the way, but I begged him to stop. "You don't know what you're doing! Not this camellia. This one is rare; you said so yourself!" He ignored me, slamming the blade of the ax into the tree's stately trunk. I winced as it took the first blow. Its branches swayed bravely, trying to hold on, pleading to be spared. But he cocked the ax back again, this time letting it fly toward the tree with greater force. I watched his anguished face. He couldn't make anyone pay for Anna's death, or for her great sadness, but he could take out his rage on the camellias. *This* camellia.

"Please!" I cried, trying in vain to make him stop.

The ax sliced through the trunk completely this time. The tree's bushy top fell into a heap on the snowy ground, its branches flailing. He fell to his knees, burying his face in his hands. At some point in the scuffle with Desmond, he'd hurt his lip, because a trickle of fresh blood dripped from his face and dotted the snowy ground.

"Father, you're hurt," Desmond said, running to his side to take a better look at the wound. "It's deep," he continued. "I'm going to get Beardsley. We need a doctor!" He turned to me. "Stay with him. I'll be back." And then he ran up the hill to the house.

I took a step closer, cautiously.

"It's time you go, Miss Lewis," he said.

I nodded.

"Don't make it any more difficult than it is," he continued. "You've found the tree. And now it's gone. No one can have it now."

A tear spilled down my cheek.

"I won't tell Desmond, the children," he said. "It would break their hearts." He rubbed his brow. "Now it's time. Please leave us."

I took a step back and turned quickly toward the path. I ran through the snow, up the hillside to the house ahead. I slipped into the servants' quarters undetected and frantically piled my belongings into the old leather suitcase. My heart ached when I thought about the children. I ran to the driveway, where Mr. Humphrey was clearing snow from the windshield of the car. "Can you take me to the train station?" I asked, out of breath.

"Of course, Miss Lewis," he said smiling at me curiously. I noticed a strange glint in his eyes. "Is everything all right?"

"I need to leave," I said, looking over my shoulder. "Immediately."

I climbed into the backseat as Mr. Humphrey got in behind the wheel. I spotted Desmond in the rearview mirror. As the car pulled away, he began to run after it. "Flora, stop!" he yelled. "Please, stop!"

Mr. Humphrey slammed the gas pedal with a surprising intensity and the wheels spun on the slick gravel, propelling the car forward with a jolt. We drove for a few minutes in silence. He eyed me through the rearview mirror a few times, before finally speaking. "It looks pretty on you," he said.

I shook my head. "I'm sorry," I said, wiping away a tear. "I don't know what you mean."

"Her necklace," he replied, still watching me in the mirror. I could see the corners of his eyes crinkle as he smiled.

I raised my hand to my neck. "How did you—"

"I was foolish," he said, grinning. "It must have fallen out of my pocket in the house. Desmond found it before I did. Of course, he didn't suspect anything. Not then. But he will."

"Mr. Humphrey," I said, feeling the blood rise in my cheeks, "I don't understand." And then I remembered seeing a silver chain in his car sometime before. *Did he have it all along?*

"Come now, Miss Lewis. You're a smart lass. Surely you've figured it out by now." He pulled a pistol from his jacket and held it up for me to see, then set it on the seat.

I covered my mouth.

"All the other girls were so easy to have," he said. "They wilted like petunias. But not Anna. No, I could never have her. She had to go and die before I could get to her. That bloody Abbott. Of course, he meant the tea for Mr. Blythe. But the teapots got mixed up." He chuckled. "The boy killed his own mother."

I tried to speak but could produce no sound.

"Desmond's probably back at the house now, putting it all together," Mr. Humphrey continued. "I thought my goose was cooked when you found the necklace in the car that day. And then that night when you saw me coming up from the orchard." He licked his lips with satisfaction. "Remember Theresa from the village? I had her down there. Buried her under the last camellia in the far row."

My hands were shaking. Why hadn't I seen this all along? The muddy boots. The lantern lights in the orchard. The burlap sack. *Dear Lord.*

"If Desmond had only asked to look inside the sack," he said. "He'd have been in for a surprise." He shook his head. "Just like his father, he'd never confront me. Cowards."

I couldn't speak. I could hardly breathe. The car was speeding along the road, and yet time had slowed, stopped even.

"I shouldn't have kept the necklace," he said. "Sloppy work on my part. But after I found her in the orchard, I snatched it from her neck. Believe me, I wanted more of her." His eyes flashed in the rearview mirror. "But Desmond was coming down from the house. I had to take what I could get." He chuckled to himself. "I think I could get ten pounds for it. I'll see about that after I'm done with you."

Terror seeped into every inch of my body, but I couldn't let myself succumb to it. Snowflakes streamed in through the window, open just a crack. I eyed the door handle. Could I escape? Could I throw myself from the car?

"I'm going to do to you what I had planned for Lady Anna," he said.

"Dear Lord!" I cried. "Please, Mr. Humphrey. You're not well. Take me to the village. We'll find help for you."

He shook his head. "The trees, they need blood."

I grimaced. "Blood?"

"For the flowers shall be anointed with her blood, and spring forth beauty."

"The words on the wall of the carriage house," I said. "*It was you.*"

"Yes. Don't you know? It's the only way they'll bloom."

"But that's not true," I said. "They bloom. You just have to give them time. You can't force a plant to flower."

"Ah, Miss Lewis, but you can," he said. "You saw for yourself. The Middlebury Pink hadn't bloomed in a decade. That flower you saw on it?" He held up his arm, bandaged at the wrist. "I had to feed it myself. It was enough to produce a single bloom, but with you . . ." He paused. "With you, the tree shall blossom once again."

"You're mad," I said.

He smiled to himself. "Lord Livingston never knew," he said. "Oh, but how he helped by bringing all the girls to me. He bedded them all, so when their bodies are found in the orchard, he'll be the natural suspect. Pretty ingenious, if I do say so myself."

I shook my head in horror.

"They think that servants don't notice," he continued.

"That we don't hear. But I watched him. I knew how he'd sneak them up to his room or where he'd meet them in the village. He'd tire of them after a few months. And then it was my turn." He fiddled with the radio dial. "It won't be much longer now. I sure liked seeing the look on your face down in the orchard that first day."

"It was you in the carriage house, wasn't it?"

"Me and Genevieve Preus," he said. "She was a feisty one." He smiled. "Yes, today, I shall have you, and then, that bloody housemaid. If I have to hear her yap anymore . . ." He shook his head. "Lady Katherine will be ready soon. I've been watching her closely." He rubbed his forehead. "What was it that Thomas Jefferson said?" His eyes met mine in the rearview mirror. "You're American, you ought to know." He thought carefully. "Yes, he said that 'the tree of liberty must be refreshed from time to time with the blood of patriots.'"

My hands trembled as I reached into my pocket and pulled out the handkerchief Mama had embroidered for me, with my initials, FAL, in the corner. I dabbed the corners of my eyes, and it somehow gave me comfort, strength, as if Mama and Papa were there saying, "Don't be afraid." I remembered what Georgia had written on the first page of *The Years*: "The truth of the matter is that we always know the right thing to do. The hard part is doing it."

And in that moment, I knew what I had to do. I leaned forward and dug my fingers into Mr. Humphrey's eyes. My stomach turned as I felt his right eye pop as I gouged my finger deeper. He cried out and took his hands from the wheel to wrench my hands away, which is when he swerved right, then left. The car pushed past a guardrail on the roadside, careening through the air over the hillside. I pulled the necklace from my neck, feeling the clasp snap. I didn't know if he'd survive, or if I would. But if he did, he would not sell this necklace for ten pounds. He would not lay a finger on it—or another girl. I hurled it out the window and closed my eyes.

CHAPTER 31

Addison

My eyes fluttered and then opened. The sun, low on the horizon, streamed through the windshield, warming me in my seat, where I sat pinned. I was grateful for the warmth, grateful for morning. The sun cut through the chills that had come over me. I felt damp all over, and when I looked down at my pants, I could see that they were soaked. How long had I been here? Days? Would Rex ever find me? Would Sean? My head ached and my legs throbbed—the parts I could feel, anyway. I touched the camellia branch that impaled the windshield and studied its intricate blossom. A few of its petals had wilted, shrinking back in defeat. "No," I whispered. "You can't die. Not yet. You're my only hope."

Nobody really talks about what happens right before you die. Does your life flash before your eyes? Do you slip into a nice, cozy dream where there are clouds made of whipped cream and soft music plays all around? Do angels sing? Does Jesus hold out his hand for you, welcoming you through the pearly gates? Are there really pearls on the gates? As I sat in the mangled car, in a moment of lucidity, I wondered if I might be in my final moments of life. Above my head, a dewdrop glistened on the camellia flower. I opened my mouth and waited until the droplet fell onto my parched tongue.

I shivered as a gust of wind rocked the car. The camellia above my head swayed, and a petal fell onto the seat. *Hold on, little flower. Hold on.*

An hour might have passed. Or a day, or maybe three. I didn't know. "She's inside the car!" someone shouted in the distance. A male voice. Deep. Hurried. I heard dogs barking and commotion overhead.

"Easy, now," someone said. "She's pinned. We'll have to use the clamps. Careful. Not too fast."

I opened my eyes for a moment, but everything was blurred.

"She's awake!"

My lips parted momentarily, and I felt pressure on my legs.

"Don't try to speak, ma'am," a man said from somewhere overhead. "You just sit tight. We're going to get you out of here, promise."

"Addison!" That voice. So familiar. "Addison, darling!"

I opened my eyes and willed them to focus until I saw his face. *Rex.*

My eyes shut; everything faded to black.

A series of rapid beeps sounded from a machine at my left. I didn't flinch when a cold hand held my arm and a needle pricked the skin. *Where am I? What's happening?* I tried to open my eyes, but the camellia orchard lured me back in, along the brick pathway—*just a few steps farther*—under the rose arbor, past the stone angel, and there, beneath the fog, near the carriage house with the rusty weather vane twirling in the breeze, the tree. *Her* tree. In my mind's eye, I took a step, feeling the soft soil under my feet. Fresh earth. The cries of so many. They could rest now. But could I?

I opened my eyes. "We almost lost you there," a young nurse said, tucking a strand of hair behind her ear. "You're safe now, honey. You've been airlifted to First Memorial in London. You were in a terrible accident, pinned in your car for four days. You're quite a survivor, you know."

A familiar song played somewhere nearby. I listened to the words: *Good day, sunshine* . . .

"That song," I murmured.

"Oh, I'm sorry," the nurse said, indicating the TV. "It's a documentary on the Beatles. I have a thing for Paul McCartney." She winked at me. "Let me just turn it off." She pressed a button on the remote control and then turned back to me with a smile.

A woman with thick tortoiseshell glasses pushed a button on the hospital bed to incline it slightly. "Hello, I'm Doctor Hollis," she said, examining a medical chart and then nodding assuredly. "You got quite a bump on the head. You've been in a coma for the last forty-eight hours. We're very happy to see you awake." She turned to the figure to her left. "This your sweetie?"

"Addison." That deep British voice. My eyelids felt heavy. I wished the nurse hadn't given me so much medicine. It blurred the line between reality and something else. Some*where* else. Heaven, maybe? Had I been in heaven? My eyes closed without my permission.

"Addison." His voice was louder now, more persistent. I felt a warm hand on my cheek. My eyes fluttered again, and with every last bit of strength, I opened them, searching the room. And then I saw him—his tan jacket, those warm eyes—and smiled, feeling the life seep back into me.

"Rex," I said, as a surge of warmth flooded my cold limbs. In an instant, I remembered the accident. I wanted to say a hundred things to him—about Sean, my past, about the camellia, the women who had lost their lives, about Lady Anna—but when I opened my mouth, air danced across my vocal cords. I gasped for breath.

"It's OK, honey," he said. "I'm here. I'm here, and I'm never going to let you go."

"But what about—"

"You don't have to worry about him anymore," he said quickly. "They got him. He's being extradited back to the U.S. as we speak. He can't hurt you anymore." He wiped a tear from his eye before it spilled onto his cheek. "I just wish you would have told me. I wish I could have protected you from him."

A tear rolled down my own cheek, and I wiped it away. "So you know," I said, shaking my head. "Of course, you did all along. Rex, I saw the file in your bag."

He looked confused. "What file?"

"The one labeled 'Amanda,'" I whispered, ashamed.

"That?" he said. "It's a character file, honey. I thought you knew that the heroine in my novel is named Amanda."

I looked down at my hands. A purple bruise appeared on my forearm.

"She's brave and strong," he said. "Like you."

"But aren't you angry at me," I said, "for not being honest with you about my past?" I bit my lip, fighting back tears. "For lying to you?"

"You had your reasons," he said. "And I respect them. But let me get one thing clear, please." He looked deep into my eyes. "Nothing about your past can change my love for you—nothing." He kissed my wrist, rubbing the spot I'd tried so hard to keep covered over the years. The nurse must have taken my watch off, but I didn't care now. The scars no longer had the same hold on me.

"Rex," I cried. "When I was fifteen, there was a little boy. He was only three years old. Sean killed him, Rex. He pushed him off a swing." I sobbed. "I wanted to save him. I wanted to so badly." Rex climbed into bed with me, cradling me. "But I couldn't. I didn't get to him in time. His name was Miles. Sean made me bury him. I never told anyone, Rex. Never, after all these years. I was afraid. Oh, Rex, I'm so ashamed."

He stroked my cheek. "No, no, you don't have to be ashamed. Please, honey. You were just a child."

I shook my head. "I have to tell the police. I have to tell them what happened."

Rex nodded. "I'll support you in whatever you need to do. My family has an attorney who can help us through this."

I sobbed into his shoulder. "I just don't want to hurt anymore."

"You don't have to," he said. "Not anymore."

He kissed me before pulling a letter from his pocket. "I found this upstairs on the dressing table. It's addressed to you."

I tore the edge of the envelope, remembering Mrs. Dilloway muttering something about a letter before she left in the ambulance.

Dear Addison,

I am in poor health, and in case I don't have much time left, it's time you knew the truth about Lady Anna. Whatever may have happened to the other girls, rest their souls, Anna died in a far different manner. You see, there is a poisonous plant that grows near the orchard. Lady Anna always said it was too beautiful to destroy, but that very plant killed her in the end. Abbott knew of it, and he had collected a few sprigs in the orchard. He asked if he could help make the tea, and I should have known what he had in mind. He hated Mr. Blythe. He hated that he had the attention of his mother. So, he poisoned the tea. He meant it for Mr. Blythe and saved a different pot for his mother, but it didn't go as he'd planned. The teapots got mixed up and his mother drank it instead. Her Ladyship loved her children more than life itself. She wouldn't have wanted her son punished or for him to carry that sort of guilt. So after her death, when he asked me if I'd served the tea, knowing full well the reason for his inquiry, I told him that I hadn't. I told him I'd poured both teapots out and made a fresh batch when I noticed a fly in one of the pots. And that was that. When an investigator tried to reopen the case and scrutinize the autopsy report, I had the documents sealed. For Abbott's sake. A son shouldn't have to live with that sort of guilt.

Yours,

Mrs. Dilloway

"Rex," I said, setting the letter aside. "How is she—Mrs. Dilloway?"

He nodded. "I got a call from the hospital this morning. She suffered a severe stroke. Only time will tell."

The nurse reappeared at the door. "Excuse me, Ms. Sinclair. I hate to bother you, but there's a paramedic here to see you. He was part of the crew who rescued you. Are you well enough for me to send him in? If not, I can tell him to come back later; it's no trouble."

I nodded. "Yes, please, have him come in. I'd like to thank him."

A tall man with dark hair walked into the room timidly. "It's good to see you awake," he said, smiling. He paused to turn down the volume of a handheld radio attached to his belt. "For a while there, we weren't sure if you'd make it." He extended his hand. "I'm John Simmons."

"John," I said, shaking his hand. "I don't know how to thank you for saving my life."

"I only wish we could have found you sooner," he said. "You're a fighter. Four days out there."

"I'm American," I said, smiling. "It's in our blood."

He grinned, reaching into his pocket. "Ms. Sinclair, the reason I'm here . . . well, I found something near the crash site and I thought it might belong to you." The necklace dangled from his fingers; he let it fall into my hand. The tarnished chain held a silver oval locket with a camellia etched into the center. *Lady Anna's necklace.* I recognized it at once from the painting at the manor.

I gasped. "I don't understand; I . . ."

"You must have lost it during the crash," he said, standing up. "Well, I won't keep you. It's good to see you making a recovery. The men at the station will be so glad to hear it."

"But," I muttered, staring at the necklace.

He walked to the door but turned back to face us again. "Oh, I almost forgot to tell you—we made quite a discovery out there in the ravine. If you can believe it, the men found a rusted-out Rolls-Royce from the 1940s nearby, with someone's remains inside."

I gasped again. "Someone?"

"Yeah," he said. "A man, likely, by the size of him. Don't mean to startle you, miss," he said. "I just thought you'd like to know that you picked a pretty good place to crash—led us to some poor soul who's been out there for decades." He smiled. "Anyway, we all wish you the best, Ms. Sinclair." He nodded at Rex with a wink. "And maybe let that husband of yours do the driving for the remainder of your stay."

"I will," I said, looking up at Rex as he squeezed my shoulder.

"I can't believe all of this," I said after the paramedic had left. I pointed to the engraving on the front of the locket. "See? It's a camellia."

"You seem to recognize it," he said, kissing the top of my head. He took the necklace in his hand to have a closer look.

"I do," I replied, remembering the way it rested on Lady Anna's neck in the painting. Those sad eyes. That expression of longing, of secrets.

He held the locket to my ear. "Listen," he said. "I think there's something inside." He fiddled with the clasp, then shrugged. "It's jammed. We'll have a jeweler look at it."

"Let me try," I said, taking the necklace into my hands again, heart racing in anticipation. What had Lady Anna kept inside? I tugged at the hook, but it held on stubbornly, until suddenly it released and the locket popped open. Something small bounced out onto the floor. Rex knelt to pick it up, then held it out in his palm for me to examine.

"How strange," he said. "What do you think it is?"

My eyes flooded with tears. "A seed," I said. "Of course. A camellia seed."

Rex looked astonished. "Really?"

I nodded, remembering the stump I'd found behind the carriage house that day with Nicholas. Of course; Anna had kept a seed in her locket, just in case something should happen to her prized camellia. Did Flora find it and save it? Had she been inside that car? With who?

"It's a Middlebury Pink," I said. "I know it."

"But how do you know if it will even grow, when it's been in the locket for decades?" Rex asked.

Over the years, I'd read several articles about seed germination, including one story about a wheat seed found entombed with an Egyptian mummy that had been successfully sprouted by gardeners centuries later. "Camellias are patient," I said. "It'll grow."

I held the locket up to the light, eyeing the inside carefully, and I detected an engraving. It read, "Darling Edward, my true north."

"You're crying," Rex said, pressing his cheek against mine.

"Rex," I said, "I feel like I've been given a chance to start all over again."

"Me too," he said. "I almost lost you."

"I clutched the locket. "I just wish the gardens didn't have to be destroyed."

He looked confused. "I'm not sure what you mean."

"The blueprints," I said, remembering how I'd shuddered when I'd seen the plans for the property. "I saw them. I saw the golf course they have planned for the orchard. Rex, I wish you hadn't signed off on all of that."

He kissed my neck. "I would *never* sign off on something like that," he replied. "What you saw, *Watson*, must have been a stray page from a development project my parents are investing in north of Cambridge."

"No," I said. "I'm sure I saw it right. There was an orchard of trees, and the manor was there."

Rex scratched his head. "Well, the 'orchard' you're referring to is a field of aphid-infested crab apples, and the 'manor' is an old barn." He smiled. "I take it you didn't look at the plans very carefully."

I felt a flush in my cheeks. "But I thought—"

"You thought I'd let my parents take a bulldozer to the gardens that my wife had fallen in love with?" He shook his head. "Besides, those very camellias inspired my new novel."

I grinned. "Really?"

"Yes," he said. "The flowers, the mystery, the manor—I couldn't have come up with this story if you hadn't found the clues."

We both looked up when we heard a knock. An elderly man stood in the doorway. His face was partially shrouded by a herringbone beret that rested low on his forehead, but when he looked up at me, I had a distinct sense that I'd seen him before—but where? He cleared his throat. "Pardon me. I was just looking for my sweetheart. I thought for sure they had her in room three thirty-four." He held a coffee cup in his hand.

"You must have gotten turned around," Rex replied. "That's on the other side of the hall, around the corner."

"I'm ever so sorry to interrupt," he said, looking down at his hands. "Crikey, I forgot Flora's creamer again. If I walk back down to the cafeteria, her coffee will be cold." My eyes shot open when I heard the familiar name.

"Here," Rex said, grabbing two coffee creamers from the tray near my bed. "Take these."

"Thank you," the man replied. "You must know American women and their coffee."

Rex smiled. "I'm married to one."

He tipped his cap at me and smiled. "Top of the morning to you both," he said with a wink before walking out the door.

I blinked back a tear. *Could it be?* Flora. The photograph of the man standing in front of the stairs at Livingston Manor. The fog was beginning to clear. "Top of the morning to you," I said under my breath.

Rex squeezed my hand. "Everything all right, love?"

I nodded, smiling up at him as I squeezed the locket in my hand. "I was just thinking," I said, pausing as my voice faltered a little, "that I know where I'd like to plant this seed."

"At the manor?"

"No," I said. "In New York, in Greenhouse Number Four at the Botanical Garden."

Rex squeezed my hand in approval.

As I lay there, I closed my eyes, envisioning the camellia tree the seed would grow into, the beautiful blossoms it would sprout. Its journey, like mine, had been a harrowing one, fraught with uncertainty. With pain. But now it would put down roots and thrive. It would live with dignity, peace, and forgiveness.

I would too.

Epilogue

T he manor dazzled under the July sun. Two years had passed, and yet it felt like a lifetime since I'd stood there looking up at the stone facade. The summer before, Rex's parents had urged us to make the trip to see the completed renovation, but I hadn't been ready then. Not yet. But then I received a letter from Katherine Livingston. She and her younger sister, Jane, planned to see the memorial plaque James and Lydia had commissioned in memory of the women who had lost their lives in the 1930s and '40s. It was time to return to the manor.

I stepped out of the cab, cautiously looking up at the front of the old house. I remembered how I'd felt when I had first arrived, unsure, frightened by the ghosts in my past. And now—I looked at Rex, remembering the way he'd stood by my side when I testified at Sean's trial, testimony that had put him behind bars, this time for the rest of his life—and I felt *so* sure.

"Addison, Rex!" my mother-in-law, Lydia, cried from the front steps. The residence had been meant as their summer home, but she and James had spent the majority of the past two years there. And I knew why—the place had a charm, a mystique like no other.

"You're just in time. The Livingstons will be here any minute. Let's go down to the orchard. You must be parched. I'll have Mrs. Brighton bring down some cold drinks."

"Mrs. Brighton?"

"The new housekeeper," Lydia said. "She started six months ago. She's doing a fine job. Mrs. Dilloway hand-selected her before she passed."

"Oh," I said quietly. "I hadn't heard." I felt a lump in my throat as we walked down to the orchard. I clutched the little sack in my hand that I'd carried with me on the plane.

"What do you think of the furniture?" Lydia asked, pointing to a set of chaise longues and various teak tables and steamer chairs. "I'm having some lighting put in next week, and James wants a grill and maybe an outdoor fireplace."

I smiled. "I think it's wonderful."

Rex's father caught up to us. "Hello, you two," he said, holding a book in his right hand. He smiled proudly. "Look what I found in the Heathrow bookstore last weekend. I recognized the flower on the cover and smiled at Rex. "What will it take to get my copy autographed?"

Rex took the book into his hands, pulled a pen from his pocket, and signed his name on the inside cover, the way he'd done at his recent book signing in New York. I never tired of gazing at the cover—"*The Last Camellia*, by Rex Sinclair"—or the dedication page inside: "To my wife, Addison, with love, always and forever." I squeezed his hand.

"Look," Lydia said, pointing to the hillside, where three people were making their way toward us. "They're here."

I recognized Nicholas immediately. His hair appeared whiter than before and his face a bit thinner. I wondered how the years had changed my own face. "Addison," he said, clasping both of my hands in his warmly. "What a pleasure to see you again." He turned to the women who stood beside him. "These are my sisters, Katherine and Jane."

"It's so wonderful to meet you," I said to the two women. "I feel as if I know you."

Jane smiled. "If it weren't for you, we might never have come back," she said.

Katherine nodded, then took her brother's hand in hers. "Just being here again," she said, "I don't have words to describe what I'm feeling right now."

I held up the bag in my hand. "Before we go see the plaque, I wondered if I might show you something first—something special that I've brought from New York."

Everyone nodded and eyed the bag with anticipation as I lifted out the little terra-cotta pot I'd cradled in my arms during the transatlantic flight. The soil, still damp from the water I'd given it on the plane, embraced a small but thriving sprout, about a foot tall, that I'd managed to propagate from the Middlebury Pink seed I'd found in the locket. "Your mother's favorite camellia," I said, holding the plant out for them to see.

Katherine gasped. "How did you—?"

"She saved a seed," I said.

Nicholas offered Katherine his handkerchief, and she dabbed her eye.

"I was able to grow a new seedling at the New York Botanical Garden, and when it bloomed last winter, we succeeded in growing this start. It will be a tree in its own right before too long, and I know just the place to plant it."

We walked ahead to the old carriage house, where the stump of the tree's ancestor remained. "There," I said, placing my hand on my belly as I knelt down.

"Everything OK, honey?" Rex whispered.

I nodded with a smile. "I think I just felt the baby kick."

"He's going to be an athlete, my grandson," James said with a smile.

"Or a gardener, like his mum," Lydia added.

"Whomever he decides to be in this life," Rex said, tucking his arm around me, "he'll be extraordinarily loved."

Lydia handed me a trowel and I dug a small hole, before freeing the sprout from its temporary clay home and setting it gently into the cool English earth. We watched the little camellia sway in the summer breeze. "Be sure to have your gardener keep an eye on it," I said. "It'll need to be staked when it gets a bit bigger, and don't let them give it too much water. It'll drown the poor thing."

Lydia nodded.

"There," I said, patting the ground softly before turning to face Nicholas, Katherine, and Jane. For a moment, I saw them as they once were: three young children standing in the garden. "What do you think your mother would say if she were here?"

Katherine took a step toward me. "I think she would say thank you," she replied. "Thank you ever so much."

Jane put her hand on her sister's shoulder. "I wish Abbott could be here to see this," she said. "It would have made him so happy."

We walked to the memorial in silence, where we quietly marveled at the names of the women on the plaque before turning back toward the house. Birds chirped all around.

Two figures, an elderly man and woman, stood on the hill near the house. My heart beat faster as Rex and I exchanged a knowing look.

The couple walked closer, and Katherine turned to Jane. "Can it really be . . . ?"

"I don't believe my eyes," Nicholas said.

Rex and I stayed behind with his parents and watched the momentous reunion before us.

I smiled, clutching the locket around my neck. The seed of peace, of reconciliation, of healing had been there all along, of course. Someone just needed to plant it.

**Newport Community
Learning & Libraries**

Acknowledgments

I dedicated this book to my mother, Karen Mitchell, not only because she suffered through my colicky beginnings (apparently I cried for three solid months) and modeled love and grace to me, but also because looking back on my early years, she introduced me to everything beautiful, important, and special in my life, whether it was the flowers in the garden, the egg nog at Christmas, or the significance of faith. It also should be noted here that she made pie for me every year on my birthday because I didn't like cake.

This book wouldn't be here without the amazing support of my literary agent, Elisabeth Weed, who launched my career in fiction with such savvy and has been there for me every step of the way (and with my publishing schedule, that is no easy feat!). I am tremendously honored to have Elisabeth as a partner in my career and especially grateful to be able to count her as a friend.

A very special thanks goes to my dear editor at Plume, Denise Roy, who stuck with me through the many, many drafts and who helped me see the light—or, rather, the beautiful garden—at the end of the tunnel. You have a very special gift. Also, much gratitude to Milena Brown, Elizabeth Keenan, Ashley Pattison, Kym

Surridge, Phil Budnick, Kate Napolitano, and everyone else at Plume. It is a privilege and a pleasure to work with you all.

A heartfelt thanks to the lovely Stephanie Sun, who has read every one of my books in the early draft stages, and who provided such brilliant feedback on this novel in particular.

Many thanks to the amazing Jenny Meyer, who has shared my stories with readers in seventeen countries around the world and who somehow manages to keep up with all of my books. I am so grateful.

To Dana Borowitz, for believing in me and for reminding me that the best things in life aren't achieved by a short sprint, but rather a steady pace and lots of endurance.

To my dear friends: Sally Kassab, for reminding me of the importance of loyalty and "showing up"; Wendi Parriera, for making me smile and always taking my side; Camille Noe Pagan, for the encouragement; and many, many others who have cheered me on in so many ways. Thank you.

Last but not least, my family: Mom, Dad, Jessica, Josh, Josiah, love you.

One mother's desperate hope for survival.
One woman's search for the truth ...

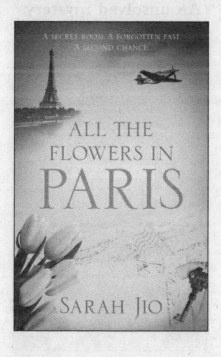

1943: In occupied Paris, Celine creates bespoke bouquets at her father's flower shop on rue Cler, whilst trying to shield her young daughter from the brutal reality of war. But when an SS officer takes an interest in Celine and her family, all their lives are put in jeopardy.

2009: Caroline wakes in Paris with no memory of her previous life. Hunting for clues to her identity in her apartment on the rue Cler, she discovers a bundle of letters written by a young widow during the Second World War. As she peels back the layers of the past, Caroline finds new purpose – but Celine's story is unfinished. Desperate to find out the truth, Caroline digs deeper, uncovering dark and dangerous secrets ...

Can learning the truth about Celine help
Caroline unlock the mystery of her past?

A sudden snowstorm.
A missing child.
An unsolved mystery.

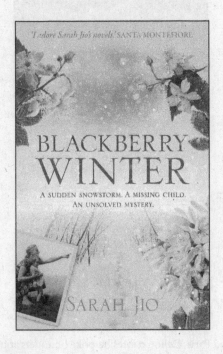

1933. Vera Ray kisses her young son goodnight and leaves to work the night-shift at a local hotel. The next morning, she discovers an sudden snowfall has blanketed the city, and her son has vanished, the snow covering up any trace of his tracks, or the perpetrator's.

2010. Journalist Claire Aldridge has been burying herself in work to avoid her own pain. When she is assigned to cover the 'blackberry winter' storm she learns of the disappearance of a three-year-old boy. He was never found. Claire vows to find the truth, but as she immerses herself in the mysteries of the past, Claire discovers that not all secrets should be revealed.

A haunting story of love, family
and the secrets that can destroy us...